DEATH WALKS IN EASTREPPS

DEATH WALKS IN EASTREPPS

Francis Beeding

Dover Publications, Inc.
New York

This Dover edition, first published in 1980, is an unabridged
and unaltered republication of the work originally published
by The Mystery League, Inc., Publishers, New York, in 1931.

International Standard Book Number: 0-486-24014-2
Library of Congress Catalog Card Number: 80-65688

Manufactured in the United States of America
Dover Publications, Inc.
180 Varick Street
New York, N.Y. 10014

CONTENTS

CHAPTER ONE

CHAPTER TWO

CHAPTER THREE

CHAPTER FOUR

CHAPTER FIVE

CHAPTER SIX

CONTENTS

DEATH WALKS IN
EASTREPPS

CHAPTER ONE

I

ROBERT ELDRIDGE sat back in his seat. The train would be moving presently. He looked at his watch. . . . Twelve minutes past seven. He had perhaps entered the train too soon. His compartment might at the last moment be invaded. Then, of course, he would have to move into another.

He hoped it had not been noticed—this anxiety of his to avoid his fellow-men whenever he caught the 7:15 from Fenchurch Street. But that was hardly likely. There was nothing to excite suspicion or even comment in his wish to travel alone. Most Englishmen preferred, if possible, to do so. There was no call for anyone to guess that he had a special reason of his own.

So far the scheme had worked well. It had been in operation now for six months, and never a hitch . . . so far. He must have brought it off something between twenty and thirty times. It was still, however, difficult to feel at ease. One of these days . . .

Why had they not thought of something less elaborate, simpler and more normal altogether? Eldridge sighed. He was, he reflected, like that. If there were two possible courses, one straightforward and the other devious, he was bound to find himself sooner or later committed to the more romantic.

The train was moving. The platform slid past. Eldridge sat up. He had never lost that boyish thrill of a great locomotive gathering itself together for a long run. Romance brought up the 9:15—that was Kipling. Romance again . . . romance at forty-seven. . . . Well, there was no fool like an old fool—so they said.

Eldridge sighed again, settled himself more comfortably in his corner facing the engine and lit a cigar—a long, dark cigar of the finest Havana tobacco. He had contracted the habit of good cigars during those lean years in South America. They were sent to him in consignments of a thousand at a time, to his office in Fenchurch Street, a few hundred yards from the station. It was true he paid a wicked price for them, but he could afford it. Come to think of it, there had been very few moments in his life when he had been unable to afford what he really wanted. He was that sort of man. He had suffered, of course, his ups and downs. But a man must take the rough with the smooth.

Eldridge stirred uneasily. For some of the rough had been exceedingly rough. That night sixteen years ago, for example, when he had slipped across the gangway of the s.s. *Malabar* bound for Montevideo. But he was not going to think of the past. The past was . . . past. And the future would take care of itself. All that mattered now was the present. In another three hours . . .

Eldridge blew a fragrant cloud of smoke and closed his eyes. The present . . . that meant Margaret. He had never really known what life was until Margaret had taken him in hand. What luck—what stupendous luck —to be loved for himself alone, at forty-seven! He had found it at first rather difficult to believe, but at last he could have no doubt of it. She did not even know that he was rich, but thought of him as working hard in the City to make both ends meet. And he had been very careful not to undeceive her. That again was his romantic disposition. For a day would come, very soon now, when he would appear to her openly in the likeness of a fairy prince. He would walk into the little drawing-room at Eastrepps, and just outside the window she would catch a glimpse over his shoulder of the gleaming bonnet of a Rolls.

That would be when he had dealt with Withers.

Very firm about the lips, Eldridge pulled a paper from his despatch-case and read it carefully. An excellent report so far as it went. Harris was doing well—the best private inquiry agent he had been able to find. He hated to employ the fellow, but Withers had somehow to be caught, and unless it were done quickly Withers might be catching him. And that would never do. Margaret had made it clear that she could not allow herself to be divorced by Withers, for then she would lose Cynthia. Withers would take the child like a shot if he were allowed to pose as a husband wantonly deceived. How Margaret had ever come to marry the man he could not think. She had been caught young, of course . . . forced into it by her revolting family. Withers had once had money.

Eldridge returned to the paper he had taken from his case. "The party has been under continuous observation for the last fortnight," he read. "Yesterday he motored to Oxford and put up at the hotel where he is at present staying. He engaged a *suite* and continues to preserve an air of expectancy."

It really looked as though they would catch him at last. A fellow with any spark of decency would have let Margaret divorce him three years ago—when she had told him outright that she would never live with him again. But Withers was waiting to divorce Margaret. If only he knew how good a case he had! . . . But he would never know—not till it was too late for the knowledge to be of any use to him.

Eldridge nodded thoughtfully. He had managed things pretty well so far. Margaret had been his for six months now. She had given him everything—the essential Margaret she had never, he was sure, allowed another to see or know . . . everything, body and soul, heart and life . . . Margaret.

There was a smarting behind his eyes as he sat crumpling the paper in his right hand. There was only another person in the world she loved except himself. Cynthia was five now. Or was it six? Six it must be, though Margaret seemed absurdly young to have a girl of six. She couldn't be more than twenty-seven at the most. He would catch Withers at last, and then let the fellow look to himself! Margaret should have her divorce and Cynthia as well.

"I shall be ruthless," said Eldridge in a hoarse whisper.

"Ruthless," he repeated, and gazed round rather guiltily, as though there might be someone to hear him.

At that moment, indeed, the door slid back, and the conductor was asking for his ticket.

Eldridge produced the white cardboard slip. That, of course, was another precaution—no season ticket for him, even though he went to London regularly once a week. It was essential that he should not be too well known on the line, and he had done his best to avoid making friends with the railway officials.

Eldridge turned away his head and gazed out of the window as the man took his ticket, punched it and handed it back to him.

The door shut with a slight click, and Eldridge was himself again.

Undoubtedly it was unpleasant—all this mummery and creeping to and fro. But it would soon be over now. Margaret and he could then come out openly. And when they did come out they would make a splash. He had the money . . .

There again he had reason to be thankful to Margaret. But for her he would have been caught in the Wilmott crash a year ago. Margaret had a head on her shoulders. She had insisted that he should get out of that Elm

Investment Society of the Hosiery Trust, though she hadn't a notion how much he had put into it. And not a fortnight afterwards the whole thing had gone sky high. Fourteen years Wilmott had got for that—the most disgraceful fraud that had been perpetrated within living memory—so the judge had said.

Eldridge set his lips firmly together. Crash was an ugly word, and he knew something of crashes—no one better. But for God's providence he might himself have been in Wilmott's shoes . . .

Sixteen years ago . . . but he was not going to think of that, though it was sometimes hard—devilish hard— with so many people still alive who had good reason to remember—all the many hundreds, in fact, who might, he supposed, be described as his victims. He had meant, when he bolted, to pay them all back some day, but there had always been something that made it difficult, even impossible. He had never had quite enough money, for one thing; for what he spent on himself—and a man must live—would never be more than a drop in the ocean. And now it was too late. For what was the use of righting wrongs years afterwards, when they had all been forgotten?

Forgotten. . . . Now and then he might hear a reference to the matter. For his victims were everywhere —there were a score or more even in Eastrepps, persons he met every day, who little thought that the respectable Mr. Eldridge was the notorious Selby, of Anaconda Ltd. James Selby, lost for years in South America, no longer existed for the world—had covered his tracks so completely that no one could possibly suspect. Sixteen years in South America changed a man, and the most striking features of Selby—thick fair hair and a plenteous beard —had been tactfully obliterated by time and the razor. It was hard on a man to be almost completely bald at forty-seven, but in this case it had saved a world of trouble.

Eldridge looked at his watch. They would be serving dinner in half an hour. Meanwhile, he had that list of investments to check. Better get on with it at once.

He reached for the despatch-case lying beside him on the seat, opened it, and for the next half-hour was absorbed in a file of papers contained in a yellow jacket. He had checked the final figure just as the door slid open and the dining-car attendant announced that dinner was served.

Eldridge closed the despatch-case with a snap and, rising briskly, walked down the corridor to his solitary table in the dining-car. Mulligatawny soup, poached turbot, roast leg of lamb—the usual railway dinner. . . . Not so bad. He ate it steadily, and even had a second slice of lamb, for he was hungry. During the meal, as was his custom, he read from a book propped up against the cruet. Margaret was anxious—and Margaret was right—that he should improve himself. And he had not, so far, had much time for reading. His eye ran resolutely down the page:

> " 'Twill vex thy soul to hear what I shall speak;
> For I must talk of murders, rapes and massacres,
> Acts of black night, abominable deeds,
> Complots of mischief, treason, violence,
> Ruthful to hear, yet piteously performed."

That was Shakespeare—fine, of course, though a trifle morbid. But Margaret had said that he should read it, and he would read anything for Margaret.

He read steadily for three-quarters of an hour, and then returned to his compartment.

Thence he stared a trifle nervously from the window. The train was drawing into Norwich, and it was always possible that at Norwich, where it stopped, someone might enter. The critical moment approached, and it would never do for him to be spotted. That was why he had always to travel after dark, which was a bore in summer-time, especially with daylight saving, but it just could not be helped. And, in any case, it added to his great content when at last, all risks successfully encountered, he had reached his desire.

The train was moving less fast through the summer night. The swift express had changed into something almost a parliamentary, had stopped three times since Norwich, and now, at long last, was approaching Banton. Sometimes it stopped there, sometimes not; it depended on the passengers. The lights of the little station flashed into view. There was a grinding of brakes. The train slowed and came to a pause. Eldridge drew back a little from the window, keeping his eyes on the platform. Two dim figures descended from the train. That was young Lord Marsham and a friend going to the big house. Lucky dog! . . . had always had everything but money, and now he had married that, as befitted the sole legitimate heir of his wicked old father.

The train was again on the move. The sky was very dark, but cloudless—the moon not yet up, though it would be rising soon. Eldridge glanced at his gold watch . . . another two minutes. He moved away from the door, picked up his felt hat and set it firmly on his head. Then he buttoned his coat, took his gloves, stick and despatch-case, and returned to the window, his hand on the catch of the door. His mouth was a little dry and his heart beat a fraction faster than usual. He always felt like that, though it was really ridiculous. There was no danger, and even if anyone saw him they would only regard it as . . . peculiar.

At last. . . . There was a grinding of brakes, and the train abruptly slowed down.

Eldridge cautiously peered through the open window. The train had fallen almost to a walking pace, but he would wait until it stopped. Margaret was always insistent on that. She was afraid lest he should fall. Precious Margaret! . . . careful of him even in the least of things.

But already he could see the hedge—thick, good stout hollies, grown to withstand the strong sea winds straight from the Pole.

The train stopped with a faint jar which caused him to sway ever so slightly. He stood quite still a moment, and looked up and down the train to make sure that no one was watching. Then, quietly pressing down the catch, he pushed open the door, slipped out on to the step and down to the ballast beneath.

He closed the door carefully behind him, then sped into the shelter of the holly trees, scratching the back of his left hand slightly as he made his way through. Screened by the hedge, he crouched, till the train should pass, in a dry ditch, where some of the dead leaves of the previous autumn still lingered. Ten yards away the lights of the express gleamed like the fantastic scales of a fairy serpent. There came at last a faint whistle from the engine far ahead, followed by a grinding of wheels. The train was in motion.

Eldridge waited till the red lamp at the end was an Indian jewel on the bosom of the night. Then he brushed his knees and stepped out into the darkness. All was well. Once more the manœuvre had been successful. No one had seen him. Now, so far as the world knew, he was still in London. The train always stopped for a moment at that spot before moving backwards into the station at Eastrepps, which stood on a branch line aside from the main track. Always it stopped in the same place, just opposite the holly hedge. And next morning he would slip away from Margaret as quietly as he had slipped from the train, climb the station stairs punctually at 11:55, and so to the platform just as the first London train drew in, to deliver up his ticket in the usual way and walk out with the rest of the passengers. And nobody any the wiser.

Eldridge set out into the night, crossing the quiet summer fields wet with a heavy dew. He skirted an acre of waving corn, soon to turn yellow with the promise of a fine harvest, and so by a hedge, where nightingales sang in May, to a little lane down which he walked between festoons of old man's beard, nettles and deadly nightshade. Then he passed down a street, where no one was likely to recognise the respectable Mr. Eldridge—a street of workmen's dwellings. He paused a moment at the end. A lamp shone upon the heavy enamel plate which bore the name of the street—Sheffield Park. He read the name absently and passed on, turning abruptly to the right into Heath Road. The salt tang of the sea wind struck his nostrils. He paused a moment, and ran a silk handkerchief between his neck and collar, for he was hot, and he hated to enter the presence of Margaret anything but cool and collected. The sea was somewhere in front, scarcely half a mile away. Upon the dark, unharvested waters far out, as it seemed, hanging in the sky, shone the lights of a passing ship. A faint refreshing wind fanned his face.

Again he paused. Something stirred in him. This was beautiful, and Margaret was near. He strode off manfully to the right. There it was at last—a small cottage. How small for such a treasure! But he would change all that.

A faint light showed through a slit between the curtains of the ground-floor window. He raised a hand and tapped softly on the window-pane, then stood waiting in the outer darkness of the porch, looking towards the door of fumed oak which he could not see. His heart was beating high. Custom could not stale his great content.

There came the sound of a catch slipping back and the door swung open.

Robert Eldridge stepped forward.

"Margaret!" he said.

II

At half-past seven on July 16th, 1930—the day on which Mr. Eldridge travelled from Fenchurch Street, Miss Mary Hewitt sat down to dinner with her brother James. The stained oak table, set of six chairs and chiffonier with its glass front were wearing bravely, but were definitely not younger than their years. The room itself was pleasant enough, papered a soft brown, with three or four good sporting prints on the walls and a fine Shiraz, blue and pink, lying in front of the double window.

The windows looked upon a small garden which consisted mostly of lawn. The roses in the flower-beds, though carefully tended, wore a stricken look, for the house faced the sea, which could be heard from time to time mumbling the sandstone cliffs upon which the house was built. At the end of the garden ran a low hedge of tamarisks.

There was no wind that evening. Far away to the right, to be just seen if you craned your neck from the window, the sun was sinking to the grey waters. But the room was full of light, and above the low sound of the sea the single note of a church clock, half a mile away, striking the hour could just be heard.

Miss Hewitt and her brother took their places in silence, which remained unbroken until, abruptly, the serving hatch shot up with a bang and startled the Colonel, so that he dropped the ring of his napkin. His red face disappeared for a moment, while his old fingers scrabbled on the carpet. Just as he rose again above the table, a pair of hands grasping two plates over-full of soup were thrust into the room from the kitchen.

"Damn that girl!" said the Colonel.

His sister sighed, and delayed to answer her brother till the hatch had shut again with a second bang behind the plates.

"I beg you, James," she entreated, "not to make these scenes in front of the servants."

"Servants!" said the Colonel, as his sister rose and placed one of the plates in front of him. "One maid with dirty thumbs, and she can't even keep 'em out of the soup."

He glared fiercely at the squat bottle of colonial burgundy standing by his plate.

"If you go on like this, James," returned his sister quietly, "we shall have no maid at all. This is the third girl we have had since Easter."

"When I was at Jullundur," said the Colonel, "I had fourteen servants—fourteen! . . . and they gave less trouble in a year than this one does in a week."

"But we are not at Jullundur," said his sister.

Silence fell for a moment. Miss Hewitt again rose from the table to take away her brother's plate. She moved quietly to the service hatch, lifted it and pushed the plates through into the kitchen.

"Wine?" asked the Colonel, laying hold of the bottle.

"No, thank you, James," replied his sister.

"Sorry, m'm," came a voice from the hatch, "but I've had a bit of trouble with the fish. I don't seem to get the hang of this 'ere stove."

"That will be all right," said Miss Hewitt nervously.

"Then it will be the cold meat, m'm?"

"Yes, Deborah, the cold meat."

"I am sorry, James," said Miss Hewitt, turning to her brother. "I suppose you heard . . ."

"Yes, Mary, I heard."

The Colonel's face had assumed a terrible expression, but his sister did not blench. She realised that he was only trying to smile.

"I heard," continued the Colonel, "and I was glad to hear. I am getting rather tired of cotton wool with pins in it."

His voice died away in a rumble.

The hatch opened again, and Miss Hewitt, taking the dish upon which reposed the remains of a sirloin, placed it in front of the Colonel. She then went to the sideboard, and, taking a dish of cold beetroot, put it beside the meat.

"Under-done," said the Colonel, waving the carvers. "I'm glad she does not over-cook the meat. Did you hear that, Maria? You can tell her, with my compliments, that she does not over-cook the meat."

He passed a plate of red beef to his sister.

"Chutney," continued the Colonel. "Where's the chutney?"

"*Must* you, James? You know what the doctor said."

"Damn the doctor!" said the Colonel, but without heat, for he always damned the doctor as inevitably as he damned the dentist, all trades-people, the secretary of the golf club, the War Office and, above all, the Pensions Department.

Miss Hewitt had returned to her place.

"That confounded Sawbones isn't going to cut out the chutney," he said, getting heavily to his feet and moving to the sideboard.

He returned in triumph bearing a dark glass jar, from which he helped himself with a liberal hand.

The Colonel, after two helpings of beef, began to feel better. Now and then he looked resentfully but not unkindly at his sister. She was silent this evening, even more silent than usual. Poor Mary! he reflected, never very bright at the best of times; ought to have married long ago; not a bad-looking girl in her day; and it was confounded hard luck that she should have wasted the best years of her life waiting for that missionary fellow. The Boxers had chopped him up in '02.

The Colonel, to cheer his sister, started to tell her about the putt he had missed on the thirteenth green. For that he must blame the Secretary. The grass had been cut only that morning, and the green was therefore much faster than usual. But no one had informed him of the fact, though he had taken a drink with the Secretary, just before teeing up.

Miss Hewitt did her best to listen, but her mind was far away, reviewing a life that had failed to offer her very much. Partly, as she secretly admitted, it was her own fault; but that did not make it any the easier. She should never, for example, have agreed to keep house for James. James was not really a bad sort, but after thirty years in India—well, what could you expect? Then there had been that unlucky investment of her small fortune in Anaconda Ltd. What had possessed her, a spinster of independent means, with five thousand pounds soundly and safely invested, to take such a terrible risk? But people did these things. Hundreds had done it in this particular case. Why, there were half a dozen she knew of in Eastrepps itself, small though the place was. The Selby crash . . . it was still a theme for the gossips.

"Mary," said the Colonel suddenly, "you haven't heard a word of what I was saying."

Her apology was cut short by a further raising of the hatch. Again Miss Hewitt rose from her seat, to receive and bring to the table a white cornflour blancmange islanded in a dish of stewed prunes. There was also a letter addressed to the Colonel. It lay on the tray beside the sweets in a buff-coloured envelope and inscribed as on His Majesty's Service.

"Sorry, m'm," came the voice of Deborah from the far side of the hatch. "There's a letter for the master. It came by the afternoon post."

Miss Hewitt laid the dish of prunes on the table.

"I had it out afterwards with the Secretary," continued the Colonel. " 'When the grass is cut,' I said, 'the members ought to be warned.' The fellow was inclined to be impertinent, but there you are—no consideration for old residents, while the young entries are coddled —positively coddled. That fellow Longstaffe, for instance—just because he can hit a ball with that unsporting steel shaft of his further than . . ."

"There is a letter for you, James," broke in Miss Hewitt.

"A letter?" said the Colonel. "Then why the deuce did I not get it before?"

He pushed his plate from him as he spoke and began fumbling for his eyeglasses, which he eventually clipped to his nose.

"A cockatoo," thought his sister. "I knew he reminded me of something."

One day she would put him in a book—that was her secret ambition.

Meanwhile the Colonel, reading his letter, had flushed an even deeper red than was normal.

"The sharks!" he burst out suddenly—"the sharks!"

Miss Hewitt, very pale, shrank back in her chair. She knew the symptoms. James was going to swear.

James swore, using an epithet which brought his sister to her feet, trembling but undaunted.

"James," she said, "I cannot permit such language in my presence. I must ask you to apologise."

"But look at this," roared the Colonel, thrusting the letter across the table. "Do you think we can live on air? Five pounds seven and tenpence deducted at source."

But Miss Hewitt had bent forward across the table, her face in her hands, creaking rhythmically with every sob that escaped from between her fingers. The Colonel paused a moment, then shambled round the table and laid a hand on her shoulder.

"Mary," he said.

But Miss Hewitt was too far gone to be comforted.

"Old girl," said the Colonel, "it's no use crying about it. Shan't be able to pay old Sawbones this month, that's all, and I'm afraid you will have to go without a new hat. We must . . . er . . . just face these things together, that's what we must do, face 'em together."

Miss Hewitt dabbed her eyes with her napkin. The Colonel wore a solemn look.

"All right, James," she said. "Won't you go back and finish your dinner?"

The Colonel stood looking at her a moment, then shook his head with decision.

"No," he answered. "The fact of the matter is I . . . er . . . don't feel quite up to the mark—confounded headache and all that. I'll just toddle off to bed, that's what I'll do."

He sneezed prodigiously; the mould quivered in its dish.

"A little hot toddy," he muttered, "and ten grains of aspirin. And I'll take my chota hazri at nine to-morrow."

He moved to the door as he spoke.

When he had left the room, Miss Hewitt pushed up the service hatch once more and ordered Deborah to prepare some hot water for the toddy. Then she wandered out into the little hall and stood a moment gazing through the glass doors which led to a small verandah on the further side of the house. The flowers in this part of the garden were protected from the fierce east winds. The dahlias were coming on nicely, and there would be quite a respectable show of hollyhocks. Miss Hewitt loved flowers and gardening, but, alas! they took up time and money.

She stood awhile, and then, taking a pair of garden scissors, went to cut some of the lilies under the drawing-room window. She grew them especially for the parish church, and always took them on Wednesday evening herself to the vestry.

Miss Hewitt, as she cut the flowers, could hear the Colonel in his room. The bed creaked suddenly under his weight. He was saying good-night to his cat Adolphus, of whom he was very fond.

It would be peaceful in the church, and thence she would go, as her custom was, to see her friend, Mrs. Dampier, on the way home by the cliff. Mrs. Dampier had a really beautiful garden . . . no such roses as hers in Eastrepps, and there was that lovely corner with the sundial where all the flowers were blue—delphiniums, lupins, campanulas, and strange exotic pansies affronting the flagged path.

Miss Hewitt picked up an old straw hat from a peg in the hall, pulled it over her greying hair, and started down the garden path to the gate. There she turned to the right and walked along a narrow lane. The Colonel's house was one of a number of small villas built along the edge of the cliff to the southeast of the golf club. A quarter of a mile behind her stood the lighthouse. Already its revolving lantern was showing fitfully against the dying sky and the first pale stars.

Miss Hewitt took her way down the path. If only she had kept her money safe . . . two hundred a year . . . a small hotel in Florence, the Lakes in summer. One could live on two hundred a year in Italy, even after the War, if one was careful. But it had all gone, every penny of it. . . . And Selby had never even been caught.

Half an hour later, Miss Hewitt, her errand accomplished, stood at the door of Tamarisk House, to be shown by a trim maid into the drawing-room. She was fond of Mrs. Dampier, but it was difficult, very difficult, not to envy her friend. Soft Persian carpets on the floor, old furniture, perfect of its kind, a black-and-gold lacquer Chinese cabinet in one corner, shaded lights on the walls —all these whispered discreetly of taste, money and security.

Mrs. Dampier was speaking. She was short, and wore horn-rimmed spectacles, amber in colour, and her skin was as fresh and clear in her sixtieth year as it had been when she was twenty. Mrs. Dampier was a character in Eastrepps, especially after her Homeric battle

with the local electric company. She had stirred the
apathetic Town Council to such good purpose that on
their appeal twopence had been taken off the price per
unit of electricity for all consumers, and for that she had
received a vote of thanks. Even Councillor Thompson,
who held shares in the electric light company, had been
forced to join in the tribute.

"You are looking tired, my dear," said Mrs. Dam-
piers. "Let us go into the garden."

She led the way out of the drawing-room along a tiled
passage to the back door.

Miss Hewitt stood by the margin of a square stone
pond. Again she felt that little pang. The old friend at
her side had not meant it, of course, but rich people were
like that. They took a pleasure in the things they owned,
and naturally liked to exhibit them. They could hardly
be expected to realise that to those who were less fortunate . . . But such thoughts were unworthy. And
yet this pond with the gold-fish and its rare plants must
have cost at least a hundred pounds. What could one
not do with a hundred pounds?

"Alisma or water plantain," Mrs. Dampier was saying.
"And here is the ladyfern. The water-lilies, of course,
will be a little difficult. One can only grow the smaller
kinds, such as the *Nymphœa odorata* or the *Rosacea
sulphurea*. I have to grow them in baskets of soil sunk
in the water."

Mrs. Dampier bent over the paved edges of the pond
planted with campanulas and saxifrages and touched with
a gesture of affection, almost such as would be used to a
child, a lovely specimen of the iris *Kœmpferi*.

"Of course," she said, "it will be two years, if not
three, before this water-garden will look really nice."

"But your roses," said Miss Hewitt.

They turned the corner of the house, and Miss Hewitt
looked across the lawn to a great bank whence a tide
of fragrance was poured from a thousand blossoms.

"Yes," said Mrs. Dampier. "My brother George pruned them in the spring when he was staying with me. He's a great gardener, you know, and they really are a success this year."

"Exquisite," said Miss Hewitt softly, every trace of envy smoothed from her mind.

They walked slowly about the garden paths talking of small matters or no matter at all.

The garden was quite dark now. A bat twittered across the lawn.

"Shall we go in?" said Mrs. Dampier.

"Why," said Miss Hewitt, "it is already ten o'clock."

"But you will stay a moment, won't you?" urged Mrs. Dampier. "You must take a glass of sherry or some orange water?"

Miss Hewitt shook her head.

"It's very kind of you, but I really must be getting home. I have to go into Norwich to-morrow by the early train. Don't trouble to see me through the house. I can leave by the garden gate."

Together they walked beyond the rose-garden to a gate set in the oaken palisade.

Miss Hewitt pulled open the gate and passed through it.

"I think your lock is broken, isn't it?" she asked.

Mrs. Dampier examined the lock.

"I must see about having it mended," she said. "I keep it locked, you know, in case anyone should want to pick my roses."

Miss Hewitt lingered a moment by the gate. She was feeling at peace once more, and turned, upon a grateful impulse, to her friend.

"Good night," she said. "It is kind of you to put up with me. I shall sleep to-night. It's this lovely garden and the flowers. They set the mind at rest."

Mrs. Dampier pressed the thin arm of Miss Hewitt affectionately.

"Good night, my dear," she replied. "It is nice of you to come. I look forward to our Wednesday evenings."

Miss Hewitt set her face to the cliff and began to walk home. She felt strangely comforted. Those roses, shining with a thousand faces . . .

She turned into the narrow lane. Soon she would be passing the bungalows. But first she had to go through Coatt's Spinney, the little wood of stunted oak trees, the unpleasant little wood. Some day it would drop into the sea, and already half the trees had been strangled by the cruel winds that swept down upon them from the north. It had been there, they said, a derelict of the land, for over a hundred years. She always felt that if, as the fishermen believed, the ghost of Eric the Red, who had harried the town in the days of Alfred, were in the habit of revisiting the scene of his ancient exploits, it was there he would walk. Usually she would hasten through it uneasily, for the trees after sunset were hardly natural. To-night, however, she didn't notice them. Her mind was full of the roses.

She did not see the shadow that moved among the trees, or hear the soft footfalls behind her.

In the middle of the wood she paused a moment. Through a gap in the twisted branches of the oaks were the sea and the first beginnings of the moon. Moonlight on rose petals—the vision flooded her mind with peace.

At that moment the blow fell. She felt nothing. But the vision was blotted out, and she lay on the ground motionless.

III

Adolphus was later than usual. He would always stay by the house till he knew that nothing further was to be expected. His master, the Colonel, was asleep, but his mistress had not yet returned, and when she came back there might be a last saucer of milk, if he were sufficiently importunate.

Adolphus had the patience of his kind, but the night was promising. The big tortoiseshell next door was already abroad; he felt it in his bones, and he was determined that to-night his affair of the previous day with that interloper should be fought to a finish. None but the brave deserved the fair, and Adolphus was the bravest cat of his acquaintance.

It was nearly eleven o'clock before he reached the little wood on the cliff—the scene of his exploits.

But there he came upon a form that he knew. For a moment he paused beside it. There was something wrong. His mistress was no longer the same. He stepped delicately to one side. Adolphus was a dainty cat, and did not wish to soil his paws.

CHAPTER TWO

I

INSPECTOR PROTHEROE—officially Station-Sergeant Protheroe, but, as there was also a section-sergeant at Eastrepps, he felt that he might justifiably adopt the more impressive title—entered the police station at nine o'clock on the morning of the 17th July, and hung his cap on the accustomed peg. He was a large man in the early forties. His face, adorned, as he considered, by a black moustache of the toothbrush variety, had no striking characteristics, except perhaps for a twisted wrinkle between the eyes only noticeable when he was put out in any way—in other words, rather frequently.

The office chair creaked protestingly as he bent to his desk and began to deal with a small pile of correspondence in the tray.

The first two letters he glanced at briefly and laid aside; the third claimed his closer attention. He ran his fingers through the short hair which was just beginning to recede from his forehead and read it again with pursed lips.

The door opened as he set it down.

"At last," said Inspector Protheroe, the twisted wrinkle parading for business between his heavy brows.

The person addressed was Section-Sergeant Ruddock, who now stood in the doorway, helmet in hand.

"Sorry, sir," he answered, moving as he spoke to his desk in the corner of the room.

"Sorry!" echoed the Inspector. "You are nearly ten minutes late, and it is your business to be here on time. You know that perfectly well."

29

Inspector Protheroe looked resentfully at his Sergeant. Why couldn't the fellow say something instead of standing there as though butter wouldn't melt in his mouth? Ruddock was like that. He never answered back, but just stood as he was standing now, as though he were waiting for you to add something rather better than usual.

"Well," said the Inspector, "have you nothing to say?"

Sergeant Ruddock blinked at his superior. He was a reddish, wiry man of middle height, and his complexion, rosy and transparent as that of a schoolboy, was absurd.

"I am sorry, sir," he repeated.

"Then perhaps you would kindly get on with your work."

"Certainly, sir. Anything in particular?"

There was nothing in particular, and Inspector Protheroe registered the fact as a further grievance against his subordinate.

"Have you," he asked accusingly, fixing his Sergeant with what he intended to be a commanding gaze, "looked into that little matter of the summons to be served on Richard Prescott?"

"I have," said the Sergeant. "I called at his house in Sheffield Park only last night. Prescott has gone away, and Mrs. Prescott does not know when he will be back"

"I want that summons delivered," said the Inspector. "You'd better call again this morning when you leave the station."

"Very good, sir," responded Sergeant Ruddock.

Again the Inspector looked resentfully at his Sergeant. Ruddock was too respectful by half. Was it possible that sarcasm was intended?

Ruddock was standing at his elbow.

"My daily report, sir."

"Thank you, Ruddock. Perhaps you will draft now an answer to these letters. Nothing of importance.

They are giving us six extra men for the summer season, and I suppose we shall have to take it lying down. With all the visitors swarming into the town, there will be work for at least a dozen. Then there's that affair of Jenkinson's dog. The woman wants to prosecute; swears that he frightened the bird off laying for the season. There are one or two other small matters. See to them, Ruddock. I must keep myself for the big case."

"The big case?" echoed Ruddock.

"The poaching on Sir Jefferson Cobb's preserves."

"Of course," said Ruddock—"the big case."

The Inspector flushed. There could be no doubt of it now. This was undoubtedly sarcasm.

"The big case," he repeated stubbornly. "Sir Jefferson Cobb, let me tell you, has written to me again this morning on the subject. An arrest will have to be made."

"Perhaps you have somebody in mind, sir," said Ruddock encouragingly.

"I have at least half a dozen persons in mind," snapped the Inspector. "Unfortunately, Ruddock, the magistrates will require evidence. Yes, Ruddock, you may not be aware of it, but magistrates require evidence."

The Inspector sat back. He, too, could be sarcastic when the occasion called.

Ruddock picked up the letters from the Inspector's desk and moved towards his own small table opposite. At that moment, however, the telephone, screwed to the wall, rang out harshly. Ruddock, at a sign from the Inspector, unhooked the receiver.

"Yes," he said. "This is Eastrepps Police Station. Sergeant Ruddock speaking. . . . One moment, I cannot hear you very well . . . not quite so loud, if you please."

Ruddock listened a moment, and turned to the Inspector.

"It's Colonel Hewitt speaking. He is asking for you, sir. Case of murder."

"What?" almost shouted the Inspector.

"Murder," repeated Ruddock quietly.

But the Inspector was half-way across the room. He snatched the receiver from his subordinate.

"Hullo! . . . hullo!"

Sergeant Ruddock moved respectfully to one side. The Inspector was obliged to hold the receiver at some distance from his ear. The Colonel's disjointed words, a series of metallic barkings, filled the room.

"Damn it, sir, don't echo me! . . . Murder was what I said. . . . Come to my house at once, 'The Hollies,' West Cliff. . . . It's on your way, and I'll take you straight to the spot. . . . No . . . nothing has been touched."

The Inspector turned to Sergeant Ruddock. His eyes were shining.

"Ruddock," he said with false calm, "tell Williams and Birchington to be ready to accompany me immediately. You will remain here at the station."

"Remain here, sir?" said Ruddock, who had already reached for his helmet.

"That is what I said," snapped the Inspector. "You will look after the office in my absence. . . . Business as usual, Ruddock."

Ruddock looked at the Inspector as though he would protest, but, thinking better of it, fell into his usual attitude of deference.

"And the big case?" he asked.

"See to it, Ruddock, see to it," said the Inspector generously. "I shall have no time for it now."

II

That same morning at ten o'clock Mrs. Dampier stepped from her garden gate. She was rarely earlier than ten-thirty. There were so many little things to be seen and decided upon before she left the house. On the other hand, she was rarely later, because it was advisable to do one's shopping before the buyers became too thick upon the ground.

It was a cool day, and the faintest of mists was hanging above the sea. But that would be gone in an hour.

Mrs. Dampier walked briskly along, mentally running over the list of things she must buy. Her daughter, with a husband and three children, would be arriving next month. It would be necessary to lay in stores.

Mrs. Dampier liked to fill her house in the summer. An empty house in a town that in July and August was packed with pleasant folk—for Eastrepps was fairly lucky in its visitors—was obviously incongruous. It seemed hardly decent to have four or five empty bedrooms when quite nice people were glad to secure an attic in the by-streets.

She stopped first at a nursery garden on the left of the road beyond the meadow. There was no doubt in her mind that Mr. Hulton's tomatoes were the best she had ever known—larger and better grown, she privately considered, than those of Sir Jefferson Cobb. They had more juice and less pith than Sir Jefferson's, and the skins were fine as silk.

Leaving the nursery, Mrs. Dampier shortly turned a corner, and found herself in the narrow Norwich Road, which became Church Street in a hundred yards, without, however, becoming any wider. It was bordered on each side by red-brick villas, the ground floors of which were shops or offices. A little further on, to the right, was a large garage, where the charabancs stood, half in and half out of the yard. Several cars were slipping, one by one, like beads on a string, round the huge bulk of the Eastrepps to Mundesley motor omnibus.

Mrs. Dampier gazed resentfully at the passing cars. She could remember the time when Eastrepps had still been a fishing village, with its flint-faced church, in all the severity of Perpendicular, standing in a little God's acre set about by Regency houses of stucco. The town

had grown out of knowledge during the last thirty years
—not as much as other East Coast places, but quickly
enough to annoy the older residents. And this, of course,
was the height of the season. Young men in blazers and
grey flannels, accompanied by young women in white
pleated skirts and brilliant jumpers, swarmed in the
streets and on the sands.

Mrs. Dampier, passing the police station, was surprised to see a small crowd of people at the entrance talking eagerly among themselves, and a moment later she
was still more surprised to see two constables emerge
abruptly from the door, push their way through the
crowd, jump on two bicycles standing by the pavement,
and pedal off very forcibly in the direction of West Cliff.
One of them had even forgotten his helmet.

The crowd, struck silent by their abrupt appearance,
broke again into active chatter, as their departing backs
swept round the corner.

For a moment Mrs. Dampier was tempted to ask what
had happened, but then thought better of it, and crossed
the road, looking carefully to right and left to avoid the
traffic. The pavement on the other side was less crowded.
There were no shops here, only the low wall of the
ancient churchyard with the great church beyond.

"Good morning, Laura," said Mrs. Dampier.

The greeting was addressed to Mrs. Cappell, with whom
she had almost collided beside the wall. Mrs. Cappell
was well enough known in Eastrepps to disregard the
fashions. Her large hat was, as usual, secured on her
head by a white veil tied under the chin. She was slim,
with long hands and pale blue eyes. To the surprise of
Mrs. Dampier, she paid no attention. She was standing
by the churchyard looking towards the porch, and her
kindly face, which had once been beautiful, was white
and strained. Mrs. Dampier realised that something had
happened, but before she could add to her greeting, a
thick-set man with a greying beard came briskly along

the walk, accompanied by a tall girl with yellow hair. They were Captain Porter, Secretary of the Golf Club, and Miss Richards, the pride of the town. She had a handicap of four, had always done well in the Ladies Open, and one day, it was hoped, would win it.

"How perfectly appalling!" Miss Richards was saying.

Laura Cappell turned her head sharply at the words.

"Good morning, Captain Porter," she said. "Then . . . then it is true?"

Mrs. Cappell had placed a gloved hand on the Captain's sleeve. To the further astonishment of Mrs. Dampier, there were tears in her eyes.

"My dear," said Mrs. Dampier, "what is it all about?"

"You haven't heard?" exclaimed Miss Richards.

"I have heard nothing," said Mrs. Dampier. "What is it, Captain Porter?"

"Miss Hewitt was found this morning in Coatt's Spinney," said Captain Porter gravely.

"Found?" echoed Mrs. Dampier.

"Our poor friend was dead," said the Captain gently.

"Murdered," added Miss Richards.

Mrs. Dampier stepped backwards, and felt the rough wall of the churchyard behind her. That was just as well, for it gave support.

"Murdered," she said swiftly, scarcely realising. "But . . . but Miss Hewitt was talking to me in my garden only last night."

"Then you were probably the last person to see her alive," said the Captain.

"She came to see me at about nine o'clock as usual on Wednesdays," continued Mrs. Dampier. "We walked about for an hour. I was showing her my new water-garden. I can't believe it. She could not have had an enemy in the world."

"I am afraid there is no doubt about it," said the Captain sadly. "She was found nearly two hours ago by her brother."

"How . . . horrible!" said Mrs. Dampier.

"It must have happened when she was on her way home from you," suggested Miss Richards. "She would pass through the spinney."

There came a loud sob from Mrs. Cappell. Captain Porter put a fatherly hand on her shoulder.

"Dreadful, my dear lady, dreadful!" he said. "But we must not give way."

"But who on earth would want to murder her?" persisted Mrs. Dampier.

"Not for her money, anyhow," said the Captain.

"How . . . how was it done?" asked Mrs. Dampier. She spoke almost against her will, sincerely grieved, but fascinated by the dreadful news.

"We have heard no details," said Captain Porter. "I thought of going up to see if I could help the Colonel at all. He must be terribly cut up. The worst of it is . . . we are not . . . we had . . . well, we didn't . . ."

"The fact is you had a bit of a scene with him at the Club yesterday, didn't you?" said Miss Richards.

"The usual scene," admitted the Captain. "The Colonel is a little difficult at times. Still, that has nothing to do with it."

"Then nobody knows how it happened?" said Mrs. Dampier.

"Begging your pardon, m'm."

A large red-faced woman had paused on the fringe of the little group. All turned with one accord.

Mrs. Applethwaite, wife of the largest grocer in Eastrepps, was obviously full of news.

"Stabbed, poor lady," she said slowly—"through the right temple it was, just above the ear. Nobody knows who did it, and if Inspector Protheroe is on the job, nobody ever will."

Mrs. Applethwaite had a notorious contempt for the local police, not unconnected perhaps with the fact that her husband had once had some slight unpleasantness with them over a matter of alleged short weight. The incident had ended with his appearance in the police court, where the justice of his cause had been triumphantly vindicated.

Captain Porter glanced uneasily at Mrs. Cappell, for Mrs. Applethwaite had not spared the feelings of her audience. Mrs. Cappell, however, had dried her eyes and there was a faint flush on her cheeks.

"Whoever it may be," she said stoutly, "I hope will be caught . . . and hanged."

There was a step on the pavement behind them. The Rev. Mr. Beelby, Vicar of Eastrepps, was coming towards the group. It opened to make way for him.

"Captain Porter," he said, bowing gravely to the ladies as he passed, "you are the very man I want. I thought of going up to 'The Hollies' to see what I could do. Perhaps you would be so kind as to come with me. This is a grievous thing. We must help all we can."

Mrs. Dampier had scarcely heard the Vicar's words. Now that the first shock had passed, she was beginning to think. Had anyone followed Mary Hewitt last night when she had left the garden? She felt sure that she had seen no one. But it had been quite dark, and her eyes were not of the best.

The Vicar and Captain Porter moved towards a two-seater which stood a little further along by the kerb.

"Is there anything we can do?"

It was Mrs. Withers who spoke. She had come upon the group as it was breaking up. Mrs. Dampier looked at her with approval. She liked Mrs. Withers, who was quiet and kind, and, as she understood, unhappily married. Also she was charming to look at—with her blue eyes and yellow hair, and Mrs. Dampier had a weakness for beauty, whether in children, women or flowers.

"I'm afraid not, Mrs. Withers—not, at least, for the moment."

They were startled by a loud laugh, which caused

all the four ladies to look round. A tall young man, dark, thin, with a weak chin and lank hair, had come suddenly among them. He was wearing a grey flannel suit. There was a rose in his buttonhole, and he exuded a scent of violets.

"Murder," he said, "murder. That will wake us all up a bit, won't it? Put some life into the place."

There was a horrified silence.

"Really, Mr. Rockingham," said Miss Richards. "I hardly think . . ."

"I don't know what you think," said the young man. "But I know what I think. . . . Everybody pleased as Punch. . . . Newspapers will be full of it. . . . We shall all be lapping it up . . . lapping it up."

"It must have been very dark in the wood," he added —"very dark and very quiet."

"Now then, sir, we must be getting along, if you don't mind."

A shortish man, wearing a black double-breasted suit, had come up and laid his hand on the elbow of Mr. Rockingham. "Otherwise we shall be late for lunch."

"Lunch, Higgins?" said the young man, eagerly. "Is it as late as that?"

"Yes, sir, in twenty minutes, sir."

The young man turned to the ladies with a bright smile.

"A man must eat, you know," he explained.

He swept off his hat, bowed and walked away, with Higgins at his side.

"Really," said Mrs. Cappell.

"Who is he?" inquired Mrs. Withers.

"That," said Mrs. Cappell, "is the Hon. Alistair Rockingham. He has been sent down here . . . for his health."

"They ought to have sent him to a home," said Mrs. Dampier. "These degenerates are really most unpleasant."

The three ladies looked distastefully after the retreating figure of the heir of the Rockinghams.

III

Christopher Bennett, Coroner for Eastrepps, was seated at his office table in Church Street, a thin little man with greying hair and pendulous cheeks which gave him a very odd appearance, owing to the slightness of his body. But a man is as large as he feels, and Mr. Bennett was being called upon as Coroner to inquire into the strange circumstances surrounding the death of Miss Mary Hewitt.

Bennett, moreover, had scored politically by the manner of this event. The poor lady had met her death in Coatt's Spinney. For years past he had been urging the Town Council to cut down those unsightly trees, and to construct in place of them a pleasant asphalt walk running all along West Cliff, where visitors might stroll of a summer's evening and admire the sea. But the opposition, led by representatives of the older residents, had been hitherto too strong for them. And now a murder had been committed in that very spot, and no one could really maintain that it was to the interest of the town that murders should be committed almost within sight of the pier. Miss Hewitt, too—so respectable a lady, sister of Colonel Hewitt. The thing had made quite a stir. There would, he believed, be representatives of the Press at the inquest, not only the local but the London Press. His directions to the jury would be reported in the *Daily Leader,* even perhaps in *The Times.*

Decidedly this was an event. His occasional inquests upon the bodies of drowned fishermen washed ashore during the great equinoxial gales were seldom noticed, except of course in the *Norwich Gazette,* and only once had the *East Anglian Record* so much as mentioned his name. But this was murder—not only murder, but mysterious and unaccountable murder The police were all at sea. Inspector Protheroe might look as knowing as he pleased, but obviously he was baffled. And now they were coming to consult him. That meant, very probably, that they wanted to manage the inquest in their own way . . . conceal the facts . . . cover up their own incompetence.

Bennett frowned heavily. He must be on his guard. He was not going to allow himself to be led by the nose. In the interests of justice, of course, he was prepared to make concessions. But he must be satisfied that they were necessary. Also there were other interests—the interests of the public, who had a right to efficient protection of life and limb in return for their rates; the interests of his ancient calling; the interests, even, of truth.

But here they were. Bennett pushed back his chair and rose, as the door of his office opened to admit Sir Jefferson Cobb, Chief Constable of the County, closely followed by Inspector Protheroe and Dr. Simms.

"Good morning, Bennett."

Sir Jefferson himself was speaking—very affably, too, for so distinguished a man.

Bennett bowed his appreciation.

"Good morning, Sir Jefferson. Won't you take the armchair?"

"Thanks."

Sir Jefferson sat down. He then produced a leather case, which he tendered with a rapid circular sweep of his large hand to the company in general, but, before anyone could have time to accept or refuse what was offered, he selected a cigar for himself and proceeded to light it.

"Sorry you don't smoke, Bennett," he said.

The Inspector and the doctor were accommodated with two office chairs, very hard and upright. The cigar smelled good, and Bennett wished he had been quicker at the uptake.

There was a moment's silence.

Sir Jefferson Cobb blew a cloud of smoke and looked genially round the little circle.

"And now to business," he said.

All four gentlemen gazed at each other, but no one seemed inclined to begin.

Bennett cleared his throat.

"Well," he hazarded at last, "what can I do for you?"

"About this inquest, Bennett," said Sir Jefferson.

"Yes, Sir Jefferson?" said Bennett deferentially. "I have fixed it for to-morrow at ten o'clock, and I have ventured to take the Parish Hall. I understand that the Press . . ."

He broke off.

"The Press," put in Inspector Protheroe, "will certainly be there."

Bennett detected an absence of enthusiasm in the Inspector, which was strange, for surely this really was a fine chance for a capable man—very different from the small poaching cases and brawls between fishermen with which the Inspector was normally concerned. Nevertheless, there was a worried wrinkle between his eyes.

"It is just as I thought," Bennett told himself—"the Inspector is at fault, and he will want to save his face."

Dr. Simms sat silent, his silk hat on the table beside him. He was ready to say a word in season; but, meanwhile, as so often, allowed his appearance to speak on his behalf. This morning, as ever, he affronted the day complete with silk hat, morning coat, spats and a buttonhole.

"Of course . . . the Parish Hall," Sir Jefferson was saying. "Very right and proper. The case has naturally excited a good deal of local interest, and the question which we have very seriously to consider to-day is whether that interest is not, perhaps . . . er . . . excessive. We are anxious, in fact, that it should not . . . er . . . extend."

"Most undesirable," said the Inspector.

"In other words," ventured Bennett, "you wish the inquest to be conducted on purely formal lines."

"Quite," said the Inspector. "I think, Mr. Coroner, that, at this early stage, if you don't mind . . ."

"On the other hand," said Bennett, "you will realise, I am sure, that I have my duties to perform. Such evidence as may be forthcoming . . ."

"Exactly," said Sir Jefferson.

"Then what exactly do you propose, gentlemen?" Bennett inquired.

The Inspector cleared his throat.

"For the moment," he said, "there is no material evidence. There are certain peculiar features of the case which will have to be investigated. Meanwhile, we think that public attention should not be drawn to them. More particularly the medical facts should not, in our view, be unduly emphasised. We do not, therefore, propose that Dr. Simms should be pressed for details, and we venture to suggest that the other witnesses should not be . . . er . . . encouraged."

Bennett looked from one to the other of his visitors.

"I am naturally anxious in no way to embarrass your inquiries, Inspector," he said at last. "But I must ask you to be frank with me."

"Certainly, Bennett."

Sir Jefferson Cobb was speaking.

"You have alluded to peculiar features," continued Bennett.

Sir Jefferson turned to the doctor.

"Simms," he said, "perhaps you would acquaint Mr. Bennett with the results of your examination."

"Miss Hewitt," said the doctor, "was stabbed through the right temple just above the ear. I found that the weapon had pierced the temporal bone. The wound was apparently inflicted by means of a knife, the blade being driven straight through in a backward direction to a depth of some five inches. Now that, Mr. Coroner, is in itself peculiar. It indicates that the murderer, whoever he was, must have been of an uncommonly powerful physique. It would also seem that he must have held Miss Hewitt closely in his left arm and driven home the knife with his right hand. Do I make myself clear?"

"I don't yet see how exactly it was done," said Bennett doubtfully.

"It's quite simple," said the doctor, rising from his chair. "Inspector Protheroe is the victim. I put my arm round his shoulder. I raise my right hand so, and I drive home the blade of the knife above the right ear, the point being directed towards the back of the head."

The doctor brought down his hand and struck the Inspector lightly as he spoke.

"It is difficult to imagine," he continued, "how all this could have happened without Miss Hewitt becoming aware of the murderer. Yet there is no sign of any struggle—just a clean wound. It could hardly have been inflicted by surprise, and yet the victim apparently made no resistance."

"The presumption in that case," said Bennett, "is that Miss Hewitt was talking to the man, and that she was acquainted with him?"

"That would seem not altogether improbable," said Sir Jefferson.

"And you do not desire this inference to be pointed at in the evidence?" pursued Bennett.

"Precisely," said the Inspector.

"Is there no other evidence available?" asked Bennett.

"Nothing definite," admitted the Inspector. "No footprints were discovered. The tragedy took place well in the middle of the spinney, and there were a good many leaves left over from last year. They had been carefully raked all round the body."

"Raked?" said the Coroner.

"Scattered," said the Inspector. "They lay pretty

evenly from where Miss Hewitt was found to the asphalt path, which runs, as you remember, sir, as far as the outskirts of the wood."

"No other evidence?" inquired Bennett.

"We have, of course, inquired into the family history of Miss Hewitt," said the Inspector, "and into that of her brother. It does not seem, however, that they had any enemies."

"In other words, Protheroe," said the Chief Constable, "you are for the moment at a loss."

"For the moment, sir," admitted the Inspector.

Sir Jefferson Cobb turned to the Coroner.

"You will realise, Bennett, that in the circumstances . . ."

"Quite," said the Coroner.

"It seems to me," continued Sir Jefferson, "that the wisest course will be to adjourn the inquest after formal evidence of death. Colonel Hewitt will, of course, expect to be heard. Then I suggest that you adjourn for a fortnight."

There was silence.

"I am in your hands, gentlemen," said the Coroner at last.

That, after all, was not so bad—an obviously perfunctory inquest, adjourned for further inquiries, would give time for the public interest to be thoroughly aroused. Bennett saw himself involved in a long and interesting case.

"Yes, by all means," he added heartily.

IV

William Ferris, correspondent of the *Daily Wire*, was on a holiday—his annual holiday with Mrs. Ferris and the children. He had chosen Eastrepps out of many other seaside places because it was small, quiet and, as his wife said, still select. He was on the whole enjoying his freedom. The residential hotel was comfortable, the food sufficiently good to make the guests wish there were rather more of it, the weather fine, the children less exacting than he had feared. Nevertheless, after a week of idleness he had begun to feel that a day devoted to doing nothing was over-long in passing, and he had read that morning in the local paper that an inquest was to be held at the Parish Hall. The professional instinct, seven long days in abeyance, had stirred within him, and his steps had led him inevitably to the scene of action.

Standing at ease on the pavement, he watched the crowd that had assembled on the steps of the building where the inquest was to take place. Rapidly his experienced eye identified the principals as they arrived— the police, the doctor, the jurors, Colonel Hewitt, conspicuous in his mourning, the representatives of the Press. Ferris surveyed these last indulgently—local men, very small fry indeed, presumably glad of even so modest a chance as this to distinguish themselves. A brace of them passed him as he was lighting a cigarette from the stump of its predecessor. They were talking eagerly, and eagerly they passed into the building.

"Possibly a story here," one of them was saying.

The word was a clarion call. For a moment Ferris looked after his brethren of the Fourth Estate, and a little later found himself presenting his card to the man at the door.

The table reserved for the Press was situated just below the platform on which the Coroner was seated. Ferris pushed his way through the crowded chairs at the back of the hall and made for the sacred enclosure. He had no intention of reporting the affair, but it would be amusing to see what these local fellows made of it. Not that there was likely to be anything of consequence . . .

He sat down at the table and looked about him. The proceedings were due to open. Already, in the next chair, a youth with untidy hair had his notebook ready and his pencil in hand.

Ferris considered him compassionately, reminded of his own beginnings. He had done this sort of thing himself in the early days. . . . And now he was Ferris of the *Daily Wire*—sometimes good for a story on the front page.

Mr. Ferris came to himself with a start.

That was the doctor who was giving evidence, and it was obvious at once that the doctor had been coached. Question and answer were alike perfunctory. That meant that the police were at fault, and that the present proceedings were merely formal. It was odd, by the way, that the victim should have been stabbed through the right temporal bone, a rather strange spot; but, as the doctor said, that particular bone was in any case thin —and especially so in later life.

The doctor stepped down, and was succeeded by an angry-looking man dressed in black, whom Ferris had identified outside the Hall as the brother of the deceased.

"Colonel Hewitt," whispered the youth with untidy hair—"a regular tartar."

Ferris nodded, and soon perceived that the description was justified. Twice already the Colonel had fallen foul of the Coroner.

Rather pathetic, thought Ferris.

"No, Mr. Coroner, my sister had not an enemy in the world. The idea is preposterous."

"I am merely putting the question, Colonel," said the Coroner. "It is my duty to ascertain whether there can possibly be a motive.

"Robbery perhaps," continued the Coroner. "Was your sister, by chance, wearing any of her jewellery?"

"No," answered the Colonel, "my sister hadn't any jewellery. It all went . . ."

The Colonel paused.

"She hadn't any jewellery," he repeated.

"Yes, sir," said the Colonel, in reply to another question from the Coroner, "she would have to pass through the spinney on her way home from Tamarisk House. How many times have I written to the Town Council about it? It's a blot on the district."

"I quite agree with you, Colonel," said the Coroner, looking, as he spoke, significantly at the Press table. "I have, as you may know, myself repeatedly urged its removal."

Ferris sat back.

"These local politics!" he sighed.

"Thank you, Colonel," said the Coroner at last. "I need not detain you further. I would wish, however, on behalf of the court"—here he glanced at the foreman of the jury—"to express our very deep sympathy with you in your terrible loss."

"Thank you, sir," replied the Colonel.

He stood a moment as though unable to withdraw, gripping the back of the chair which had served as a witness stand.

Ferris watched him curiously. The Colonel's face was very red, and there was something that glistened in his watery blue eyes. At last, very deliberately, he turned and walked to the three steps leading down from the platform. In silence he descended to the floor of the hall, and with head erect moved steadily, looking neither to the right nor to the left, to a seat near the door.

"Certainly pathetic," Ferris thought, and decided that he might have made something of the scene. But he doubted whether these local fellows would be equal to the occasion. This sort of thing had to be carefully handled, and they probably lacked the technique.

"I do not propose, gentlemen," the Coroner was saying, "to call any further evidence at this stage. I shall accordingly adjourn the inquest for fifteen days in order to enable the police to make further inquiries."

"Doon't yew go sa faast, Mr. Coroner."

A voice that had overridden many storms boomed out from a far corner of the hall.

"I hev' got a bit of evidence for yew, and oi shell be out with the fleet in tew weeks' taime."

It was John Masters speaking, coxswain of the Eastrepps lifeboat, a fisherman, as his father and forbears had been before him, the only man in England who had twice received the King's gold medal for saving life at sea. He was coming forward down the gangway, between the chairs, as he spoke, in his blue jersey and serge trousers. He had never worn anything else, not even when he had gone to Buckingham Palace. His face was tanned a brick red, and his eyes were mild and brown.

He made to ascend the steps to the platform.

"One moment, Mr. Masters," said the Coroner.

Inspector Protheroe was whispering. The court waited.

"Yes . . . yes," muttered the Coroner.

"I don't think I need take your evidence to-day, Mr. Masters," he announced. "Perhaps you would kindly step round to the police station and see Inspector Protheroe about it."

"Shall oi hev to come back and give moi evidence in tew weeks toime?" asked Mr. Masters, gazing up at the Coroner.

"Of course," said Mr. Bennett, "if the Inspector considers it important."

"Important!" said Mr. Masters. "Whoy, of course that is. Oi hev seen the mairderer."

"What's that?" said the Coroner.

"Oi hev seen the mairderer," repeated Mr. Masters.

"You saw the murderer?" said the Inspector.

"Oi hev said it twice," responded John Masters, "and oi'm willin' to say it a third time—on ooth from that

haire chair. But oi'm not a-goin' to lose a day's fishing out of givin' yew a bit of evidence. So yew'd better let me say it now and hev done with it."

The fisherman, with his rolling gait, was already
climbing the steps. Inspector Protheroe glared at him,
and the Coroner looked down in freezing discourage-
ment. But Mr. Masters, seemingly unaware that he
was in the least unpopular, turned with a friendly gesture to the Coroner's clerk.

"Show me that Boible, maister," he said.

There was a pause, while the Coroner silently registered his defeat.

"Very well," he said, "I'll take your evidence," and
he motioned to his clerk to administer the oath. Mr.
Masters took the oath.

"This is how it was," he began. "Oi was a-walkin'
along the cliff by the loighthouse . . ."

"One moment, Mr. Masters," said the Coroner coldly.
"It is four days since this murder was committed. Why
did you not go to the police at once with this . . . er
. . . evidence?"

"Haven't oi been away with the fleet since the day that
were done?" demanded the witness.

"Proceed," said the Coroner.

"Oi was a-walkin' along that haire cliff by the loighthouse," repeated Mr. Masters, "when oi see a man not
werra far from the top of the path. I didn't take noo
particular nootice of him at the toime, not hevin' no
reason to do. But thinkin' of it afterwards, oi remembered as how he was a-comin' from Coatt's Spinney,
loike."

"At what time was this?" asked the Coroner.

"Well, oi can't tell yew," replied the witness, "but that
must hev been naire about half-past ten. That wasn't
roightly dark."

"You were walking home at the time."

"Oi was walking," replied Mr. Masters.

"And you say that you saw a man," persisted the Coroner.

"Oi hev seen the mairderer," said Mr. Masters.

"How far away was this man when you saw him?"

"He were about a hundred yards down the path."

"And where exactly did you see him?"

"On the cliff naire the loighthouse."

"Some distance away?"

"That was about seventy yards, oi should reckon," said Mr. Masters.

"You said just now that the man was a hundred yards down the path. On the next occasion he may be nearer still."

"He were a hundred yards boi the path and seventy yards as the crow floy," said Mr. Masters. "The path do a koind of a zig-zag thereabout."

"Then the man was only seventy yards away?"

"Seventy yards as the crow floy and a hundred yards by the path," said Mr. Masters.

"Did you see what this man was doing?"

"He was just a-walkin' along. Once he stopped and started a-brushin' of his knees."

"Can you describe the man?"

"Koind of a short man, with a baird."

"You can swear to the beard?"

"Oi guessed that were a baird. It were dark and wavy and it grew in the place where a baird ought to grow."

"Was there nothing that struck you as odd or suspicious in his conduct?"

"He were a-walkin' along the cliff, and he brushed his knees."

"It didn't strike you as suspicious that he should brush his knees?"

"Noo. Werra loike his trousers was dusty."

"There is one last question," said the Coroner. "Are you sure it was not later than half-past ten?"

"O'im roight sure.   Oi was in bed by a quarter to eleven."

"Thank you," said the Coroner.   "You can stand down."

"The inquest is adourned till to-day fortnight," he added to the court at large.

Ferris sat back from the table.   In front of him lay a sheet of paper covered with the hieroglyphs of his profession.   Once too often an itching hand had gone to the upper waistcoat pocket, and instinct had proved too strong for him.

"Not such a bad story, after all," he reflected, with a legitimate satisfaction.   Pathos . . . humour . . . and sensation—a little mild of course.   But it could be worked up, and the *Daily Wire*, as he had that morning observed, was badly in need of a feature.

CHAPTER THREE

I

MARGARET WITHERS stood near the French window of her sitting-room in "White Cottage," looking distastefully at an open telegram. She read it again, then folded it and, with sudden decision, pulled aside the curtains and looked out.

Why had Dick chosen this day, of all days, to visit her? Why did he ask to enter by the drawing-room window? Finally, and above all, why was he nearly an hour late, though he had said in his wire that his business was urgent?

She glanced at her watch. Nearly seven, and Dick had said he would call at six. She moved away from the window and sat down in an armchair near the empty fireplace.

It was foolish to worry about Dick. Nevertheless, he was her cousin; they had lived together in childhood, and it was only natural that she should worry. She would see nothing of him for months, then he would turn up, stay several days, and disappear again as suddenly as he had come. And each time she would notice the change in him. Each time he would be more cynical, looser of habit and speech, more evasive concerning his plans. Not that she had ever dared to inquire too closely into them since that dreadful year when he had been cashiered from his regiment, to live shortly afterwards in retirement at the expense of his country.

And now he had chosen this day, of all days, to announce his coming—with Robert due to arrive that evening. Margaret moved uneasily in her chair. Dick must know nothing of Robert. Her secret would never be safe with Dick, even if they could count on his good-will. And that was doubtful. Dick had always hated her . . . friends. He would dislike Robert. He might even turn the situation to his advantage—an ugly thought, but he was ever more desperate for money, and she had begun to fear asking how he came by the little he had.

Robert would be already at Fenchurch Street, about to step into the train, and there was no means of putting him off. For this was their regular day of meeting for that essential twenty-four hours of companionship. Once a week—she could not allow more frequent visits. It was, above all, necessary to be prudent. For the same reason she lived without servants.

Soon, perhaps, she would be free—free for Robert and safe with Cynthia. This second chance had come to her out of the blue; it must on no account be missed or spoiled. She must hold on to it with both hands. For she really loved Robert. Not a doubt of it—his strength, his quiet enthusiasm, his determination to succeed; above all, his dependence upon herself.

She rose and looked into the glass above the mantel-piece, examining herself critically and without prejudice —oval face, fair hair still bright, blue eyes set wide apart, chin still firm. She picked up a powder puff and used it delicately. There were slight shadows beneath the eyes. She must try to sleep better. But Robert had no need to worry. She would keep her looks for many years to come.

There came a tap on the pane behind her. She swung round and moved swiftly to the French windows. They opened as she reached them and the curtains swung aside.

" 'Fraid I'm late," said a voice, speaking rather too precisely.

Dick Coldfoot stood before her.

"Well, Margy," he said, stepping forward. "Pleased to see me?"

He moved towards her.

"He's really a darker edition of myself," thought Margaret.

His hands were on her shoulders.

She flinched instinctively as his mouth touched her cheek. He dropped his hands and looked at her with that quizzical frown that used to annoy her so much in the old days.

"No," he said, "not quite. Only a drop taken—just enough to keep me going. But a brotherly salute isn't much catch, is it? Sorry, Margy."

"I never . . ." began Margaret.

"You never do," he interrupted. "You just suffer in silence when the rolling stone sits down on the doorstep."

"You came by the window," she observed drily.

"So I did—to be sure," he answered.

He continued to look at her, swaying a little on his heels. His face was flushed, his eyes were bright.

"Why have you come?" asked Margaret after a moment's hesitation.

"Awkward, isn't it?" he demanded.

"I don't understand," began Margaret, but she felt the roof of her mouth growing dry.

"Let me see," he reflected. "He is due to arrive soon after half-past nine. We shall then be one too many. But there is still time for a chat. And perhaps I might even smoke one of his cigars."

He sat down, as he spoke, in the armchair.

"Come on, Margy," he said, looking up at her. "Don't stand there trying to look like Cleopatra or Helen of Troy on an off day. The cigars would be in that little cupboard over there, I should imagine. Or don't you allow him to smoke in the drawing-room?"

Margaret stood a moment looking down at him. Then she moved to the cupboard, opened it, and took out a box of cigars. It had come, the moment she had dreaded. She must meet it, and she would win.

"I'm not going to pretend I don't understand, Dick," she said, handing him the box.

He nodded smilingly, took a cigar and lit it.

"That's right," he said. "It's always better to face facts."

"In that case," she continued, "you will perhaps tell me why you are taking this interest in my affairs. They have nothing to do with you."

"I think," said Dick slowly, puffing at his cigar, "that you do not really mean that, Margy. If you will reflect a moment, you will soon perceive that this particular affair—for I presume that you have only one that really matters—has a good deal to do with me—indirectly, no doubt, but a good deal."

"I suppose you have come for money."

"Well, what of it?" he asked.

"You know exactly how much money I have got," went on Margaret steadily.

It was wonderful, she thought, how she could control her voice, as he sat there, destroying her happiness, thrusting himself into her dreams.

"You know quite well that I can't afford to support you and Cynthia," she continued. "It is as much as I can do to make both ends meet."

Dick laughed.

"I am not asking you to support either of us," he replied. "We can get all the money we want . . . elsewhere."

"He cannot give me a penny," retorted Margaret. "And I would not take his money in any case."

"I know quite a lot about Robert Eldridge," he replied—"more than you think, perhaps. Love is blind, and you doubtless believe everything he tells you. But it's no use Eldridge pretending to be lacking in the goods of this world. Why does he go to his office only once a week? If he were really the poor, industrious fellow he makes himself out to be, he would be clamped to the office stool morning, noon and night."

"I know nothing of his business," said Margaret.

"I go by what I see," Dick retorted. "Your . . . friend has all the money he needs. And I give you credit for having guessed as much. I should be sorry to think that you were proposing, at your time of life, to throw yourself away on a pauper."

Margaret stepped towards him; but half-way, rather hopelessly, she paused.

"Yes," he said, "better stay put; though it would not be the first time my face had been slapped by little cousin."

"I never want to see you again," said Margaret.

"As you please," he answered sullenly. "There's no necessity for you to do so. All I need is a cheque delivered monthly. A man must pay for his pleasures—Robert Eldridge included."

"Dick. . . . It's impossible. I cannot and I will not ask for a penny."

Coldfoot rose and threw his unfinished cigar into the fireplace.

"Look here, Margy," he said. "This isn't pleasant for me. Do you think I like to see you wasting yourself on a man like Eldridge?"

He looked at her in a swift blaze of admiration.

"Gad, Margaret, you might have done better than that! But you're sweet on this fellow, and he shall pay. He isn't going to get you on the cheap. Besides, I want the money, and I've got to have it pretty quick."

"It's the old trouble," said Margaret to herself. "He is jealous—always has been. He hates Robert, and it's useless to plead."

"Dick . . ." she said at last. "I could spare you . . . ten pounds."

"You're not going to spare me anything. I want twice as much as that, paid monthly, and it will represent a very small proportion of what any man should be glad to pay for the pleasure of your company."

"Not a penny from Robert."

"Look here, Margaret, you haven't grasped it yet. I've said that I want the money. Either Eldridge shall pay up or I shall apply elsewhere."

"What do you mean?"

"I shall go to Withers."

"No."

"Withers badly needs certain evidence. He is not as rich as Robert Eldridge, who goes to London only once a week, but he will be good for a decent figure."

"You can't do it, Dick."

"It is Eldridge or Withers, and I hope it will be Eldridge, for your sake. I hate 'em both."

He paused and added violently:

"Don't be a fool, Margy. Eldridge will do anything you ask him. You needn't even mention me. And it must be done at once. I shall come for my answer to-morrow at lunch-time—understand?"

She looked at him, her anger exhausted, and now only anxious that he should go. Her nerve was breaking. She would do anything—anything to get this man out of the house, to be rid of the sight and sense of him.

"You shall have your answer," she said. "And now go, for God's sake."

He turned to obey. At the window he paused and looked at her uncertainly.

"There was mention of a tenner," he began.

Without a word she crossed the room, unlocked her writing-table, pulled out a small bundle of notes and handed them to him.

He took them awkwardly.

"Well, so long, Margy. I am going now.

"Look here," he added. "I don't want to make trouble, but it's Hobson's choice, old girl . . . you know that, don't you?"

"Will you not go?" said Margaret.

He stood regarding her a moment; then, turning, left the room quickly by the French windows.

In the garden he paused and wiped his brow a little absently with his hand. It had been a nasty business —even nastier than he had thought. But beggars could not be choosers, and in any case Margy would lose nothing by it in the end—had everything to gain, in fact, by bringing that fellow Eldridge to heel, letting him understand that she must be handsomely used. Margy was a damn fine woman—worth a prince's ransom, not to be had for nothing. And it was high time she began to get something out of life. After living with John Withers for six years she deserved anything good that might be coming to her.

Dick Coldfoot came to a stand outside "The Three Fishermen." Thinking again of Eldridge, he waved a hand vaguely at the world. A mean fellow. What would he not himself have given for Margaret? Some day perhaps, when she had her divorce . . . well, he meant to try his luck again. He would dispose of Eldridge, and Eldridge, in any case, was just a passing fancy. He left her too much alone.

Pushing into the bar, he ordered a double whisky and a small soda.

There was only one other person there, a thickset man in a neat dark suit. He was sipping a glass of ale, as though it were some rich wine of Burgundy.

Coldfoot nodded.

"Hullo!" he said. "I have seen you somewhere before, haven't I?"

The man smiled.

"My name is Higgins," he said.

Coldfoot nodded as he drained his whisky and ordered another.

"I've got you now," he responded. "You are looking after young Alistair Rockingham, aren't you?"

The two men looked at each other.

"A bit of a responsibility, isn't it?" said Coldfoot.

"It's not all honey and pie," admitted the stranger. "I have to keep pretty close to him most of the time. But he is all right at present. I have locked him up for the night."

"And come in to have a quick one," said Coldfoot.

Mr. Higgins nodded.

"And very welcome, I'm sure," said Coldfoot, tapping on the counter with a half-crown.

"The next two are on me, see?   I don't like drinking alone.   It's not my way."

The barmaid brought two fresh glasses.

"Well," said Mr. Higgins, "here's luck."

"Luck," repeated Coldfoot.

And they drank together.

II

The Hon. Alistair Rockingham, turning a somewhat touzled head, his bright eyes gleaming from the white pillow, was trying hard to be patient. The man Higgins might even yet return. It was wiser to wait until the banging of the front-door sounded all clear for the evening.

It was hard to be patient. This was the third time in a week that Higgins, on some pretext or other, had got him into bed by nine o'clock in the evening. Higgins was tiresome—always at his elbow, locking him up with or without provocation. And all because he had happened to have a nervous breakdown. Other people he knew had suffered in that way, and nothing disagreeable had come of it. On the contrary, they went off to the South of France, Monte Carlo or Nice, where they had a fine time, at the end of which they came back in the pink of condition and nobody any the wiser.

He had always wanted to go to Monte Carlo. He pictured it as full of rooms with crystal chandeliers and gleaming mirrors. And there would be gardens with exotic flowers and marble terraces, where languid girls strolled and postured in the half-light—very different from this depressing English town, which somehow made you feel that you really had no right to exist. And there would be no Higgins at Monte Carlo. That would be quite impossible.

There, at last, went the door. The house quivered under the shock of it. Higgins had departed and it was growing dark.

Rockingham raised his head from the pillow. In another five minutes he would be able to leave the house. Flinging off the counterpane, he moved quietly in his bare feet across the room towards the chair on which his clothes were lying and began to dress.

He knew, of course, why Higgins had put him to bed. Higgins wanted to slip away to "The Three Fishermen" and meet his friends. Higgins was deep.

"But I am deeper than Higgins," said Rockingham to himself, as he pulled on his trousers.

"Deeper than Higgins," he repeated a little later, with a bright smile into the mirror before which he was knotting his tie.

He looked at himself complacently. The soft shirt, blue coat, grey trousers and crêpe-soled shoes admirably expressed his temperament—distinguished but informal. He moved on tiptoe to the window, and from the shadow of the curtains looked down into the garden at the front of the house. It was, he decided, already sufficiently dark—light enough to see what he was doing, but dark enough to prevent other people from seeing.

The window was high up, thirty feet from the ground at least. That again was Higgins. Higgins did not want him to use the window except as a window . . . not as a door, of course; especially not as a door when the real one was locked.

He had no intention, however, of using the window. He knew something better than that.

He moved to a corner of the room near his bed, went down on his hands and knees, and, lifting the carpet, fumbled a moment at a crack between the boards. Thence he pulled out a key, wrapped in a handkerchief. He slipped the key into his pocket and replaced the handkerchief between the boards. Then he crossed the room again and looked once more out of the window. There was no one in the garden, and the risk of being spotted was small, for the house stood back a little from the Norwich road in its own grounds. Satisfied that no one was watching, he crossed to the door of the room and stood listening. Not a mouse stirring—the servants either asleep or gone to the pictures. The moment had come.

Softly he inserted his key in the lock and turned it. It made scarcely any noise. And that, of course, again, was due to his genius for detail. Ten days ago at lunch he had upset the salad oil. They had thought it was an accident, but he had mopped it up with his handkerchief, and in that handkerchief he had since been keeping the key.

Rockingham smiled. Undoubtedly he was clever. Who but himself would ever have thought to see whether the keys to the other rooms on the floor might fit the lock of his own room? No one, except himself.

He slipped through the door and locked it behind him.

He stood a moment in the passage listening, his head a little on one side. Next he tiptoed to the stairs and began very cautiously to go down, stepping as close to the wall as possible. That was how burglars went downstairs, for the boards were less likely to creak if you stepped on them close to the wall.

On the second landing he paused. But again no sound came to his ears, and he passed thence to the landing of the first floor and moved to the window at the far end. He pushed it up and swung a leg across the sill. Just beneath him was the roof of a verandah, and at one corner of this a drain pipe, down which it was easy to slide. It was equally easy to get back by the ivy at the other end, but he preferred to descend by the pipe. It wasted less time.

He dropped lightly from the pipe and stood a moment by a rose-bush panting a little. Then he groped beneath the bush and pulled out a small cheap clothes-brush which he had stolen from the housemaid's room the day on which he had obtained the key. That, again, was clever, for it wouldn't do to walk about Eastrepps with soiled trousers and green mould on the elbows. It might excite suspicion. Besides, he hated to be soiled or untidy, and girls were quick to notice things like that.

Rockingham dusted himself quietly, and, putting back the brush, moved towards the boundary hedge till he found the gap in the wire. He passed through the gap, walked through the long grass of the neglected garden of the empty house next door and opened the wooden gate marked "Tradesmen's Entrance," through which he slipped into the road outside. There he looked to the right, and, after a moment's hesitation, turned quickly to the left, where there was a side track. This track ended, as he knew, in a waste patch, and on the further side of the patch was another road, which led to the highway over the cliff that ran to Sheringham.

He had reached the end of the waste patch, and was about to take the road to the cliff, when he stopped and looked towards a lamp some fifty yards away. Here was a bit of luck. That girl had only just left the house.

She was walking down the street away from him. Fortune was smiling at last.

He moved off in swift but decorous pursuit. It was
a pity she walked so fast, but in any case he could
hardly speak to her until she was near the cliff road. It
was safer there—not so many houses.

He liked the way she walked—very light and sure.
What should he say to her when he drew level? He
wished to be really clever and polite. He would raise
his hat, of course. He had always liked raising his hat.
It gave one a pleasant, courtly feeling. And then, of
course, he must say something, and the first remark
was important. It must convey both admiration and
respect, show at once that he was neither a rake nor yet
a novice, and, however tactful and original one might
be, there was always the risk of a snub. Only the other
day quite the best remark he had ever made had gone
woefully astray. "Gentlemen," he said, lifting his hat
to a really lovely creature with yellow hair, "prefer
blondes," to which she had instantly replied: "Yes, and
blondes prefer gentlemen."

That was the sort of girl he liked—all her wits about
her and plenty of spirit. Unfortunately, however, he
had been unable to think of any suitable retort.

The girl in front was dark. He could see, in the light
of a street lamp, the shadow of her hair beneath the
close-fitting hat. She passed out of the yellow circle
and disappeared into the blackness beyond. He crossed
the circle himself. The long summer twilight had faded,
and it was now very dark beyond the lamplight.

For a moment he paused on the edge of the circle.
He did not like it to be quite so dark as that. But the
girl in front was getting quite away—making towards
the main road to Sheringham, which at this point ran
some hundreds of yards inland. Already she had passed
the straggling line of cottages in which the coastguards
lived. Beyond her was the open cliff and fields void of

light and life, until the first houses of West Runton began.

Rockingham looked nervously to right and left, but hastened on.

Here it was darker still, for the street lamps had ceased a hundred yards behind. There was nothing to fear, and yet he was afraid—not of anything outside in the wide spaces between earth and sky, but of something that would happen to himself. He did not exactly know what it was. He never remembered, but it would happen again if he were left alone in this empty place. . . . Higgins . . . where was Higgins? . . . It would have been better, perhaps, to have remained in his bed.

Something was going to happen. He did not know what it was, but Higgins knew. His parents, up in Scotland, knew. But no one would ever tell him. He had asked them again and again, but always they had put him off. And once, when he had asked his mother, she had burst into tears, which in someone so careful of her complexion had deeply astonished him.

His graceful quarry had disappeared into the dark. She had led him into this, and now abandoned him to his fate. He stood, silent and afraid.

It was on him now. He would know in a minute what he must do. It was bringing him to his knees. But he would resist . . . resist. Pressing both hands to his forehead, he staggered forward.

Later that evening—how much later he did not know —Rockingham found himself in an open field about twenty yards from the road to Sheringham. His hands and knees were damp with dew. He looked at his watch . . . nearly eleven o'clock. How had he come to be abroad so late? He would be missed. Higgins was usually back at the house by eleven, and invariably came to see how he was sleeping.

Rockingham began to run home, lightly and easily, as fast as his legs would carry him.

III

Inspector Protheroe looked at the station clock. . . . Twelve minutes past ten. He sat back in his chair, reading over the pages he had written. The Inspector frowned. There was nothing much in his report. That was what had made it so difficult to write; but Sir Jefferson Cobb would want to see it on the following morning. Then he rose, put on his cap, left the station and started to walk home to his cottage on the main road to Sheringham. He had told his wife that he would be late, and there was no need for him to hurry, his supper would be waiting for him—cold, of course, and she would have left the teapot on the hob.

Things were not going well. He had always hoped that some day his chance would come—a really important case, big with prospects of promotion. And now had come the biggest chance of all. Murders were rare in these days—never more than four or five in the year—and this one had been taken up by the London Press. But he had failed to make any progress, and Sir Jefferson Cobb had decided to call in Scotland Yard. The Yard, of course, could do no more than had been done already, but local opinion must be satisfied.

For the first few days Inspector Protheroe had enjoyed the publicity and prestige of his position. The eyes of the town were upon him. He was a man whose goings and comings fluttered the district. But his reputation was falling. He read it in the eyes and whispers of the people he passed in the street. Only the night before, opposite "The Three Fishermen," there had been the suspicion of a laugh as he had passed. He must not, of course, allow himself to be affected by such incidents, but they showed how the wind was blowing, and Sir

Jefferson Cobb liked to be popular. He intended to call in Scotland Yard, even though it meant depriving the local men of a fair chance.

"Not that I have anything to fear from the Yard," the Inspector told himself, as he walked towards his cottage. He had done everything that a man could do, and in his last report, just completed and signed, he had recapitulated the facts. Sir Jefferson had asked him to do so. That report would be shown to the man from London, and he had made it clear that, though he had felt bound to seek the advice and assistance of his immediate superior, Superintendent Artley, of Norwich, all the really useful work had been done by himself. He had interrogated the fisherman, John Masters, for over two hours, but had obtained in substance nothing more than Masters had said at the inquest. He had searched Coatt's Spinney from end to end, but nothing had been found. He had interviewed Colonel Hewitt on three separate occasions, each more unpleasant than the last; for the Colonel, now that the first shock was over, had completely recovered his bad temper, and had as good as told him to his face that he was incompetent. Not that the Colonel mattered one way or the other, especially as the old man had been able to tell him nothing. All he had found out from the Colonel was that Miss Hewitt had lost her money in the Selby swindle sixteen years ago, and everyone in the town knew that.

If only he had been able to act promptly and decisively. . . . *At 11:30 this morning, Inspector Protheroe, accompanied by Police-Constable Williams and Police-Constable Birchington, arrested Thomas Dark as he was leaving his house in Blank Crescent. The grounds on which the arrest was effected are not yet divulged, but it is an open secret that our popular and energetic Inspector is not the man to let the grass grow under his feet. Important developments may be expected.*

Inspector Protheroe thrust his chin forward and walked a little faster. Perhaps even yet he would prove his mettle. After all, there was no real reason to be out of heart. He had done pretty well for himself—risen from the ranks to his present position. His little house on the East Cliff, standing in its own small plot of ground, thanks to the East Anglian Building Society, would soon be his own; and his wife, for all wifely purposes, was a paragon.

Inspector Protheroe sighed. She was a good wife—not a doubt of it. But she managed his home and family with an efficiency which at times was rather overwhelming. He was lucky to have such a wife, with three growing children to feed and discipline—perhaps too lucky.

This murder, coming out of the blue, might even yet make a difference. He was still the man in charge, and, though the days of his brief authority were numbered, he did not mean to fall back into the old groove. He must attract attention, get himself transferred to a busier district. Eastrepps was no place for a man of parts—too respectable, no crime whatever in the real sense of the word. This murder in Coatt's Spinney could only be regarded as a bright exception.

"And one swallow," said the Inspector to himself, "does not make a summer."

His thoughts ran on. Jane was a good wife, but too contented by half. A man sometimes needed a wider outlook than the home, liked to get loose, see new men and cities. Only once had he really got away, on the great occasion when he had gone to Paris. He had been sent over to identify old Arrowsmith, who had absconded with the funds of the Eastrepps Goose Club. How he had made his wife laugh at his descriptions of the funny French police! Yes, my dear colleague . . . but certainly, my dear colleague. . . . What queer things he had eaten, and how bad all that wine had been for his stomach! Yet, for all his qualms, he had enjoyed it immensely. Those French policemen knew a thing or two, very smart in their foreign way; and they had certainly done him well—taken him on his one free evening to a music-hall, surprisingly called a casino. And the show . . . well, one couldn't see that sort of thing in England—not even in London; but it was surprising how soon you got used to it. And they had all been very lovely. Yes . . . that undoubtedly had been an occasion.

Somewhere to his left—he had cleared the town and was rapidly approaching his home—a dog was barking, but it was not exactly a bark. What noise was it that a hound made in following a line? Speaking—that was the word. And yet it was not altogether like a hound. He would recognise that dog if he heard it again. . . . After rabbits, perhaps. There were a good many rabbits still along the cliff.

Inspector Protheroe, who had paused a moment on hearing the dog, moved on again. His thoughts felt vaguely back after the broken thread.

The Casino de Paris . . . a girl with slim legs, dancing under the shifting lights. . . .

He turned off the road to take a short cut across the field at the end of which stood his small house. He must pass between two thickets of gorse as he left the highway, and it was necessary to go carefully in order to avoid them. Midway between the thickets he stumbled, nearly pitching headlong into the thorns. He recovered his balance and looked down, but it was too dark to see what stood in his way.

He pulled his torch from his pocket and flashed it on the ground at his feet.

Across the path lay a slim leg clad in a thin silk stocking. He brushed a large hand over his eyes, then slowly allowed the beam of his torch to travel upwards. Good heavens! this was real—a young woman lying under a bush. And she had not moved, though he must

have kicked her pretty sharply. He bent down and laid
his hand on the leg, pressing it gently.

"Miss . . . miss," he began.

For a moment he remained, bent motionless, till, suddenly thrusting his torch between his teeth, so that the
light might shine on the bush, he stooped yet lower and,
disregarding the thorns, lifted the slight figure in his
arms, carried it into the open and laid it gently on the
ground. Then, taking his torch into his hand, he flashed
it into the face of the girl.

The blood had only just ceased to trickle from a deep
incision in the right temple.

CHAPTER FOUR

I

SIR JEFFERSON COBB for distraction stroked the end of his nose with a feather pen, one of many that lay upon the narrow jade tray in front of him. His eye, for assurance, ran over the library table—a fine piece, specially made—none of your antiquities for him. Every kind of tool for writing, erasing, blotting, sealing, stamping, opening and closing of correspondence lay to his hand. His legs were extended at ease within a capacious knee-hole. To right and left of them were double rows of drawers which purred when you shut or opened them, and from which Sir Jefferson could produce at a moment's notice exactly the letter, document or receipt he wanted. Sir Jefferson at his desk, symbol of the order, method and style which he had created for himself, was twice Sir Jefferson. He was looking thoughtful, not exactly thinking, but hoping that the thoughts would come, though who would be expected to think at four o'clock in the morning, with the light of dawn indecently suggesting that at such an hour he looked his fifty-seven years, and more, that he was unshaved and wearing a dinner-jacket? The big desk this morning somehow failed to produce that Napoleonic feeling.

He had always intended to call in Scotland Yard to investigate the murder in Coatt's Spinney. Local opinion had demanded it, and local opinion must be respected. Then had come the shock of yesterday. A second murder, again committed in the late evening and in the same way. He had acted without hesitation or delay. He had been informed of the murder at eleven o'clock. At 11:15 he had rung up the Yard and at 11:30 the Yard had rung up him. Chief-Detective Inspector Wilkins was on his way to Eastrepps in a fast car with two of his men, Superintendent Johnson and Sergeant Allquick. Sergeant Allquick, driving the car, had fulfilled the promise of his name, reaching Eastrepps at ten minutes past three A.M.—something not far short of a record, for it was a hundred and thirty-nine miles from Hyde Park Corner. They had gone immediately to the scene of the crime, searching the ground with torches for footprints or other clues. Then they had come to the library to discuss the situation in all its bearings. And they were still discussing it.

Sir Jefferson looked across approvingly at Chief Inspector Wilkins—an able fellow, shrewd, alert, with an ironic mouth and humorous dark eyes—not in the least like a policeman. Wilkins was tactful. He gave credit where it was due, having, for example, expressed his appreciation of the promptness with which the Yard had been summoned. He had also commended Protheroe for having on his own initiative gone to interview the family of the murdered girl. *No time wasted and no harm done,* had been the comment of Wilkins, after a first rapid survey on his arrival—which was handsome so far as it went.

But Wilkins was speaking.

"Now, Protheroe," he was saying. "I think we will just run over your information about Miss Taplow."

Inspector Protheroe produced his note-book.

"The facts," he said, "are these. Miss Taplow was the only child of Mr. and the late Mrs. Taplow of 'Fernside,' East Cliff Road. They have lived here for the last fifteen or sixteen years. She was unmarried, and has stayed continuously with her father since she left school three years ago."

Wilkins glanced towards the Chief Constable of the County.

"Did you know her, Sir Jefferson?" he asked.

"Perfectly well," replied Sir Jefferson. "She has dined in this house lots of times. Old Taplow comes here every year for the shooting . . . Colonial Office . . . retired . . . good fellow."

Sir Jefferson paused, and his voice dropped a full tone. "This will knock him all to pieces . . . his only child."

"A sad business, Sir Jefferson," said Wilkins.

He turned back to Inspector Protheroe.

"You, of course, ascertained from her father whether he had noticed anything abnormal in his daughter's behaviour. Was it, for instance, usual for her to go out alone in the evenings?"

"Her father, sir, assured me repeatedly that he had noticed nothing exceptional. His daughter seldom went out alone after dark, but every other Wednesday evening she attended the meetings of a literary club. She invariably walked home, and always came the same way."

"Did she come the same way yesterday evening?"

"She would usually pass quite near to the spot where the body was found."

Wilkins looked again towards Sir Jefferson.

"Miss Taplow was not engaged to be married . . . no love affairs?"

The Chief Constable shook his head.

"Not so far as I know," he answered slowly. "There were two or three men who took an interest in her in the old days. But they made themselves scarce when her uncle died."

"I see," said Wilkins. "The will not up to expectations."

"It was taken for granted that she would inherit her uncle's fortune. Old Sir James Taplow was a sugar planter—made his money abroad and used to throw it about a bit. Everyone thought him very rich, and it came as a shock when they found he was penniless."

"Indeed," said Wilkins.

"Penniless," repeated Sir Jefferson. "The old man had lived on his capital for twenty years, and he had also, I understand, put a good deal of his money into an investment trust run by that blackguard Selby. I lost a bit in that myself. So did a good many people round here . . ."

"Yes . . . yes," interrupted Wilkins quietly. "But Miss Taplow—had she, to your knowledge, or to her father's knowledge, any enemies?"

Sir Jefferson shook his head.

"None, to her father's knowledge," said Inspector Protheroe.

Wilkins was silent a moment.

"Sir Jefferson," he said at last, "there is often, I am sorry to admit, in cases of this sort a certain—shall we say?—rivalry or lack of co-operation between the local police and Scotland Yard. I feel sure that in the present instance we are going to work together quite frankly and openly."

He looked directly at Inspector Protheroe.

"All our cards are on the table," interposed Sir Jefferson.

"Haven't you formed any sort of opinion yourself?" asked Inspector Protheroe.

"My only ideas are such as must have already occurred to you all. I was inquiring just now into the private affairs of Miss Taplow, but, as you must have felt at the time, such inquiries are almost certainly beside the point. The murder of Miss Taplow can hardly have anything to do with her personal history. Her murderer was very probably the murderer of Miss Hewitt. The two crimes appear almost certainly to have been committed by the same hand. As to that, the medical evidence seems to me conclusive—in each case a clean knife-wound through the right temporal bone running backwards towards the base of the skull. Private and personal motive, therefore, seems to be eliminated

—though we cannot, of course, omit to obtain all possible information. One never knows what may or may not have a bearing. Clearly, if there is a personal motive, it must be one that applies equally well to both victims— an elderly lady and a young girl, both of them without an enemy in the world. On the whole, I think we can assume that this will prove to be murder without a motive in the ordinary sense."

"You mean that we are dealing with a homicidal maniac?"

"On the face of it that seems the only possible assumption. We have now to think over carefully the facts in our possession. We have to thank Inspector Protheroe for putting us in possession of them so promptly."

Inspector Protheroe looked extremely gratified.

"Frankly," Wilkins continued, "there is only one point that has struck me as at all helpful."

Inspector Protheroe leaned forward eagerly.

"It has probably struck you," continued Wilkins, "that there is one circumstance common to both crimes."

"The manner of death," began Sir Jefferson.

"That, of course," agreed Wilkins patiently; "but there is something more significant. Miss Hewitt, according to what you have told me, was murdered on an evening of the week when she invariably visited the Church and afterwards her friend Mrs. Dampier and walked the same way home. Miss Taplow was murdered on an evening of the week when she invariably attended a meeting of her literary society and walked the same way home."

"In both cases it was a Wednesday," added Inspector Protheroe.

"That may or may not be a coincidence," responded Wilkins. "The important point is that both victims were murdered when they were at a spot in which they were always to be found at the times and on the dates in question."

"And what do you infer from that?" asked Sir Jefferson.

"I infer that the murderer was well acquainted with the habits of both his victims. That narrows the field of inquiry."

"There is also the evidence of Masters," said Inspector Protheroe.

Wilkins looked gravely at the Inspector. There was the suspicion of a twinkle in his eye.

"Yes?" he prompted.

"Masters saw the murderer," said Protheroe.

Wilkins waited.

"You remember," insisted Protheroe eagerly, "the man with the black beard."

"To be sure," said Wilkins, and now he was smiling openly. "But beards, I am afraid, are hardly evidence. When a person is seen near the scene of a murder in a black beard, we may assume one of two things. Either he put it on for the occasion, or took it off after his attention had been called to the fact in the local Press."

"Er—yes," said Inspector Protheroe, feeling that he had ceased to shine as brightly as before.

There came a slight sound from the terrace. Inspector Protheroe, feeling sensitive, swung quickly round.

Sergeant Ruddock was standing respectfully at the open window.

"Well, Ruddock?" he asked sharply, "what is it?"

"I beg your pardon, sir," said Ruddock, "but I am still on the big case, and seeing a light here, I thought I would try to have a word with Sir Jefferson."

Wilkins looked with interest at the newcomer.

"Have you anything to report, Sergeant?" he asked.

"Yes, sir, we've got him."

Sir Jefferson scrambled to his feet. Inspector Protheroe made an inarticulate noise in his throat which might have meant approval, censure, or mere astonishment. Wilkins said quietly:

"You've got the murderer?"

"I beg your pardon, sir. This has nothing to do with the murder. Inspector Protheroe entrusted me with other work."

Wilkins smiled.

"I see," he said. "This is the big case?"

"A matter of poaching in Sir Jefferson's preserves," the Sergeant explained.

"That will do, Ruddock," said Protheroe. "You ought to know better than to come breaking into an important conference on so trivial a matter."

"Sorry, sir. I saw a light in the window as I was coming up from the woods, and I thought Sir Jefferson would be interested."

"Sir Jefferson has no time for poachers this morning, Ruddock."

"I'm afraid not," said Sir Jefferson.

"So you've got him, have you?" he added eagerly.

"Name of Harris, sir," replied Sergeant Ruddock.

"Ruddock," said Protheroe, "you're wasting our time."

"Er—yes," said Sir Jefferson, "come to me later, Ruddock."

"Where did you catch him?" he added, as Ruddock turned to go.

"Over in Fellbrigg woods," said Ruddock, "red-handed. And he put up a bit of a fight."

"Splendid!" said Sir Jefferson. "I always suspected Harris. I must see old Trelawney about this—best man on the bench. . . . Has the right feeling about these cases. . . . It was good of you to come, Sergeant; but we can hardly talk about it now—eh, Protheroe? Where have you put the fellow?"

"He's at the station, sir."

"Capital!" said Sir Jefferson, "capital!"

"And now that we have finished with the big case . . ." Wilkins began.

"Exactly," said Sir Jefferson.

"You can go, Ruddock," said Protheroe—"unless you have anything to suggest concerning the minor mystery on which we happen to be engaged."

Inspector Protheroe sat back contentedly. His sarcasm was improving.

"No, sir," said Ruddock, "I have nothing to suggest."

"Inspector," said Wilkins, "I think we all need a little rest. I shall start my investigations at nine o'clock this morning. You will see that the scene of the crime is kept clear. Meanwhile, I think we shall need extra help. In a case like this the ordinary routine work of detection requires a pretty considerable force. But I will look into that later."

Sergeant Ruddock was gazing uncertainly at the great man from London, as one who had, albeit with diffidence, an idea.

"Well?" said Wilkins encouragingly.

"I know nothing of the second murder," said Ruddock respectfully. "I only heard of it just now when I left Harris at the station. But if I might make a suggestion, sir . . ."

He glanced uneasily at Wilkins.

Wilkins nodded.

"Certainly," he said. "You know the local conditions. What do you suggest?"

"I am pretty well acquainted," continued Ruddock, "with most of the people here, and I might perhaps be permitted to make a few inquiries myself, especially among those who live near the scene of the crime. Someone may have seen or heard something which may give us a clue."

Wilkins smiled.

"In cases of this kind," he repeated, "there are invariably scores of persons who come forward with information. In my last case in the Yard I interviewed

over a hundred people who claimed to have actually seen
the murderer. Not one of them had ever been within a
mile of him."

He added quickly, seeing Ruddock to be chapfallen:

"But inquiries must, of course, be made. That is part
of the routine to which I was referring. There will be
work and to spare for all of us—eh, Inspector?"

He turned to Protheroe as he spoke, but Ruddock
again intervened:

"Wouldn't it also be as well, sir," he pursued, "for
some sort of special watch or patrol to be kept on the
streets?"

Wilkins regarded him curiously.

"What I mean is," continued Sergeant Ruddock, "that,
as there has been a second murder, we should be prepared for . . . for . . ."

Sergeant Ruddock faltered. He had dared to make a
suggestion, and the eyes of his superiors were fixed
steadily upon him.

"For a third. Is that what you mean?"

"God forbid!" said Sir Jefferson.

"Yes, Sir Jefferson," said Wilkins. "But Ruddock
has only said what many in Eastrepps will be thinking
to-morrow. We shall certainly have to arrange for special patrol measures, and I think, Protheroe, that the
local men will be best for this work."

"A most sensible suggestion!" put in the Chief Constable. "There was a good deal of feeling in the town
over the first murder, and it is essential to give people
the impression that something is being done. Public
confidence must be restored."

"Perhaps you would make the necessary arrangements, Protheroe," said Wilkins.

Inspector Protheroe swallowed heavily. He had
never thought to receive suggestions indirectly, of course,
from Ruddock.

But Sir Jefferson Cobb had risen to his feet and was addressing Wilkins.

"Well, Chief Inspector," he said, "I will fix you up with a bed, and we will meet again at midday."

They moved together to the door of the library.

"Another fine day," said Wilkins, looking through the open window to the smooth lawn outside.

The sun was already up; the birds very busy and the air fresh with the scent of earth and flowers.

"What's that?" asked the Inspector suddenly.

Protheroe, near the door, swung round sharply. From outside near the house came the sound of someone crying.

The Chief Constable moved towards the window. Before he reached it, however, a girl appeared, slim and dark, in the frame of it.

She stood a moment, in silhouette; then, with hands thrust forward, stumbled into the room.

"I can't bear it," she wept. "I've seen him . . . I've seen the murderer."

II

Sergeant Ruddock moved steadily down Oakfield Terrace at a little past three in the afternoon. He was tired, but elated. He had dealt successfully with the big case, which in Protheroe's hands had been dragging on for months, and he had talked as one policeman to another with Chief Inspector Wilkins from Scotland Yard. His suggestions, though elementary, had been well received.

It was very hot. His helmet was sticking to his head. Already he had visited five houses—all within a few yards of the spot where Miss Taplow had met her death the evening before. None of the inmates had been able to afford him any useful information. Presumably Protheroe, Birchington and the rest were similarly engaged. Ruddock smiled to himself. Protheroe was carrying out a plan which his own subordinate had suggested. And it was hot . . . and Protheroe was subject to heat as butter. It was good to think of Protheroe plodding from house to house. . . . Protheroe would go on plodding all his life, till at last, perhaps, his plodding brought him to the office of a provincial superintendent, with a small pension, to end his days in a cottage, with tomatoes in a frame and geraniums in the window. Dogged does it—it was a favourite maxim with Inspector Protheroe. He was dogging it now.

Sergeant Ruddock pushed open the gate of a small detached villa some distance from its fellows—for he was now on the outskirts of Eastrepps, where it straggled untidily towards East Runton—and, walking up the garden path, made to ring the front-door bell. He paused, however, before he did so, becoming aware of voices. They were men's voices, raised in anger, coming from an open window on the left.

"I have got to live," said one of them.

"*Je ne vois pas la necessité,*" came the other, in French, but with a strong British accent.

"One of Margy's tags," sneered the other.

Sergeant Ruddock removed his helmet, wiped his forehead with a large brown silk handkerchief, which he then passed round the sticky leather lining. He knew French. He could translate what the man had said. That correspondence course had been worth something, after all—that and the gramophone records.

Learn while you listen.

I do not see the necessity—that's what the man had said; and the man, presumably, was Mr. Robert Eldridge, who did not see any reason why his visitor should continue to exist. This was interesting.

Sergeant Ruddock stood a moment in reflection. Then his hand moved again to the bell, but once more dropped to his side without ringing it. The voices were growing louder.

"Blackmail," said one of them. "I could put you in the dock for this."

There came the creak of a chair pushed violently backwards. Sergeant Ruddock crept to the window, which came nearly to the ground, and looked around the edge of it.

Eldridge had risen, and was standing in the middle of his study. Another man, whom Ruddock had never seen before, was lounging on the chesterfield. Eldridge was in a passion, his fists shut, his face the colour of beet. And the other man evidently did not like the look of him. He continued to lounge, but warily, and the apparent ease with which he talked was obviously assumed.

"I expect to receive that cheque before the fifteenth," he said. "That is my limit."

He delivered this with a watchful eye on Eldridge, and, as he finished, jumped up from the chesterfield, but only just in time, for Eldridge, so to speak, had already put his head down.

"Now then," said the other sharply, "pull yourself together. That sort of thing won't do you any good."

The speech ended in an oath strangled at birth. Eldridge had got his man. The two faces, white and red, were very close, the one blind with rage and the other quick with fear. Then Eldridge suddenly dropped his hands and stood shaking, while the other man staggered back to the chesterfield.

"I almost wish I'd done it," said Eldridge.

"This will cost you another tenner per month," said the other, still white, but quickly beginning to recover.

Eldridge passed a hand over his forehead.

"Get out," he said. "Get out quickly. I shall send the money. But you'd better not tempt me any further now."

The other man had already picked up his hat, which lay on the chesterfield. Sergeant Ruddock thought it was time to move. He slipped to the porch and rang the bell.

The door was opened so quickly that the Sergeant shrewdly suspected that the housekeeper, who appeared on the threshold, had, like he, been more nearly interested in what was taking place in the study than she should have been.

"Good afternoon, Mrs. Brandon," he said pleasantly.

"The police," said Mrs. Brandon, recoiling at sight of the uniform.

Sergeant Ruddock smiled.

"Merely making a few inquiries," he said. "It's about . . . about what happened last night. I should like to see Mr. Eldridge a moment, if I may."

Mrs. Brandon stared at him vaguely.

"I beg your pardon," she said, "but I'm a little hard of hearing."

"I should like to see Mr. Eldridge a moment," repeated Ruddock.

Mrs. Brandon drew aside to let him enter. At that moment there came the sound of a door opening in the hall, and the Sergeant caught sight of Eldridge, followed by the man he had seen with him in the study. Eldridge stopped on seeing Ruddock, while the other stepped quickly back.

"Hullo! What is this?" exclaimed Eldridge.

"The police," muttered the stranger.

Sergeant Ruddock quickly explained his errand.

"Excuse me, sir," he said. "We are all hard at work on these murder cases, and I am making a few inquiries in the neighbourhood. I ventured to call. Someone may have heard or seen something last night."

There came the sound of footsteps on the garden path behind him as he spoke.

"I am, of course, entirely at your service," replied Eldridge. "But I am afraid I can't be of much use to you personally. I was away from home yesterday evening." He broke off.

"Excuse me a moment," he added. "Here is a telegram."

Ruddock turned to perceive young Townshend from the post office, very smart in his uniform, who, lodging his red bicycle against the side of the porch, handed an envelope to Eldridge.

Eldridge opened it and read the message slowly.

"No answer," he said to the boy.

"Mrs. Brandon," he added, raising his voice and speaking over his shoulder to the housekeeper, "I find that I must go to London to-morrow morning."

"Yes, sir. Nothing serious, I hope."

"Just some urgent business that I . . . that I was unable to finish off completely yesterday. I shall be back in the evening—no . . . I shall return on Saturday morning by the usual train."

Eldridge looked at the telegram and nodded.

"Yes," he repeated, "I shall return on Saturday."

For a moment he had forgotten his surroundings. Here was a stroke of luck. He would be able to finish off his business in London and return on the evening train. That meant he would be able to pass an extra night with Margaret, following the usual plan. His thoughts were shining suddenly with Margaret, till, looking up from the telegram, he caught the eye of her so-called cousin fixed upon him privily. The man knew, of course, what was passing in his mind—knew that he would be with Margaret on the following night. Well, he was going to buy the silence of this dirty blackmailer till he and Margaret were safe; then he would send him to the devil.

He put the telegram in his pocket.

"Now, Sergeant," he said, "I am at your disposal."

He turned to Ruddock, waving him towards the study.

"Thank you, sir," said the Sergeant, moving towards the door.

"By the way," said Eldridge, "do you wish also to have a word with—with this gentleman?"

The word "gentleman" seemed to choke him.

"Mr. Coldfoot," he added more easily.

"Not unless he is staying with you, sir," Ruddock replied.

"I am not staying with Mr. Eldridge," said Coldfoot. "You will find me at 'The Three Fishermen' if I can be of any use to you."

"Thank you, sir," said Sergeant Ruddock.

"Now, Sergeant, what can I do for you?" inquired Eldridge.

Coldfoot had departed, and Eldridge, closing the study door, was indicating a chair.

Ruddock did not immediately sit down, but stood a moment looking round the room, a pleasant room furnished with leather armchairs. A few books, mostly novels or sporting yarns, were lying about. A collection of native weapons hung between the windows—an Indian *machete* among others—and next to them a German steel helmet, with other trophies of the Great War.

"I see you notice my little collection," said Eldridge. "I picked up some of these things in South America, and some were given to me."

"Very interesting!" said Ruddock absently.

"Well, Sergeant," continued Eldridge, "you are making inquiries, I understand."

"Yes, sir," said the Sergeant. "The murder took place not far from here, and we thought perhaps that someone in the house . . ."

Mr. Eldridge glanced towards the window.

"Out there, wasn't it?" he said. "My housekeeper tells me that you found the poor girl lying in the gorse not far from the cliff."

Ruddock looked keenly at Eldridge.

"You were not at home, sir, I think you said."

"I was away in London," Eldridge replied. "I am usually away in London on Tuesdays and Wednesdays."

"Indeed, sir?"

"They are my working days," said Eldridge. "I still have to keep an eye on things at the office."

There was a short silence.

"Of course my housekeeper was here," Eldridge continued. "Perhaps you would like to talk to her? But I'm afraid it wouldn't be of much use. She's a little hard of hearing."

"If it is not giving you too much trouble, sir."

He rose to ring the bell, which was answered almost at once by Mrs. Brandon.

"No trouble at all," said Eldridge.

"Mrs. Brandon," said Eldridge, "Sergeant Ruddock would like to know whether you heard or saw anything unusual yesterday evening. Let me see . . . when exactly was the crime committed?"

"Between ten and eleven o'clock," said Sergeant Ruddock.

"No, sir," replied Mrs. Brandon nervously. "I can't say that I did. What a terrible thing it was, to be sure! Poor young thing! Walking back home, she was, like she always does."

"You say she always walks home, Mrs. Brandon?" said the Sergeant.

"Every other Wednesday night. I catches sight of her usually from my sitting-room, which is on the first floor at the back of the house. Punctual to the minute, she is usually—just about half-past ten o'clock. You could set your watch by her."

"And did Miss Taplow always come home the same way?"

"Always," said Mrs. Brandon. "She is secretary to a literary society. They meets once a fortnight, and she comes home across the common afterwards."

"And you saw or heard nothing last night?"

"I saw her cross the common," replied Mrs. Brandon slowly, after a short pause, "and that is all I did see."

"She was alone?"

"There was no one with her."

"You saw her distinctly?"

"Pretty fair. There was a bit of a moon last night, and she passed less than a hundred yards away."

"At half-past ten?"

"That is always her time, and the poor young lady must have been killed only a few minutes later."

She lifted a corner of her apron to her eyes.

"You heard nothing, Mrs. Brandon?"

"Nothing," said Mrs. Brandon. "It was all quiet . . . quiet as the grave. Oh, Lord! why ever did I say that?"

Mrs. Brandon stood facing the two men. A tear was running down her left cheek.

Eldridge rose and put a hand on her shoulder.

"Come, Mrs. Brandon," he said, "you mustn't give way, you know. You may be sure the murderer will be brought to justice."

"That won't bring the poor young lady back to life," said Mrs. Brandon, sobbing and unashamed.

"Thank you," said Sergeant Ruddock. "I needn't trouble you any further, Mrs. Brandon. You may be sure we shall do our best, and Scotland Yard have sent down one of their best men."

He turned to Eldridge.

"Don't trouble to see me out, sir. I know the way."

He moved with Mrs. Brandon into the hall. By the front door he paused a moment.

"You're quite sure you heard nothing?" he asked again.

"Nothing, Sergeant, nothing, except there was a dog barking—a queer excited sort of barking it was. And the animal must have been making a pretty fair noise, or

I shouldn't have noticed it, being a little hard of hearing."

"Anyone own a dog round here?" asked the Sergeant.

"Not that I know of," said Mrs. Brandon.

"And that is positively all you heard?"

"Yes, Sergeant."

"Good afternoon, Mrs. Brandon."

"Good afternoon, Sergeant."

III

On the afternoon of the following day Chief Inspector Wilkins was seated in the police station. This, for the time being, was his headquarters. It was four o'clock in the afternoon of a blazing day. The heat had fallen on Eastrepps suddenly—a blast of hot air from the dragon south. The Chief Inspector disliked heat. Heat upset his digestion and made even the easier brain-work, the routine thinking as he called it, more difficult.

He sat back on the hard wooden armchair and considered the situation. The routine was being strictly followed. Superintendent Jenkins from London, assisted by Sergeant Allquick and Superintendent Artley from Norwich, had been resolute and pertinacious in their inquiries. The same was equally true of Inspector Protheroe and the quiet Sergeant Ruddock. These men were confining their activities to Eastrepps, but the Norfolk Constabulary was meanwhile at work in half a dozen villages round the town—Mundesley, Banton, Sheringham, and the rest of them. The results, however, were meagre. The East Anglian mentality, the Inspector owned, was difficult. Folk were reticent, almost taciturn, indifferent to the stranger. They kept themselves to themselves, and were proud of it.

Inspector Wilkins sighed. He felt the need of counsel, of someone with whom he could exchange ideas, on whom he could sharpen his wits. The local men were as good as one could expect, but the force still went for brawn

rather than brains. Some day, perhaps, it would see
its error—come round to his way of thinking which he
had so often, but in vain, urged upon the staff authorities.
Enviously he thought of the scientifically trained men
with whom he had talked in the beer-halls of Berlin and
of the nimble-witted officers of the Sûreté. The Yard
had done pretty well on occasions, but at times like this
one wished for a little leavening of the wholesome lump.

Chief Inspector Wilkins pulled himself together. He
must concentrate, go through the facts again. Wanted
a person of unsound mind, of average height, but of great
physical strength, preferably with an intimate knowledge of the daily habits of Miss Hewitt and Miss Taplow.
Neither too tall, nor too short—that was how John
Masters, interviewed at three o'clock that morning, before putting forth on the deep, had described the man
whom he had seen in the neighbourhood of Coatt's
Spinney on the evening of Miss Hewitt's death. Masters
was a character—maddeningly exact, but entirely non-
committal. Not that he could blame Masters. It had
been dark—not absolutely dark, but still dusk, deep-
ening into night, and Masters was to be commended for
seeing anything at all, let alone the black beard of which
so much had since been heard.

Masters undoubtedly had seen the man. Chief Inspector Wilkins could distinguish at once the genuine
witness who had seen things from the persons who
thought that they had. He was surprised there had so
far been no volunteers in the present case prepared to
describe the murderer or swear to some unusual sight
or sound. Usually it required a staff of experts to deal
with them.

There came a sound of footsteps from the station
porch. That was Protheroe.

"Well?" said Wilkins.

Protheroe entered the room.

"Sit down, Protheroe," said Wilkins. "You look a bit warm."

"Eighty-eight in the shade—so they say," said Protheroe, as Wilkins rose to make way for him.

"Don't move," he added graciously.

"I'm in your seat," said Wilkins.

Protheroe sat down and looked kindly upon the man from Scotland Yard—a nice fellow, polite and anxious not to lord it over the local police.

"Sorry I could not let you have my report before," continued Protheroe. "But I thought it better to wait till I had something to tell you."

"Quite," said the Chief Inspector. "But I like to receive routine reports as soon as possible, even though there may seem to be nothing of interest."

Protheroe ran a moist handkerchief between his collar and his neck. Then very deliberately, he produced a note-book and began to flutter the pages. Wilkins carefully suppressed any sign of impatience.

"Acting on your instructions," began Inspector Protheroe, "I have conducted a house-to-house inquiry in Norwich Road, Birchington Avenue, Goldsmith Road, Hannington Place, Gunton Street, Market Street and Blind Man's Alley. I have interviewed a hundred and thirty-one occupants or lodgers in the houses abutting on the afore-mentioned streets."

Chief Inspector Wilkins sighed. This was the language of the Force, and Inspector Protheroe knew no other.

"It was not till I reached No. 41, Norwich Road, that I obtained any information of interest," continued Inspector Protheroe.

"Yes?" prompted Wilkins.

"There," said the Inspector, "I obtained information which may, or may not, be to our advantage. No. 41, Norwich Road is let for the season to Lord and Lady Steyning. His Lordship and Her Ladyship do not in-

habit the house. They have took it—taken it—on behalf
of their eldest son and heir, the Hon. Alistair Rockingham.

"Rockingham," he repeated, "family name of the
Steynings. I looked it up."

"And then?" said Wilkins.

"The Honourable Alistair Rockingham," continued
the Inspector, "arrived at the house on June 15th, and
he has been staying there ever since. The Honourable
Alistair Rockingham is suffering from a nervous breakdown."

Chief Inspector Wilkins came to attention.

"A nervous breakdown," repeated Inspector Protheroe.
"He is at present in the care of his personal valet, Joseph
'iggins . . . er . . . Higgins. Higgins informs me that
he—I am referring to Higgins—was for seven years attendant in a private home for mental cases, kept by Dr.
Kirkwood, of 'The Larches,' Sydenham, and that he was
specially engaged by Her Ladyship. It seems that Rockingham has for some months exhibited symptoms of"—
here he consulted his note-book—"incipient mental de-
rangement. I am quoting the words of 'iggins . . . er
. . . Higgins."

Wilkins nodded.

"His doctors—I am referring now to Rockingham—
have ordered him perfect rest and seclusion near the sea
in a quiet neighbourhood. Eastrepps was chosen as
being a locality in which the noble family is entirely unknown. I got all this from Higgins."

"His doctors?" said Wilkins. "Did you think to ask
who they were?"

"I did," said Protheroe with an air of one who could
be relied upon to do the proper thing. "One of them was
Sir Hilary Braxted, the well-known mental specialist.
And I understand that the Honourable Alistair Rockingham is partial to female society. It was that which
first made them think he was not quite right in his head."

"Indeed," said Chief Inspector Wilkins.

"Unduly partial, I may say," pursued Inspector Protheroe. "It came to a 'ead . . . er . . . head at the Duchess of Clandoyle's Ball on the 2nd of June last, when the Honourable Alistair frightened his partner in the conservatory. Then his parents judged it better that he should take a rest. It appears that they first tried the little village of Felpham in Sussex, but the patient complained of the loneliness, and apparently threatened on more than one occasion to take his life. So his parents, fearing fatal consequences, caused him to be transferred to Eastrepps."

"Thank you, Protheroe. I think I have all that quite clear. And now we come to the point. Where was this Mr. Rockingham on the night before last, and on the night of the murder of Miss Hewitt?"

"That," said Protheroe, "is not so promising."

"I thought there would be a catch in it somewhere," said the Chief Inspector.

"Higgins swears that his . . . er . . . charge was under lock and key. It is the invariable practice of Higgins to conduct Mr. Rockingham to bed at 9:30 P.M. precisely. As a valet he personally supervises the undressing of his master, and locks him securely into a bedroom on the top floor of the house. Mr. Rockingham is not called till eight o'clock on the following morning."

"I see," said the Chief Inspector. "So we must assume, if we are to assume anything at all, that Rockingham somehow succeeded in leaving his bedroom upon the nights in question."

"Yes," said Protheroe. "That was my idea. Higgins is prepared to swear that he locked Mr. Rockingham into his room on those two nights as on every other night."

"What sort of man is Higgins?"

"Seems thoroughly reliable," replied Inspector Protheroe. "But I have not yet been able to check his h'antecedents."

"Thank you, Protheroe," said Wilkins. "This information may very possibly be of value, and I am sure you will agree that, pending further inquiries, Rockingham should be watched. Perhaps you would arrange for a man to be posted in the grounds. Can you spare a couple of men to take on the job turn and turn about? Otherwise . . ."

"Very well, sir. I'll see to it."

"Meanwhile," continued Wilkins, "I think it would be well to make further inquiries at the house in Norwich Road and even have a look at the premises. We have got to be sure that Rockingham really was locked in his bedroom on the nights in question. You might perhaps talk to the servants."

"I've already done that—a cook and a couple of housemaids. Of course I had to be careful, but I was able to satisfy myself that, as far as they know, Higgins never lets Rockingham out of his sight. No life at all for the poor young man, they said."

"Did they say anything of his habits?"

"A bit soft in the head, but quiet and pleasant; always raises his 'at when he meets them out of doors—a perfect gentleman, and no harm in him at all, as far as they know."

Protheroe ceased, and for a moment Wilkins was silent.

"Well, Protheroe," he said at last, "I would be grateful if you would get your men on the job."

"Perhaps I should inform Sir Jefferson, sir."

"I'll do that myself," responded Wilkins. "I shall be seeing him in a moment. That hysterical maid of his who broke into our conference last night has come to her senses at last, and may be able to tell us something. The doctor says I can see her now. That girl was properly scared."

"So is a good many that I could name," responded Protheroe. "It wouldn't take much to start a panic in the town. Already the visitors are leaving."

"Well, Inspector, it's up to us to put heart into them."

"Hullo, Ruddock! Any news?" he added, as the Sergeant appeared at the door.

"Nothing, sir, I am afraid," said Ruddock. "I have spent the morning visiting the houses near where the second murder took place. Nobody saw or heard anything on the night it was committed."

The Chief Inspector glanced at a large-scale map of Eastrepps, spread on the desk in front of him.

"That's hardly surprising," he said. "I see that the nearest house is at least two hundred yards away."

"Occupied by Mr. Robert Eldridge," said Protheroe.

"Nothing for us there?" asked Wilkins.

"Nothing, sir," said Ruddock. "Mr. Eldridge himself was away from home. His housekeeper heard a dog bark at the time of the murder. And that was all I got out of my morning's work."

"We shall want something better than that," said Protheroe, smiling at the Chief Inspector as one expert to another.

But his smile was not returned. Wilkins had already moved to the door.

"Don't forget to have those men posted, Protheroe," he said, and passed out into the street.

Sir Jefferson Cobb lived on the outskirts of Eastrepps, a good mile and a half from the police station. The Inspector, deciding to take a taxi, walked towards a rank which stood about a hundred yards away, near to the church. The street at that hour was thronged with trippers returning from the sands, but for so large a number of persons there was extraordinarily little talk. Young men in flannels, girls in summer frocks, obvious parents driving their progeny, seemed oddly silent. There was little laughter and no sense of ease.

There came an unexpected movement among a group
of persons walking on the pavement on the further side
of the street, and Wilkins, looking across the road, saw
a youngish man with a flushed face and fists ready for
action. Beside him stood a girl who had laid an unregarded hand upon his arm, evidently wishing to re-
strain him. Opposite the pair a youth with dark hair
was shrinking from the man with the fists; and, as
Wilkins crossed towards them, another man, thickset
and wearing a dark double-breasted suit, thrust himself
between them.

"It's all right, sir," said the man in the double-breasted
suit. "There was no unpleasantness intended to your
young lady."

The youth with dark hair was smiling nervously.

"None whatever," he said. "You mistake me, sir.
My dear young lady, you mistake me. You resemble
closely someone I know—a most remarkable likeness."

"Come along, Tom," said the girl. "There's no need
to make a fuss. He was only raising his hat."

"Then the sooner he learns to keep his hat on his head
in your presence, my dear, the better for him. Resem-
blance indeed! If he isn't careful he won't resemble anything at all when I've done with him."

"Do you hear that?" he continued, addressing himself
to the man in the double-breasted suit. "Tell that damn
loony of yours, and get it well into his silly head, that
I will knock his face in if I catch him at it again."

The man with the dark hair laid a hand on the shoulder
of his companion.

"Higgins," he said, "no violence. You must on no
account permit any violence."

"That's all right, sir," said the man addressed as
Higgins. "It's time you were getting home."

Higgins resolutely moved forward, firmly gripping
the arm of his charge.

Wilkins stood a moment on the pavement looking after the receding pair.

"So that," he said to himself, "is the Honourable Alistair Rockingham."

For an appreciable time he did not move. Then he turned abruptly and went back to the police station.

Sergeant Allquick was in conversation with Sergeant Ruddock.

"Allquick," said the Chief Inspector, "put a call through to the Yard. I want all possible information on the Steynings, Lord and Lady, and their eldest son, the Honourable Alistair Rockingham."

"Very good, sir."

An hour later, Chief Inspector Wilkins, on returning to the police station after his interview with the hysterical maid, found a neat typewritten slip on his desk. It began with an extract from Debrett, and a certain amount of information, to the extent of perhaps a dozen lines, was added.

The Inspector read it carefully; then sat a moment gazing in front of him.

"Now that is very interesting," he murmured to himself.

IV

William Ferris picked up his Scotch and splash, delivered to him five minutes previously by the landlord of "The Three Fishermen," and moved across the bar parlour to a seat near the man in the dark blue suit facing the door. He meant to keep as near to that man as possible during the next few days. For this was Chief Inspector Wilkins, one of the so-called Big Five at Scotland Yard. The Big Five, of course, existed only in the Press, but the public had got used to the term, and one was expected to employ it.

Ferris had never had the pleasure of meeting the

Chief Inspector in the flesh, but he had seen him more than once in the witness-box at criminal trials. Wilkins had a reputation for usually getting there in the end, but in this instance the end seemed as yet far off. Either the police were utterly at a loss, or they were keeping their knowledge of the case very much to themselves.

Mr. Ferris looked about him. At the other end of the tap-room sat a couple of fishermen in blue knitted jerseys, with wide trousers and tanned faces. Near them was an obviously indoor man, perhaps a clerk or a post office official. On the other side of the Chief Inspector was a personage, corpulent and fifty, with a gold chain spanning a full stomach, and side whiskers, wearing respectable broadcloth. There was also a sprinkling of tourists of the sort which Eastrepps did not encourage, for they wore ready-made suits, and one carried a straw hat under his arm.

Then there was the man in tweeds made as loosely as the fellow himself, with the powerful shoulders and the handsome air. He must have been a good-looking fellow before he had run to seed, and he still presumed upon it. At present he was trying his charms on Florrie the barmaid. But Florrie, for all her good humour and readiness to please, had seen too many of his like before. She smiled mechanically at his jests, chided him without heat for his compliments, and kept him at a distance with the experienced affability of her calling.

"A good girl," thought Ferris, and proceeded to admire for himself her plump hands upon the beer handles, the chestnut hair correctly piled, in defiance of lay fashion, upon her head, the amused but wary blue eyes.

Ferris was on his mettle. He had received a telegram from the *Daily Wire* that morning instructing him to "cover" the Eastrepps murders. That, of course, was only right and proper, for the Eastrepps murders were peculiarly his own. He had been first in the field. This was his pigeon, and he intended to bring it down, even though it meant risking a snub from the famous Chief Inspector.

"Good evening, Chief Inspector," said Ferris.

The Chief Inspector cocked an eye in his direction.

"Good evening," he replied.

His tone was civil but cold.

"Taking a rest from your labours, I see," said Ferris.

The Chief Inspector nodded and raised a tankard of ale to his lips.

"You are on the Press," he said, setting down the tankard and looking shrewdly at the representative of the *Daily Wire*.

Ferris smiled.

"Guilty, m'lud," he pleaded.

"Better be careful what you say to me," he added facetiously.

"Anything you would like to know?" asked the Chief Inspector.

Ferris bent forward eagerly.

"I'm not fool enough to believe you would tell me anything vital," he said, "unless it were likely to be useful to the police. But I'd like you to remember me if you should need publicity at any time. I'm here for the *Daily Wire*, and I am out for an exclusive story. If I can help you in any way . . ."

He paused, and the Chief Inspector considered him a moment.

"Help?" he said at last.

"I go about a bit," said Ferris.

"Very well," said the Chief Inspector. "It's a bargain. If you should pick up anything useful, come straight to me. The labourer is worthy of his hire. Frankly, Mr. . . ."

"Ferris."

The representative of the *Daily Wire* hastily produced a card from his pocket and thrust it at the Chief Inspector.

"Frankly, Mr. Ferris, our evidence so far is not exactly plentiful. All we can do for the moment is to suspect anybody whose behaviour seems at all . . . unusual."

"Is there anything I could send over the telephone this evening?" Ferris inquired.

The Chief Inspector again considered his man.

"Mr. Ferris," he said, "you know the feeling of the town. Why not try to be a little unusual? Instead of working up the panic and barking at the police, try a more decent line. Say something to reassure the public. The ordinary routine inquiries are being made, and an immense amount of work has already been done. See that we are fairly handled. It will pay you better in the end."

Ferris held out his hand. The Chief Inspector took it without enthusiasm.

"It's a bargain," said Ferris.

"So you've been going about a bit, have you?" resumed the Chief Inspector.

"I'm doing what I can," replied Ferris. "I have interviewed the coroner and the parson. I tried to have a word with the brother of the first victim, but . . . but . . ."

"It was he who had the word, I think," said the Chief Inspector pleasantly.

"There is some talk of a servant girl having seen the murderer," continued Ferris.

The Chief Inspector assumed a blank official air.

"Yes," he said, "you made some reference to her in your message this morning."

"It was Richards of the *Advertiser* got hold of that story. He had it from the cook."

"And he had it wrong," said the Chief Inspector. "You might emphasise in your next that in a case like this there are always numbers of people who see the murderer. Unfortunately, they seldom agree. John

Masters informed us that he was of medium height and
had a black beard. I have no doubt that he was also
tall, and short, and clean-shaven."

"And the servant girl?" persisted Ferris.

"She did not mention a beard," said the Chief Inspector. "Presumably he had shaved during the interval."

"I am told," continued Ferris, with whom it was a
principle not to recognise any humour but his own, "that
she was assaulted on her way home and knocked off her
bicycle. Also that she is something to do with the local
big whig—Sir Jefferson Cobb."

The Chief Inspector looked quizzically at Ferris.

"Is it possible that I am being interviewed?" he said.
"However, if you want a story——"

"Yes?" said Ferris eagerly.

"It was rather dramatic," said the Chief Inspector.

Ferris edged a little nearer.

"We were holding a preliminary conference, shortly
after my arrival from London, at Sir Jefferson Cobb's
place. It was about four in the morning. She came in
from the garden, poor thing. She had been undoubtedly
frightened—in fact, it was some time before the doctor
would allow her to be questioned. I only saw her this
afternoon. Of course, when it came to the point, she
had not very much to say for herself. A man had
accosted her in the street, and she assumed at once it
was the murderer. Her description, however, was even
vaguer than usual in such cases."

"Was the girl actually assaulted?"

"She did not wait for that," said the Chief Inspector
quietly. "She just scrambled on to her bicycle and rode
away."

"So it might have been anybody?"

"Yes," said the Chief Inspector, "it might have been
anybody, and that is the moral of the tale. I hope you
will bring it properly home to your readers. You might

even say that Chief Inspector Wilkins has investigated the incident, and attaches no importance to it whatever."

"So I said to him, I said, 'You keep out of my way, you bloody, thieving Dutchman. These are my mackerel,' I said. 'You go and take that lumbering sea cow of yours back to Dutchland.' "

It was one of the fishermen speaking, at the further end of the room.

The Inspector sat back and returned to his beer. Ferris looked at his watch. There was a small table on the other side of the room. He crossed to it and sat down. He would write his message here and now, and telephone it later to the *Daily Wire*.

The swing door of the tap-room opened as he started to write. A thick-set man, wearing a double-breasted blue coat, came into the bar, and crossed the room. The man in tweeds by the counter, catching sight of him, put a hand on his shoulder.

"There you are, Higgins," he said. "Same place, same time, same drink—as you see."

"Good evening, Mr. Coldfoot," responded the newcomer.

The Chief Inspector glanced up from his paper. He had been waiting for Higgins. He wanted to be sure that his plans were being carried out. Higgins, again examined by Protheroe, had been quite positive that Rockingham could not escape from his room, and a further search of the premises under Protheroe's direction had revealed no sign of evasion. Protheroe could be trusted on these points. He was thorough in his ponderous way.

The Chief Inspector himself desired to remain in the background, but his instructions to Protheroe had been explicit. Higgins was to make no change in his habits; he was to lock up Rockingham as usual in his room at half-past nine and leave the house. If Rockingham were in the habit of escaping it seemed simpler to catch him in

the act—the house being under continuous observation
—than labouriously to reconstruct his proceedings.

"They say that he comes a-walkin' up from under the
sea, a-swearin' by his gods and a-strikin' to left and
roight with his great axe. Eric the Red he was in his
toime, and if yew ask me . . ."

The voice trailed off and became inaudible as the Chief
Inspector lifted his newspaper.

There was a sound of clinking bottles, and a door
slammed somewhere within the house. The inn would
be closing soon.

"Time for another," said a voice.

That was Coldfoot speaking. A loose-looking fish,
thought Wilkins. Staying here, it seemed, at "The Three
Fishermen." Had a reputation for drinking too much;
not a very pleasant fellow. That seemed to be the general
verdict.

"Yes, Mr. Coldfoot"—it was the landlord speaking—
"I will send it up to your room." He came round the bar
as he spoke and moved to the centre of the tap-room.

"Time, gentlemen, please," he said.

There was a general movement. The fishermen drained
their glasses, rose and moved towards the door.

At that moment, however, the door was suddenly
thrown open from the outside. A policeman in uniform
stood on the threshold. There was a general recoil as
the man entered.

It was Sergeant Ruddock. He looked swiftly round
the room till his eye lighted on Wilkins.

"There you are, sir," he said. "Best come at once."

There was dead silence, broken by a high thin shriek.
It came from the barmaid Florrie.

"His hands . . . look at his hands!" she said.

All eyes were fixed upon the Sergeant. His hands
were streaked with red.

"Yes," said Sergeant Ruddock, startled out of his
usual calm, "there has been another one."

CHAPTER FIVE

I

ELDRIDGE looked quickly to right and left, and started
for the station. It was his usual hour—the best in the
day if you wanted to go unobserved. At 11:30 in the
morning everybody was either at work or on the sands.

It had been a stroke of luck—that telegram calling
him to the office yesterday. And the luck had held, for
he had been able to finish off his work in the early afternoon and to slip back, as he had intended, that same
night to Margaret in Eastrepps. No one had seen him
going from the station to Margaret's house in the dying
light—no one except a policeman on his beat, and that
did not matter, for the man was a stranger. Besides, it
had been dark, and the policeman had been talking to
someone.

Eldridge continued on his way trying to suppress the
feeling of guilt which always attended these manœuvres.
Why should he not be walking abroad in Eastrepps—
even in so poor a part of the town as Sheffield Park? It
was true that he was not yet supposed to have arrived
from London, but the chance was infinitely remote that
he would meet someone who not only knew him, but
knew also that he was supposed to have spent the night
in town.

There at last was the station perched above him on its
high embankment. His burden grew lighter as, with
another cautious look to right and left, he approached
the wooden stairs. Nobody over used these stairs. They
were a short cut to Sheffield Park and the other roads
which lay in that part of the town, and nearly all the

passengers left the station by the broad road which led
to the main streets and shops.

Eldridge, as he climbed the steps, descried a plume of
smoke to his right, half a mile away, perhaps. That was
the London train, punctual as usual. He moved a little
quicker. Invariably he timed his approach, so that he
arrived at the top of the steps just as the train was drawing in to the platform.

He slipped through the unguarded wicket at the head
of the stairs. This was the season of the great invasion,
and usually the train was packed. To-day, however, to
his astonishment, not more than a couple of dozen people
got out, mostly men—the majority in plus fours, carrying bags of golf-clubs, slung over their shoulders, but
the minority, strangely enough, wearing cameras and
bowler hats. Yet this was July, and here was the first
train from London, the fastest of them all (Fenchurch
Street 8:40, Eastrepps 11:27).

Eldridge quietly joined the passengers. He moved
in their company towards the usual exit, handing the
return half of his ticket to London to the man at the
barrier, and breathing the smallest sigh of relief when, at
last, he stood in the little square in front of the station.

"Taxi, sir?"

"No, thank you," said Eldridge.

Margaret had of late been unkind about his figure.
It was not at all a bad figure for a man of his age, but it
would do him good to walk—better than Swedish exercises, anyway.

He made off down the inclined plane to Goldstone
Park, which led to the Norwich road and so into Church
Street. He had the better part of a mile and a half to
cover before he reached his house. He continued on his
way unaccompanied and unobserved till he reached the
Eastrepps Tennis Club on the Norwich road. Three or
four couples were playing on the new courts. That was
a pretty girl—a good service she had too. . . . Re-

minded him of Margaret. Every woman he met reminded him of Margaret.

"I beg your pardon," said Eldridge suddenly.

He had run into a man.

It was a man he knew.

Colonel Hewitt, in black, was staring at him resentfully.

"Lovely day," said Eldridge.

The Colonel still stared at him, his red face drawn and troubled.

"Heavens!" he said. "Is that all you have to say? Here is a murderous madman loose in the town, and you tell me it is a lovely day! Is it possible you haven't heard?"

"Of course," said Eldridge gently, "your sister and then Miss Taplow."

"You haven't heard," said the Colonel, and it sounded like an accusation.

Eldridge took a pace backwards.

"Not another!" he exclaimed.

"John Masters," said the Colonel. "They found him last night . . . murdered. Don't you read the papers?"

"Not this morning," stammered Eldridge.

"Killed last night," repeated the Colonel. "Stabbed in the same way as . . . as Mary . . . the bravest fellow in Eastrepps struck down like a dog, out there."

He pointed vaguely in the direction of the Golf Club and the lighthouse.

"He was going home from seeing his sweetheart," continued the Colonel. "And the police, as usual, are completely baffled."

"How perfectly appalling!" said Eldridge, after a pause.

"The third murder in less than three weeks," said the Colonel.

"Terrible!" said Eldridge.

"Terrible, indeed."

A stranger had joined them unobtrusively, a smallish man in a ready-made suit of grey flannel and a rather bright tie with spots.

The Colonel turned and looked the stranger up and down.

"I know you," he said. "You're that person on the *Daily Wire.*"

"That's right," said the little man. "My name is Ferris."

"Well," said the Colonel, "what do you want? This, by the way, is Mr. Eldridge, one of our local residents."

Ferris extended a hand.

"Pleased to meet you, Mr. Eldridge," he said.

There was an awkward pause. Mr. Eldridge did not much like the look of his new acquaintance. And why was the man staring at him so intently?

"I was hoping to catch you," said Ferris at last, turning to Colonel Hewitt. "I thought perhaps you might be willing to go over the ground with me. You know the place so well."

"It's all in the newspapers," said the Colonel. "Masters was killed on the zigzag path that runs down the cliff over there. His cottage is not far from the bottom."

"That would be not far from . . . Coatt's Spinney."

The Colonel flinched.

"Perhaps a quarter of a mile," he said.

Eldridge had ceased to listen. He had all at once an uneasy feeling that he had seen this man Ferris before. He remembered vaguely that flannel suit and forward droop of the shoulders. Yes, by George, he had it now! He had seen the fellow last night, talking to the policeman as he had been walking down Sheffield Park. Luckily, however, the man was a stranger; he could have had no idea that Robert Eldridge was supposed to have been away in London at the time.

"What I can't understand"—it was Colonel Hewitt

breaking in on his reflections—"is how you managed to travel this morning all the way from London without hearing a word about it. It was in the London Press, and the placards are shrieking it everywhere."

"There must have been quite a lot of correspondents on the train," added Mr. Ferris, looking intently at Eldridge.

"Er . . . yes," said Eldridge. "At least a dozen—all slung about with cameras."

"Ghouls," said the Colonel.

He turned suddenly and, raising his arms in a wild gesture, strode off down the street, leaving Ferris and Eldridge together.

Ferris looked after him a moment.

"Poor old boy!" he said. "The death of his sister has broken him to bits."

Eldridge again found himself under inspection.

"Funny you didn't meet any of those newspaper men on the train," said Ferris.

"Not at all," replied Eldridge shortly; "I had a carriage to myself."

"I see," said Ferris.

Eldridge looked down the empty street.

"Pretty bad for the town,"

"It's a stampede," said Ferris. "There will be precious few visitors left this time to-morrow. And I don't wonder at it. I've seen a few panics in my time. Once they start they get entirely out of hand."

"There's a madman loose," said Eldridge. "There's no sense in these awful crimes. That is what makes it so difficult."

"But mark you," said Ferris, "the police are doing their best. That man Wilkins is pretty thorough, and he is going through the local residents with a fine toothcomb."

"But with a madman it's almost impossible. He may be quite normal at ordinary times."

"There is someone in this town," said Ferris, "who cannot account for his movements on the three evenings when the crimes were committed. Sooner or later the police will find him."

Eldridge looked at Ferris a moment without speaking. His face was rather set.

"Yes," he said at last. "I hadn't thought of that."

II

Shopping was easy that morning, thought Mrs. Dampier, as she made her way into the fishmonger's. The town was quiet—too quiet. It was true that she had been almost run over by a taxi piled with luggage when crossing Church Street, but apart from this misadventure, everything had been curiously calm. There were few people in the shops, and still fewer on the pavements—which was strange for ten-thirty on a Saturday morning. The marble slab of Mr. Wilcox was piled with all the riches of the sea. Only one other customer stood beside it—a large lady with a pale face and many feathers in her hat, who appeared to be considerably reducing a large order for fish.

"No," she was saying, "just a couple of pounds of whiting and a dozen kippers. That's all I can take this morning. I wish I could make it three dozen as usual, but it's no use buying for the future, the weather hot as it is."

"But you're usually quite full up this time of year, Mrs. Rackham."

It was Mrs. Wilcox speaking, as she counted and packed up the kippers.

"Full up I was," replied Mrs. Rackham, "till last Thursday, but there's no holding the folks since John Masters met his death. It will be ruination for us all —if it goes on."

"I want a small lemon sole," said Mrs. Dampier.

"Certainly, m'm."

"You'll send it up in time for luncheon, won't you?"
Mrs. Wilcox nodded absently.

"I am sorry your visitors are going," said Mrs. Dampier to Mrs. Rackham, as they moved together towards the door.

"But that isn't the worst of it," said Mrs. Rackham. "Those who are leaving have paid for the full week. But those who were coming for next week—two parties, one of eight and one of four—have cancelled their rooms. And you needn't think that I'm the only one to suffer—not by any stretch of the imagination. There isn't a boarding-house in the town that isn't hit as badly as I am. It's hard—cruel hard! And what are the police doing, I should like to know, swarming about all over the place and letting folk be murdered in their beds?"

Poor Mrs. Rackham! reflected Mrs. Dampier as she left the shop. It certainly was hard luck on the lodging-house keepers. Not that Mrs. Rackham's view of the situation was very accurate. People were not being murdered in their beds. They died in the roads, at night in the darkness, when the sun had set. They died swiftly, silently. Three murders in less than three weeks . . . no rhyme or reason in any of them. What had poor John Masters done to deserve this frightful death, coming upon him on the narrow cliff as he walked to his cottage by the edge of the sea? His end was perhaps the most mysterious of the three—unless, thought Mrs. Dampier as she moved towards the chemist's, to renew her stock of *eau de Cologne,* it was his evidence at the inquest that had been his death-warrant. Had he not stoutly maintained that he had seen the murderer—the man with a black beard? Dozens of people in Eastrepps had heard him say it, and his evidence had been reported not only in the local Press, but also in the big London dailies.

"Good morning, Mrs. Dampier."
It was Mrs. Cappell speaking, her head, as usual,

enveloped in a blue veil tied about her large hat. "Isn't this simply too depressing?"

She waved her hand at the empty street.

"Good morning, Laura," responded Mrs. Dampier. "I hear that all the visitors are running away."

"Most of them have gone already, so my nephew tells me," answered Mrs. Cappell. "He has just come down to stay for a few days, and he tells me that the golf-course is a howling desert. It is usually so crowded at this time of year that you have to put your name down on the time-sheet the day before. But nobody is staying this season—except the police and all these journalists."

A disconsolate quintet of minstrels—three men with blackened faces carrying banjoes in cases, followed by two girls in crumpled white pierrot dresses, passed as she was speaking.

"It must be pretty bad for them," continued Mrs. Cappell, looking after the little band.

"Poor things!" she said, "they won't get much out of the local residents."

They were silent a moment.

"Well," said Mrs. Dampier at last, "the bus will be starting in five minutes, and I don't want to miss it."

She hastened away to buy her *eau de Cologne* and to take her seat in the bus, which was waiting at the corner of the churchyard.

A quarter of an hour later she was back again among her roses. She sat, as was her custom, in the little summer-house, built at the end of the terrace, whence she might look out across the expanse of beds and lawn to the blue delphiniums about the sundial and the dark trees beyond. How peaceful and remote was this gentle place, with all the stress and terror shut outside! Her mind ran discursively over the things she had seen and heard—fantastic horror by night and by day, the distresses and anxieties of the hundreds of poor folk who would all suffer in their small way from the panic that had come upon the town. Meanwhile, she had the good fortune to be sitting here, away from it all. Mr. Bennett the Coroner, Sir Jefferson Cobb, the Chief Inspector from London, and the rest—they must move about, haggard in the hot sunshine, tracking down the Evil, as one enterprising paper had named it, while the frightened trippers fled in scores and minstrels played their jazz on the deserted sands, and no one ventured to stir abroad after nightfall. Here it was very peaceful and very quiet. The bees were at work, and the sun slept on the wall where the peaches were beginning to swell. There would be a good crop this year, and she would keep them for her grandchildren. They loved peaches.

A gong sounded, remote and musical.

Mrs. Dampier rose, and with a small sigh moved towards the dining-room and the lemon sole.

III

"Now let us get this quite clear," said Chief Inspector Wilkins. "Constable Birchington was on duty in Norwich Road from 9 P.M. until 11:35 P.M., when I met him on my way to the house. Is that correct?"

"Yes, sir," said Constable Birchington.

"And you walked up and down the whole time, keeping your eye on the house?"

"Yes, sir," said Constable Birchington.

"Between what points?"

Birchington laid a thick finger on the map of Eastrepps spread out in front of the Chief Inspector.

"Between there and there, sir," he said.

Wilkins marked the places indicated with two crosses.

"You saw nothing?"

"Nothing, sir. I kept my eye specially on the bedroom window, but it was dark the whole time."

The Chief Inspector looked pensively round the table at Eastrepps police station, and then turned to Protheroe, who, next to a new man from the Yard, Matthews by name, was sitting on his left.

"Now, Protheroe," he continued, "you, I understand, were with Matthews in Elm Avenue, on the other side of the house."

Protheroe nodded.

"You saw nothing whatever until I arrived?"

"That is so, sir," said Matthews.

The Chief Inspector sighed.

"This means that the house was under continuous observation?" he said. "And yet this fisherman, John Masters, was murdered at West Cliff at 10:35 last night. There can be no doubt of the time. Sergeant Ruddock came upon the body almost before life was extinct."

Sergeant Ruddock spoke gently from his place at the table.

"Yes, sir," he said.

"You might run over your evidence again, Ruddock, if you don't mind."

"Certainly, sir. I was taking a walk along the shore under the west cliffs, meaning to return home by the zigzag path that climbs to the golf course not far from the lighthouse and some few hundred yards from Coatt's Spinney, where the first murder was committed."

Chief Inspector Wilkins nodded.

"I had got two-thirds of the way up the path," continued Ruddock, "and was going slowly, for it was very dark. It was just before the storm broke last night, and there were heavy clouds. I heard a thud and a light crash or crackling, as though something had fallen into the gorse bushes about twenty yards ahead. I hadn't got my torch with me because, as I say, I was off duty, but I went in the direction of the sound as quickly as I could, and there I found John Masters. He was lying half on the path and half in a gorse-bush, stabbed, like the others, in the right temple. Only this time the murderer must have cut an artery, I think, for there was a lot more blood than when Miss Taplow met her end. He died, sir, in my arms. As soon as I saw he was dead I left the body and ran up the path, hoping to catch the murderer, but I hadn't gone thirty yards before I put my foot in a rabbit-hole, fell down and twisted my ankle."

Sergeant Ruddock touched the heavy ashplant on which he had been leaning for support that day.

"I understand, sir," he continued, "that you examined the path last night."

Chief Inspector Wilkins cut him short with a gesture. "Yes," he said, "I examined the path."

Had he not looked over every inch of it? But there had been nothing except for one footprint, smudged and indefinite. In this dry weather it was not even possible to tell how long it had been there. And Rockingham had been in his house asleep in his bed the whole time. The Chief Inspector had made instantly sure of that. The moment Sergeant Ruddock had brought the news to "The Three Fishermen" he had hurried round to the house in Norwich Road, accompanied by Higgins. They had entered Rockingham's bedroom to find him sound asleep, his clothes folded neatly on the chair, just where Higgins swore he had left them two hours before.

So that was one line gone west, and a very promising line it had been. Where else was he to weave his web? He sat a moment, gazing at the stolid faces of the men around him—red Protheroe, with his thick moustache; pale Matthews, the best of his trained shadowers; heavy Birchington; nondescript Sergeant Ruddock.

The door opened, and Sergeant Allquick appeared and saluted. The Chief Inspector rose at once.

"Good!" he said. "How long will they be out?"

"A couple of hours. Higgins will take him for a walk along the front. Our men will keep them both in sight, and warn us if they seem likely to come back."

"Good!" said Wilkins again.

"Matthews," he added, "I think you'd better come along with me. You, too, Protheroe."

They left the station and were driven to the house in Norwich Road. Matthews and Protheroe, on a word from the Inspector, took up their positions of the previous evening. Elm Avenue joined the Norwich Road at right angles, and the house occupied by Rockingham, No. 41, stood at the corner. There were plenty of trees, the Inspector noted, especially along the hedge or fence bordering the garden of the house.

He pointed to a door marked "Tradesmen's Entrance."

"Yes," said Matthews. "I kept my eye on that door most particularly. It is locked, and it certainly did not open last night."

They approached the house, and the Inspector showed his card to a maidservant. Wilkins briefly explained the object of his visit, and the three men passed up the two flights of stairs till they reached the bedroom. The door was then locked, and the Inspector started his search.

First he noted the single window, forty feet from the ground, which Constable Birchington had kept under close observation on the previous evening. The room was then swiftly but very thoroughly searched. There were three chairs, two small tables, a wardrobe, a sofa and the bed. A rather worn Axminster carpet and a cheap Persian rug by the bed itself covered the floorboards. Rockingham's clothes were hanging in a large wardrobe in one corner of the room. These were closely inspected. Finally the rugs were rolled up. The Inspector stepped forward to look at the pedestal table by the bed.

"Hullo! a board loose."

It moved under his foot, and he bent to examine it—a loose plank just by the bed in the corner between the table and the wall. It came up easily, and the Inspector put his hand in the cavity revealed. He drew out a dirty handkerchief, oily to the touch, wrapped about something hard. Unfolding it, he displayed to Protheroe a key, oily like the material in which it was wrapped. He held the handkerchief to his nose.

"Olive oil," he said. "Does this fit the door?" he asked, tossing the key to Matthews.

Matthews caught it and tried it.

"It does," he said.

They passed into the corridor. There were three other rooms, and all were locked. Matthews tried the key in the first door. It opened at once, disclosing a children's nursery, the furniture covered with dust-sheets. Wilkins took the key from Matthews and tried it in the other doors. It opened them all.

Wilkins passed to the end of the corridor. The window there gave upon Elm Avenue. The wall again ran sheer, but this time for only half the distance. Twenty feet below there was the slightly sloping roof of a verandah; while between that and the window from which the Chief Inspector was gazing was a window on the landing below.

Wilkins moved quietly down the corridor to the head of the stairs. These he descended one by one till he reached the eighth, then he stopped and stood looking at the dust which had accumulated a little in the corner of the step where it joined the wall.

"Fetch me a pair of his shoes," he called over his shoulder.

"But he must go up and down every day," objected Protheroe.

"Not walking close to the wall," said Wilkins. "He did that to avoid making a noise."

Protheroe went off, and returned with a pair of crêpe-soled shoes.

The Inspector again looked at the dust, and then carefully superimposed the right shoe, which coincided very closely with the mark. Still without a word, he moved down the stairs. There was another mark, again close to the wall, on the twelfth stair, fainter than the one above.

"Matthews," said Wilkins, "go and ask the housemaid when she last swept the stairs."

Meanwhile the Inspector continued his examination. The stairs yielded nothing further, however, and he had reached the landing on the first floor when Matthews returned.

"The girl says that she last swept them yesterday, though they may not look like it. It is what she calls a dusty house."

Wilkins nodded. He was standing at the window of the first-floor landing. The roof of the verandah, sheeted with zinc, was six feet below. The Chief Inspector examined the window and the frame carefully. He noted that it moved very easily, and that there was a faint trace of oil in the grooves and round the catch.

"Olive oil," he said again. "Just like a madman—artful, but like a child. Lays a clever scheme to get away which leaves behind it a trail like the King's highway."

Thoughtfully he swung himself over the still and on to the roof of the verandah. There was a large ivy plant at one end, with its twigs and leaves broken here and there and dusty only in patches. The thick trunk writhed down the side of the verandah till it reached the ground.

"Easy as lying," said the Chief Inspector.

"Go down to the garden," he called up to Matthews and Protheroe, who were watching him from the window.

Their heads disappeared.

The Chief Inspector then examined the roof with care. On the opposite side to where the ivy climbed he found a drain-pipe running from the gutter. The pipe was rusty, and in the rust were a number of long smooth smears. The Inspector lay flat and peered over the edge. The smears ran all the way down the pipe.

The Inspector rose and, crossing again to the ivy, examined it more closely.

"Down by the pipe and up by the ivy," he said.

He crossed again to the pipe, and swinging his legs over, slid down it till he reached the lawn, landing with one foot in a small rose-bush. Something moved as his weight came upon it. He bent down and picked out a clothes brush.

Matthews, at his elbow, stood watching him. The Inspector, holding the brush gently between finger and thumb, nodded sharply.

"Test this," he said to Matthews.

Matthews sped away.

The Inspector looked about him.

The lawn in this part of the garden ran beneath overspreading trees to a thick hedge bordering the wire fence which ran parallel to Elm Avenue. Wilkins followed the line of the hedge. There were marks here and there, and in some soft earth a dozen paces further along he came across the clear print of a crêpe-soled shoe. Wilkins paused a moment and then started forward again. But again he pulled up short. The hedge along which he was walking was backed by some wire netting, which in one place was loose and lifted easily. Moreover, there were the marks of someone who had evidently passed beneath it. Wilkins crawled through on his hands and knees and found himself in the overgrown garden of a deserted house. The grass was tall, and the trail of someone who had passed through it was clearly visible.

"Who lives in this house?" Wilkins asked of Protheroe, who was following his progress with respectful interest.

"It has been empty more than a year," responded Protheroe.

The Chief Inspector followed the trail through the grass. It took him round the corner of the empty house and so to its tradesmen's entrance, which, like that of the house occupied by Rockingham, gave on the Elm Avenue. The key was in the lock of the door, and it turned sweetly under his hand.

"Olive oil," said the Inspector.

He opened the door and found himself in Elm Avenue just as Matthews drew up beside it in the car.

"The prints are Rockingham's," he said briefly. "I have compared them with a good one which we found in the bedroom."

Chief Inspector Wilkins pointed to the door.

"Were you watching that door last night, Matthews?" he asked.

Matthews shook his head.

"Not the whole time," he answered crossly. "I walked up and down the Avenue, of course, but I cannot swear that I kept my eye on that door all the evening."

"Protheroe?"

Chief Inspector Wilkins had raised his voice.

Protheroe bounded towards him through the tall grass like an ungainly rabbit.

"No, sir," he said, "I had no instructions to watch that door."

"Then that is how he got out," said Wilkins.

Matthews scratched the back of his neck.

"But he was in bed at eleven-thirty last night," he objected. "You saw him all tucked up and sleeping like a lamb."

The Chief Inspector smiled.

"The murder was committed an hour before," he said. He paused a moment and added:

"Take back this handkerchief and key and put them where I found them. Be careful that nothing is moved or altered in the room. I will see you later at the station."

"Where will you be, sir, in case anything should turn up?"

"I must find a magistrate," said Wilkins.

He nodded at Protheroe, who was looking at him inquiringly.

"Yes," he said, "I'm going for a warrant."

IV

"Sit down, Sergeant. You look tired, and no mistake. It's the 'ot weather, I suppose, and being run off your feet with all these murders. What you want is a nice strong cup o' tea. And I thought you might be able to do with a grilled kipper to it."

"You spoil me, Miss Scarlett," said Sergeant Ruddock as he sat down. "And I really don't deserve it."

"Come now, Sergeant," said Miss Scarlett indignantly. "Maybe you do and maybe you don't. You're much too modest about yourself, and if some of us 'ad their deserts . . . But you haven't even took off your boots."

Sergeant Ruddock shook his head.

"I'm sorry, Miss Scarlett," he said, "but I have got to go out again after tea, and I am pretty sure to be late again to-night."

" 'Ow you do work, to be sure," said Miss Scarlett, setting the kipper in front of her lodger and pushing a large plate of bread and butter, cut thick in the way he liked, towards him. "And everybody saying that the police are a lot of lazy 'ounds."

"Indeed!" said Sergeant Ruddock. "Is that what they say?"

"Lazy 'ounds," repeated Miss Scarlett indignantly. "I 'ad it from Wilcox, the fishmonger. 'Well,' I said to him this morning, 'that's a nice remark to pass. And where would you be without the police?' I said. 'And what about my customers?' he said. 'There's 'ardly a visitor left in the town,' he said. 'And the fish,' he said, 'going bad on me, and the season slipping away.' "

"And what did you say to him?" asked Ruddock, boning his kipper with a practised hand.

"I gave him as good as he gave me," replied Miss Scarlett, "and I do think that I made him see reason in the end. 'What do *you* know of the police?' I said. 'Only what you gets from the papers. And what do they know?' I said. 'The police,' I said, 'works cruel hard. And catching criminals is a bit above weighing fish,' I said."

Miss Scarlett had taken up her favourite position on the other side of the table near the mantelpiece. She looked complacently around the room. The six high-backed chairs, with detachable seats of green leather, the fumed-oak dining-table, the sea pieces on the wall, the sideboard with its cupboard of glass and china, were all hers—bought from the savings of her Pimilico days before she had been ordered to the sea for her health. Now she need keep only such lodgers as she pleased, and of all she had ever had Sergeant Ruddock, with his modest and polite way of living, pleased her most.

"Not but what Wilcox 'adn't some right on his side," she admitted. "For everybody is leaving the town, and, as he very well said, if this sort of thing goes on something will have to be done. We don't pay rates and taxes to have murderers running loose in the streets. You may say, 'What's three murders among so many?' But once people gets it into their heads that they aren't safe, they sees a criminal behind every hedge. You can't really blame the visitors. I don't know as I'd come here myself for choice—not unless I was one of these newspaper men. For them, of course, it's meat and drink."

"Plenty of them about," agreed Ruddock.

"Swarming," said Miss Scarlett. "You can't open a newspaper without seeing columns on Eastrepps. Might be a good advertisement, if it weren't so bad for the town."

Ruddock smiled.

"I don't read the papers much myself," he said.

"There was a piece about you in one of them this morning," continued Miss Scarlett. "Photograph and all."

"Photograph?" said Ruddock in a mild astonishment.

Miss Scarlett looked a little conscious of herself.

"Well," she explained, "there was a young man who called to ask if I had a photograph, so I made so bold as to lend him the one that you has in your bedroom. He had it copied, and was back with it in an hour. I hope I didn't do wrong?"

"Certainly not, Miss Scarlett," said Ruddock. "But the Press must be pretty hard up for news."

"There you go again!" protested Miss Scarlett. "Always wanting to 'ide your light. Wasn't it you that as good as seen the 'Evil'?"

"The Evil?" said Ruddock.

"That's what they call him, you know—the Eastrepps Evil."

"Well," said Ruddock. "I merely twisted my ankle. They could hardly make a story out of that."

"And I never inquired about it this morning. I do 'ope as how you are using that stick I gave you?"

"Yes," he said kindly; "but I don't really need it now. Those cold-water compresses were very good indeed. But what do the newspapers say?"

"I'll read it for you, if you like."

"I've got to go for another conference at the station in ten minutes," the Sergeant warned her.

But Miss Scarlett was reading:

" 'I understand that he'—that's you—'was walking up the zigzag path leading to the top of the cliff, when he heard a dull crash, such as might have been made by heavy body falling to the ground. The gallant Sergeant'—that's you—'lost no time. Unarmed though he was, he ran forward through the darkness, already suspecting that he was on the track of the

Evil. His suspicions were only too soon confirmed, for, lying in the path, he came upon the body of John Masters, who had been struck down almost within sight of him, and who practically died in his arms. Leaving the body as soon as he was satisfied that life was extinct, Sergeant Ruddock sprang forward in pursuit of the murderer. In his haste, however, he tripped and fell, and on recovering his feet found that he had twisted his ankle. The murderer had made good his escape. The Sergeant, though he was in some considerable pain from his ankle, lost no time in reporting to Chief Inspector Wilkins, who, as is well known, is in charge of the case.' "

"There is a lot more about the Chief Inspector," added Miss Scarlett.

"Now I wonder where he got all that from?" said Sergeant Ruddock.

Miss Scarlett studied a large red rose on the carpet.

"He got it from me," she said at last defiantly. "Mr. Ferris his name was, and I thought it was high time that credit was given where it was due. 'He's too modest,' I said, 'that's his great fault.' And then I told this Mr. Ferris what I thought about it. 'When one 'as a 'ero in the 'ouse,' I said . . ."

Ruddock waved a deprecatory hand.

"You shouldn't have done it," he protested.

"I'd do it again and welcome," said Miss Scarlett.

Ruddock smiled a little wanly.

"I understand now," he said, "why Inspector Protheroe was a little short with me this morning."

"Who cares for him?" asked Miss Scarlett indignantly.

"It is my duty to care," said Ruddock gently.

"But, never mind," he added, pushing his plate away, and rising. "They will have something better to talk about to-morrow morning."

Miss Scarlett gazed at him with wide eyes.

"Is it—no, it ain't—a clue?"

"A clue it is," Ruddock replied. "And that is why I am going to be late to-night. Important developments may be expected."

v

The car containing Chief Inspector Wilkins, Sir Jefferson Cobb and a slim girl with yellow hair pulled up silently at the meeting of the Overstrand and Norwich Roads. All three got out and stood for a moment in the shadow of the trees.

"Now, Annie, you quite understand?"

It was Sir Jefferson Cobb speaking.

"All you have to do is to walk up and down the Norwich Road till you hear a whistle. Our men won't lose sight of you for a single moment."

"Where will they be, sir?" asked the girl.

"In the gardens opposite No. 41."

The girl looked uncertainly at Sir Jefferson.

"Miss Smart," began Chief Inspector Wilkins.

The girl turned to him quickly.

"We shan't let the man get within ten yards of you," he continued. "You will be quite safe, and, in any case, you are not going to let us down. I'm sure of that."

Annie Smart looked at the Chief Inspector doubtfully.

"No, sir," she said at last.

She hoped she looked braver than she was feeling. It was all very well for these men to talk of being safe and all the rest of it. But it was always possible that something might go wrong, and that last awful murder had been committed almost under the noses of the police. Her mind went back to the dreadful evening three days before, when she had gone out to meet her young man. She would see again the tall stranger who had walked after her in long silent strides. He had lifted his hat to her and said something. And then she had run blindly, with the Evil, as it seemed, at her heels. Luckily Mrs. Chesham's house, where her aunt was cook, had been only a few yards away. Thither she had bolted, and her aunt had kept her all night. Who would have dared to go back to Sir Jefferson Cobb's house, more than a mile away, in the dark middle of the night? So she had waited till dawn, and then, creeping home, had found the police in her master's study. No wonder her nerves had given away!

And now she was to be used as a decoy—after having been bothered, too, with a lot of questions which she had been quite unable to answer. How could one be expected to describe the Evil? She had felt it behind her in the dusk. That was enough. The Inspector seemed to think she ought to have stayed to have a look at it. He was a hard man, the Inspector—kind in his way, but he seemed to think it was wrong to have anything in the shape of nerves, and when all was said and done, a girl had a right to her feelings.

And now he was speaking.

"Please wait here with Sergeant Allquick. He will tell you when to start."

Well, it was too late now to draw back.

"Yes, sir," she responded faintly.

Still, it was rather a tall order. She had read somewhere how big-game hunters would tether a kid or a fawn as a lure for savage beasts. It was a wicked cruel thing to do.

"I hope that girl is all right," said Chief Inspector Wilkins as he moved off with Sir Jefferson Cobb down the road.

"You may trust Annie," Sir Jefferson assured him heartily. "She is naturally a bit scared, but she will carry on. She's properly covered, isn't she?"

"You needn't worry about that," said the Inspector shortly.

"What are your other arrangements?"

"I've got four men in front of the house," replied the Chief Inspector, "and two men in the Avenue watching the verandah and the water-pipe. Matthews and I will be at the tradesmen's entrance of the empty house next door. Is that you, Sergeant?"

Ruddock was saluting in the shadow.

"Where is Inspector Protheroe?" asked the Chief Inspector.

"He is in the Avenue, sir," replied Sergeant Ruddock.

"Tell him to watch the back door of No. 41 and to keep his ears open. If he hears or sees anything, he should come straight to me. I shall be at the back door of the empty house. Is that clear?"

"Yes, sir," said Ruddock.

The Chief Inspector and the Chief Constable walked together down a narrow lane which led by a roundabout way to the avenue. It was a quarter-past nine.

"You really mean to arrest him if he leaves the house?" said the Chief Constable.

Wilkins did not answer for a moment.

"Perhaps," he said at last.

"You haven't really a scrap of evidence," Sir Jefferson objected, "except that he is in the habit of escaping from his room, and that he likes raising his hat to any girl he happens to meet."

"That is all—for the moment," said Wilkins. "That is why I said 'perhaps.' This is an experiment."

"You mean he may assault the girl. Be careful, Wilkins."

"No. I promised her that he shouldn't get within ten yards of her," said the Inspector. "And now, sir, I think we had better get to our posts."

They had reached the point where the lane ran into the Avenue. There they turned to the right, and a few steps brought them opposite the back door of the empty house. Here the Chief Inspector was met by Matthews and two men from Norwich.

"Perhaps you would stand over there, sir," said Matthews to the Chief Constable.

The Chief Constable did as suggested.

"I am going to make the round," said the Chief Inspector.

He walked away silently, keeping in the shadow of the trees on the further side of the Avenue. He had rubber soles to his shoes, and made no sound. Presently he reached the corner of the Avenue and Norwich Road. There he paused and looked to the right. The road was deserted, its tarred surface smooth and shining faintly in the light of two street lamps. The Chief Inspector, after a moment's hesitation, crossed the road till he was in the shadow of the gardens of the houses opposite. A head came up as he approached the boundary hedge.

"All right, sir."

It was Constable Birchington speaking. "The young lady is walking up and down."

The Chief Inspector nodded and drew himself further into the shadow of the hedge. He stood still for a moment or two. Would it work?

A light step sounded behind him some ten yards away. Annie Smart was coming along the pavement and passed within a few feet of him. "Good girl!" thought the Chief Inspector. She was walking with her head up, and now and again she glanced towards the house opposite. The Chief Inspector himself looked across the road. No. 41 was in darkness. The girl's footsteps died away and silence fell. The Inspector looked at his watch. Ten o'clock. Was it going to fail?

But Annie Smart was returning. Her figure showed dark and slim under the street lamp. She paused in the light of it.

"Good girl!" repeated the Inspector to himself.

There was a slight sound as of a window being lifted. The Chief Inspector's head came sharply round. A

light had flashed on in Rockingham's bedroom. The
girl shrank back against the lamp-post, then squared her
shoulders firmly and walked on slowly down the Avenue towards the second lamp-post.

There was a man at the window of No. 41, and he was
watching her intently. He had a hat on his head. The
girl passed under the second lamp and deliberately
paused in the full light of it.

A low whistle came down from the man at the window.
And now, by Jove! he was raising his hat.

The girl turned still more towards the house. She
was looking up at the window. The man beckoned. She
took a few hesitating steps, which brought her into the
middle of the road.

"Down in a minute, my dear."

It was the man at the window calling softly. Abruptly
he disappeared, and a moment later the light in his room
went out. The Inspector turned and walked quickly
back to his post at the back door of the deserted house,
passing Inspector Protheroe, who clutched him by the
arm.

"Look, sir," he said.

The Chief Inspector stared over his shoulder. The
lean form of Rockingham hung a moment from the
window ledge and dropped lightly to the roof of the
verandah. Then it crossed to the corner of the roof
where the pipe started to the ground.

The Chief Inspector waited no longer, but moved
rapidly to where Matthews and his men were standing
on guard. They stood together by the door for what
seemed an interminable time. At last, very faintly, there
came to the Chief Inspector's ears the sound of someone
moving through the rank grass on the farther side of
the door. Someone was fumbling at the lock. Someone was breathing heavily. The door opened. A tall
man passed furtively through.

Chief Inspector Wilkins stepped forward and laid a hand on his shoulder.

"George Alistair Rockingham," he began.

A white face looked for an instant into his own. A shoulder twisted under his grasp. Rockingham had torn himself free and was running down the Avenue. The Chief Constable and the two men from Norwich appeared from the shadow of the trees on the further side.

Wilkins stood watching the hunted man. The circle was closed, and he could not escape. Rockingham had seen that already for himself. He paused in the lamplight, turned back towards Wilkins and for a moment looked this way and that. His face was ghastly, the mouth working, the head up, like that of a beast surprised.

The two men from Norwich were closing in upon him, and Wilkins himself took a step forward.

Wilkins, describing afterwards what happened next, said it was as though something had struck the man an invisible blow. One instant he was standing plainly in the lamplight, and the next instant he had dropped to the ground, a low, almost indistinguishable figure, on all fours.

Wilkins ran forward. A snarling face with bared teeth turned towards him obliquely as he advanced, and suddenly, with the head thrown back, it gave tongue.

The Honourable Alistair Rockingham was on his hands and knees, barking like a dog.

"God save us!" said Matthews from the further side.

"That completes my case," said Chief Inspector Wilkins.

CHAPTER SIX

I

Chief Inspector Wilkins was walking up and down the arrival platform of Eastrepps Station. He was rather dreading the next quarter of an hour. Lord and Lady Steyning were due to arrive, and he had arrested their only son on a charge of murder. A painful business. Otherwise, however, nothing could be better. He had laid the Eastrepps Evil, and congratulations had come to him over the telephone from the Chief High Commissioner. This case would add appreciably to his reputation.

Meanwhile, he must do all he could for the Steynings. He had, indeed, received a note to that effect from the private secretary of no less a person than the Home Secretary himself. He was asked to help them in every possible way consistent with the demands of justice. Presumably they would wish the necessary steps to be taken as quietly as possible. Rockingham would henceforth be kept where he should have been put in the first place. The doctors who had allowed him to run loose must be feeling pretty nervous about it. But they would doubtless be able to make out a good case for themselves. They usually did.

Chief Inspector Wilkins smiled. He had been cheered on his way to the station. Quite a small crowd, in fact, had followed him, and it was rather nice to be popular —especially after several days of the cold shoulder.

The mystery was solved. The trippers who had left would come back, or their places would be taken by others. The town would soon recover. People would be taken to see the spot where John Masters had met his death; they would be brought to gaze upon the pipe down which Rockingham had slithered. And once more the tennis courts which he had passed on his way to the station would be astir with flannelled figures, and the landladies of Eastrepps would again take heart.

"Good morning, Inspector."

Wilkins turned, and saw a man who seemed familiar. What was the fellow's name? He remembered it now —Richard Coldfoot, often at "The Three Fishermen," excitable, and not a pleasant companion.

"Feeling no end of a chap this morning, I suppose," the man continued.

"Is it as obvious as all that?" said the Chief Inspector pleasantly.

"Why not?" responded the other. "This is a fine feather in the cap of Chief Inspector Wilkins, and he can hardly fail to know it."

"The case is not yet finished," said Wilkins shortly.

He turned away rather pointedly to meet the train, which was now coming into the station.

The train drew up. There were only a few passengers on board, and the Chief Inspector had not long to wait. The door of a first-class compartment opened. A tall man in a grey suit stepped out and turned to help a lady to the platform, fashionably but rather too youthfully dressed.

The couple stood a moment looking back towards their compartment, whence they were joined by another man, short and bearded, with a light overcoat on his arm.

The Chief Inspector knew this second man—Sir Hilary Braxted, the mental specialist. He approached the group and took off his hat.

"Lord Steyning?" he said.

The tall man nodded. He had a kind but weak face, not improved by a straggling, yellow moustache and a pair of watery blue eyes set rather too close together.

Lady Steyning, on a nearer view, was dark, with hair to match, and had once been good-looking.

Wilkins introduced himself.

"I am Chief Inspector Wilkins," he said.

"Quite," said Lord Steyning under his breath. "Quite," he added aloud.

"I have had a letter," began Wilkins.

"Of course," broke in Lady Steyning. "I rang up Johnny Carstairs myself only yesterday," she added, turning to her husband.

The Inspector noted this familiar reference to the Home Secretary.

"We want to help you clear up this dreadful . . . misunderstanding," continued Lady Steyning. "It is impossible that my boy should be guilty."

"I am afraid, madam," said the Inspector, "that the facts, when you know them, will convince you that I had no other course but to arrest him."

He looked aside at Sir Hilary Braxted. Sir Hilary caught the Inspector's eye, and for a moment they looked at one another.

"Good morning, Sir Hilary," said Wilkins.

"Good morning, Chief Inspector," said the doctor.

"There is some terrible mistake," said Lady Steyning. "Sir Hilary here will tell you . . ."

She broke off. There were tears in her eyes.

Wilkins turned to Lord Steyning.

"I think," he suggested, "that it would be more convenient if we continued this conversation at your hotel."

"Certainly," said Lord Steyning under his breath. "Certainly," he repeated aloud.

The ticket collector stared at them curiously as he took the tickets. So those were the parents of the murderer. He whispered a word to Bill the porter, who gazed at them with round eyes and passed it on to the taximan outside.

Lord and Lady Steyning with the Inspector and Sir

Hilary Braxted entered a closed car sent by Sir Jefferson Cobb and were driven off.

"What was that?" asked Lady Steyning suddenly.

Something had struck the car as it gathered speed. The Chief Inspector glanced out of the window. Three or four louts were standing on the edge of the road. One of them was shouting something. The Chief Inspector hastily pulled down the blind.

"Nothing," he said.

Lady Steyning was sitting very upright in the back of the car.

"Abominable!" said Lord Steyning under his breath. "Abominable!" he repeated aloud.

"I am afraid," said Wilkins gently, "that this case has attracted a good deal of attention."

The remainder of the journey passed in silence, unbroken until Wilkins had closed the door of a private sitting-room in the Grand Hotel, overlooking the sea.

It was Sir Hilary Braxted who spoke first.

"I understand," he said, looking very directly at Wilkins, "that you have been instructed to give us such assistance as is in your power. We in our turn are ready to help you in every way."

Wilkins bowed.

"I am, as you probably know," continued Sir Hilary, "medical adviser to the family."

"When shall we see my son?" broke in Lady Steyning.

"You can see him at once," Wilkins replied. "But perhaps it would be best to have our conversation first. He will be taken to Norwich later in the day."

"As you please," said Lady Steyning, and signed to the doctor to continue.

"I would ask you to be very frank with us," continued Sir Hilary. "We wish to know on what evidence you have made this arrest. Let me say at the outset that Mr. Rockingham has been my patient for a number of years, and I can assure you, speaking as an expert, that it is in my view quite impossible that he should be guilty of the very terrible crimes that are laid to his charge."

The Chief Inspector made a deprecating motion with his hands.

"I am sorry, Sir Hilary," he said; "but the facts in my possession are overwhelming. I have, of course, no medical knowledge. I can only base my conclusions on such evidence as I have been able to obtain. I think you will agree with me when you hear it that I could scarcely have acted otherwise."

"You are charging him with murder," said Lady Steyning.

She stopped abruptly, looking very white and clearly unable to go on. Sir Hilary brought her a glass of water, but she waved it away and sat back stiffly in her chair.

"Go on, Chief Inspector," she said. "What have you got against my boy?"

Wilkins cleared his throat. "In the first place," he said, "I am able to prove that your son, who was locked in his bedroom every night by his personal attendant, Higgins, found means to leave the house in 41, Norwich Road whenever he so desired. Secondly, he has been identified in the street by a housemaid in the employ of Sir Jefferson Cobb, the Chief Constable of the County, who is prepared to swear that your son—er—accosted her three nights ago at about ten in the evening. At half-past ten John Masters met his death on the path near the lighthouse. Thirdly, the accused, when arrested and searched, was found to be carrying a large knife known, I think, as a Swedish knife; the blade is very sharp and pointed—just such a weapon as could have been used in the commission of the crimes. He acknowledges that he bought it in the town two days after his arrival when, to use his own words, he had given that fellow Higgins the slip. The ironmonger who sold it to him has identified him as the purchaser."

"Speaking as his medical attendant," interrupted Sir

Hilary, "I maintain with confidence that if Mr. Rockingham had been found with fifty knives, he has neither
the will nor the strength to commit a violent crime.
There is still, moreover, nothing that connects my patient with the murders."

"I am sorry to say that there is one very definite circumstance," said the Inspector. "I regret to mention it,
but it must be brought out sooner or later. Upon the
occasion of the murder of Miss Taplow a dog was heard
to bark some five minutes before her body was found.
She had not been dead more than a few minutes."

There was silence for a moment. The doctor's face
was expressionless, but Lady Steyning had covered her
eyes.

"God have mercy on us!" said Lord Steyning under
his breath. "God have mercy on us!" he repeated
aloud.

"Believe me," said the Inspector in a low voice. "I
realise this must be inexpressibly painful to you, but
we must face the facts. It was part of my task to inquire into the personal history of anyone in Eastrepps
whose conduct seemed in the least degree unusual. My
attention was called to your patient, Sir Hilary. I at
once made the necessary inquiries, and was informed of
the affliction to which he is liable. It is now my painful
duty to acquaint you with the fact that your son upon
his arrest the night before last had some kind of fit and,
falling on his knees, began to bark with the same peculiar
and unmistakable note which had been heard three days
previously when Miss Taplow met her death."

There was a long silence. Lord Steyning had laid a
hand on his wife's shoulder.

"You must not give way, Marion," he said under his
breath. "You must not give way, Marion," he repeated
aloud.

Sir Hilary Braxted was staring steadily in front of him.

"I knew, of course," he said, "of these symptoms.

There are certain moments when he does, unfortunately, have these fits as you call them, Chief Inspector, but I can assure you that they are not in the least degree dangerous to human life."

"I submit, sir, with deep respect," replied Wilkins, "that other members of your distinguished profession may think otherwise."

Sir Hilary sat silent, fingering his beard.

Lady Steyning had lowered her hands, and was gazing straight at Wilkins.

"Of course," said Wilkins gently, "you quite realise that in this case the usual consequences, should your son be found guilty, would almost certainly—er—not follow. He will, of course, go for trial, but the verdict is bound to be such as to cause his detention, as we say, during His Majesty's pleasure."

"Broadmoor—that is what you mean," said Lady Steyning.

Then, with a little sigh, she fell forward in a faint across the table.

II

William Ferris rose from the breakfast-table and began to fill the first and best pipe of the day. He had every reason to be pleased with himself. Had he not been the first journalist in London to write about the crimes in Eastrepps? Had he not invented a phrase with which all England had run for the last three weeks? The Eastrepps Evil—it was on everyone's tongue, and that very morning a cheque for twenty pounds had fallen from an envelope sent personally from his Editor, with instructions to prolong his holiday for another week or even ten days if he liked.

Ferris moved into the sitting-room.

He and his family were now almost the only guests at the boarding-house. The trippers had flown upon the third murder, and Mrs. Snell, the landlady, had talked of ruin and the breaking up of the home. Ferris had even had trouble with his wife fearing for her children, and he had been compelled to assure her patiently every day that the Evil walked abroad only at night, and that people were quite safe provided they kept to the house after dark.

But now the Evil was laid. As a citizen, Ferris rejoiced, but professionally—well, Othello's occupation was gone, and he could not help feeling a little blank. Was there anything further he could do? Chief Inspector Wilkins had refused to give him any particulars of the arrest of Rockingham or the case for the Crown. But one might always try again. "After all," reflected Ferris, "the police had every reason to be kind to him, for he had certainly been kind to the police."

Ferris, with a pleasant word to his landlady, all smiles that morning, for she had received news of visitors anxious to recover their rooms, passed out of the front door, and so to the Police Station in Church Street. Here he found Sergeant Ruddock writing in the station room. The Sergeant was in plain clothes.

"Good morning," said Ferris. "Any chance of a few words with the Chief Inspector?"

The Sergeant shook his head.

"No, sir, I'm afraid not," he replied. "Chief Inspector Wilkins is at the Grand Hotel, talking things over with Lord and Lady Steyning and Sir Hilary Braxted, and he is going straight to London by the afternoon train."

Ferris nodded thoughtfully. Lord and Lady Steyning and Sir Hilary Braxted had no interest for him. He had "covered" them the night before, describing, in the manner of his profession, two degenerate members of the high aristocracy smitten with grief at the dreadful charge overhanging their son and heir.

"Busy, Sergeant?" he inquired.

Ruddock was alone in the office.

"Clearing off some routine work," he replied.

Ferris apparently considered this as an invitation. For he sat down.

Ruddock, signing a form, looked up pleasantly.

"Take a seat," he said. "It was nice of you to write so kindly about me in the *Daily Wire*, but I rather wish you had pitched on somebody else."

"Protheroe, for example," said Ferris, with a grin.

"It would have been more tactful," said Ruddock.

He rose as he spoke.

"Home," said Ruddock.

"Come by way of my rooms," suggested Ferris. "There is a bottle of the old and bold in the sideboard cupboard."

"Thank you," said the Sergeant.

They left the station. The town, though it had not yet filled again, was returning to business. The residents were about their shopping, and on the other side of the road Ferris caught sight of Eldridge stepping out of the lending library.

"See that man?" he said, turning to Ruddock.

"That's Mr. Robert Eldridge of Oakfield Terrace," said Ruddock.

"I nearly made a fool of myself over him," continued Ferris. "Inspector Wilkins as good as asked me to tell him of anything unusual which I might happen to come upon in the course of my inquiries. Well, I saw this man Eldridge, in Sheffield Park on the night when John Masters was murdered."

"Why shouldn't he have been in Sheffield Park?" said Ruddock pleasantly.

"No reason at all," replied Ferris, pushing open the door of his lodging-house and motioning Ruddock to enter. "But I happened to meet him again on the following morning. He was coming from the railway station."

"Indeed?" said Ruddock, as they entered the sitting-room. "And why shouldn't he be coming from the railway station?"

"No reason at all," replied Ferris, "but he was talking to Colonel Hewitt at the time."

"And why shouldn't he talk to Colonel Hewitt?" inquired Ruddock.

"No reason at all," replied Ferris, "but he had given the Colonel to understand that he had not heard of the murder of John Masters because he had been in London the night before."

Ruddock lifted the tumbler which Ferris had placed before him.

"I see," he said. "You had seen him in Eastrepps, and he was pretending to have been in London. That is interesting."

Ferris and Sergeant Ruddock drank together.

"Well," said the Sergeant, setting down his glass, "why didn't you come to us about it?"

"There was nothing against Eldridge," said Ferris, "and one can never be quite sure. Chief Inspector Wilkins had rubbed it into me how easily a person can be mistaken on a question of identity. I could have sworn it was Eldridge I had seen in Sheffield Park, however, and I should probably have mentioned the matter to the Inspector at our next meeting. Then came the arrest of Rockingham. It all just shows how necessary it is to be careful."

Sergeant Ruddock emptied his glass.

"Did Eldridge realise that you had seen him?"

"I believe he did. He looked a bit sheepish when he found me gazing at him rather pointedly. But that, again, is only my impression. What do you make of it, Sergeant?"

"Well," said Ruddock slowly, "if we hadn't arrested Rockingham . . ."

"Exactly," said Ferris.

"It would be worth investigating," concluded Ruddock.

"What about another spot?" suggested Ferris.

"No, thanks. It's very good of you," said Ruddock, "but I really must be going."

He rose as he spoke.

"Nothing for me, I suppose?" said Ferris.

Ruddock shook his head.

"Rockingham will be brought before the magistrates the day after to-morrow at Norwich. I expect there will be a week's remand."

"In that case," said Ferris, "I shall be getting on with my holiday."

Ruddock smiled.

"I am sure you deserve it," he observed. "And please don't think me ungrateful for what you said about me in the *Daily Wire*. But it doesn't do for a mere sergeant to be too much in the public eye."

"Still," said Ferris brightly, "I shouldn't be surprised if I haven't given you a bit of a leg up, after all."

Sergeant Ruddock smiled.

"Well," he admitted, "perhaps you have."

III

Mrs. Dampier decided to take her after dinner coffee out of doors. It was hot, oppressively hot—with a promise of storm in the air, as on the night poor John Masters had met his end.

Poor John Masters!—a fine man, come of a line of seafarers, one whose heart was upon the wide waters. There had been none like him in Eastrepps for a hero so long as she could remember. Had he not won the King's gold medal twice for saving life at sea? Moreover, he had supplied Mrs. Dampier with lobsters, the best that ever came upon the beaches.

And now he was gone, like her friend Mary Hewitt,

and that charming Miss Taplow—struck down by the madman, Rockingham, whom she had seen so often shambling along Church Street with little Higgins in tow.

But the nightmare was ended now, and Mrs. Dampier, as she sipped her coffee, was conscious, though she would never have admitted it, of an immense relief. She had never shared the general panic, but it was nice to think that Eastrepps was itself again. The pleasant little town, perched upon the edge of England, with the hungry sea at its feet and nothing but keen winds and harsh waters between its houses and the Pole, would soon recover from this evil dream. The visitors would be coming back, and the minstrels again perform before audiences free of care on the sands. Mrs. Rackham would soon be ordering her three dozen of kippers at the fishmongers. Life would go on as before, and the town would no more be butchered to make a pressman's holiday.

Mrs. Dampier finished her coffee, and, rising from her chair in the summer-house, began to walk slowly towards her roses. They were drooping a little in the heat. She must tell Johnson about it. He must water them longer to-morrow. But they were very lovely, a superb mass of blossom, banked for twenty feet from the edge of the lawn to the top of the pergola that ran behind. Here in her garden beauty was caught in a net of shining petals, and to guard against unlovely invasions, the lilies and lupins stood about like sentinels, with the tall hollyhocks stiff as grenadiers towards the gate. To her right shone ever so faintly a still pool, with little newts and tiny Japanese fish that darted silently about their business in the cool depths. And beyond the pool was a gracious company of trees.

Here was the delectable garden which she had made for herself. She had watched it grow for thirty years. She had loved it, and she found it beautiful and good.

She moved gently away from the roses to the top of

the garden, where there was a tall hedge of sweet-peas, and beside them a gate leading to the road. It was not latched, and she remembered that the broken lock had not been mended. She would see about it in the morning.

She moved forward to shut the door properly. It was made of oaken slats, which, though green, were still strong and serviceable. Suddenly she stopped. There were footsteps outside. Then came a soft knock, as though someone, before beating upon the door, had slipped a cushion between his fist and the wood. A single dull thud was followed by a long sigh. Something fell against the door heavily, so that it shook, and with a slight whimper of hinges swung open towards her.

A man was trying to enter the garden.

His face shone a moment in the light of a street-lamp, white and set, with dark lines spraying out across his forehead.

He stumbled towards her and dropped, a falling shadow, at her feet.

"Sanctuary," she thought. "He has come here to be safe," and a great fear smote her suddenly as a sound of breathing, short and harsh, drew her eyes from the man on the ground.

Opposite her stood a dark figure. His eyes burned in a swarthy face and about his chin was a black beard. His arm was raised. Something gleamed in the lamp-light.

"Don't . . . don't . . ." whispered Mrs. Dampier, as he struck home with savage force.

IV

Robert Eldridge, with Margaret at White Cottage, had ceased to recognise himself. Was this the man who travelled weekly to Fenchurch Street, who wore a black coat with striped trousers, spats and a hard collar? With Margaret he was transformed—a conquistador, a hero home from the West. Or he was clad in a wide tunic, trimmed with a key-pattern in gold; his head was crowned with honeysuckle. She was in his arms by a purple sea, as in the film he had seen at the Tivoli the other day. Love on an Island. . . . This was his island —this room in which the hours slipped away with Margaret as in another life than his own.

"Bob," she said, "you're exceeding your allowance."

But he pulled her closer to him and kissed her again.

"One day in seven, Margaret," he said. "We must make the most of it."

After a time she drew away a little impatiently, he thought.

"Dear," he asked, "what is it?"

She put a hand up and played with the lobe of his left ear, a gesture which filled him with a delight admittedly foolish.

"Bob," she said, "I do get so tired of waiting. I just sit here day after day and wonder how long we shall have to go on like this. Then, of course, there is Dick, who threatens to spoil it all. This is the greatest thing in our lives, but, just because it ought to be so fine, all this secrecy and fear is unbearable. I never want to see again this flat land, the grey sea and this beastly little town."

He rose from his chair, took a turn down the room and back again.

"I know how you feel," he said. "But we shall not have to wait much longer."

How lovely were her arms as they stretched towards him to lie across his shoulders!—like the necks of two white swans, he thought, and wished he could write poetry.

"Only a very short time now," he continued. "I can promise you that."

He swung away again, and, reaching up to the mantelpiece, found and lighted a cigarette.

"Nobody wants to live here less than I do," he went on.

"I thought you rather liked the place," she said.

"I did like it once upon a time—in fact, I still have nothing very definite against it. But somehow these last few days . . ."

He broke off.

"Yes?" she prompted.

"I have taken a dislike to it," said Eldridge.

"Anything in particular?"

"The fact is," he said after a pause, "I've had a bit of a fright, and I suppose I haven't yet had time to shake it off."

Margaret's eyes grew wide with alarm.

"What is it?" she asked. "Why didn't you tell me before?"

"I haven't seen you until to-night since it happened."

"But, Bob, please tell me what it is?"

Eldridge paused a moment.

"It has to do with these awful murders," he began.

"Well?"

"Has it ever struck you, my dear, that they have happened always on a night when you and I have been together?"

"I hadn't noticed it, Bob. But what if they have?"

"It was an odd coincidence. Suppose the police had come to know that on each of these occasions I had not been in London as we pretended, but in Eastrepps. I might have been asked to account for my movements."

"But, my dear, all this is very hypothetical. Why should the police worry about your goings and comings?"

Eldridge looked at Margaret. She was smiling—just a little bothered, but quizzical. He wondered what she would say if she knew that there were at least a dozen people in Eastrepps alone who could get him ten years' penal servitude. The ghost of Selby stirred in him. His thoughts slipped back to the day when he had stolen from his well-appointed office to a waiting hansom—there had still been a good many hansoms on the streets in those days—and driven quickly to the docks. He saw again the stagnant lake, with its stinking reeds and the fetid smell of the oil-fields. Robert Eldridge, the real Eldridge, was dying slowly under the corrugated-iron hut, in a temperature of 112° Fahrenheit. Soon he would bury Eldridge and steal his name.

He passed a hand across his forehead. That chapter of his life was closed. Yet, for a moment, it had become so vivid that his very sense of time had been confused.

"As a matter of fact," he continued slowly, "the case is not altogether hypothetical. John Masters, you remember, was killed last Friday night. I spent that night with you, and I am afraid that someone saw me coming here."

"Anybody in particular?"

"It was one of the reporters who have been hanging about the place for some time."

"Where did he see you?"

"In Sheffield Park."

"Why shouldn't you be in Sheffield Park?"

"No reason at all, but I met him again the next morning when I was pretending to have just arrived from London."

Margaret pursed her lips.

"I see," she said. "And you think that he noticed the . . . er . . . discrepancy."

"I am pretty sure he did. I was talking to Colonel Hewitt at the time, and I could feel this journalist fellow asking himself why on earth I should pretend to have been in London at an hour when he had seen me in Eastrepps. Then I realised that I had done the same thing on the nights of the two previous murders—a pure coincidence, of course, but rather startling."

"I hadn't noticed it myself," said Margaret.

"Nor had I till that moment. But if the police had noticed it—well, it would have been distinctly awkward.

I might have had to admit coming here to you in order to clear myself of having . . . of having . . ."

Margaret laughed.

"Committed the murders, you mean?"

Eldridge sat staring in front of him.

"Still worried?" she asked, crossing to where he sat.

"Not now," he said, taking her hand and smiling back. "There isn't any reason to worry now. They have arrested Rockingham, and all inquiries are at an end. But I don't mind telling you that another such coincidence . . ."

He broke off suddenly.

"What's that?" he exclaimed.

They listened a moment. Someone was crying in the road outside. Then came a patter of footsteps and the sound of windows being thrown up.

Margaret crossed the room, pushed open the French shutters. The sound came louder now—voices and a man shouting on the high chanted note of the hawker.

Eldridge, glancing at his watch, found it was already past midnight.

"I will go and see what it is," he said.

"You forget," answered Margaret, "you are not supposed to be here. I will go myself."

She slipped through the French window as she spoke. He heard her footsteps on the path outside, as he stood half hidden by the curtains. The shouting was still audible, but it was already dying away in the distance. It had been succeeded by a vague hum and the sound of several people moving hastily through the night. Then the garden gate clicked. That was Margaret returning. He heard the rustle of her skirt as she moved to the window. He saw her white face clearly as she entered.

"Why, Margaret, what's the matter?" he asked.

She handed him a single sheet, damp from the press.

"Another coincidence," she said. "The Evil is still at large."

CHAPTER SEVEN

I

"WAKE up, John!"

"Give over, Bertha," said William Ferris.

"Wake up," repeated his wife.

Ferris realised that he was being shaken, not too gently, by the shoulder. He sat up and thrust a thin fist into a dull eye.

"What is it?" he asked.

"Listen!" said his wife.

Ferris listened.

A loud, familiar call was sounding in the street outside.

Ferris, fully roused, swung his legs over the edge of the bed. His feet groped for his slippers. The call was passing beneath their window.

" 'ORRIBLE DOUBLE MURDER IN EASTREPPS THIS EVENING! . . . 'ORRIBLE MURDER! . . . 'OR-RIBLE MURDER! . . . 'orrible murder! . . ."

The voice died away as the man passed. Already Ferris was out of bed. He crossed the room and thrust his head into the night, to find that it was one of a score similarly displayed. Windows were opening all down the street. Some distance away was a lamp-post, and passing beneath it he distinguished a second newsboy following the first who had aroused him.

"Caught napping," said Ferris to himself.

" 'ORRIBLE MURDER," shouted the newsboy, throwing back his head. He looked to Ferris like some beast from

145

the forest—chin unshaven, mouth open, neck on the stretch, eyes black against a white face.

"Bertha," called Ferris, "give me some money."

Bertha fumbled in a large bag. She stood behind Ferris, being in her nightgown, and not wishing to be seen from the street. She was too slow for her husband. He snatched the bag, pulled out the first coin that came to his fingers and tossed it down into the street below.

"I'll stick it on the railings," said the newsboy, "but you had better look lively, or someone will pinch it."

Ferris made for the door.

"John," called Bertha after him, "you have thrown him half a crown."

"Caught napping," said Ferris to himself again, as he darted down the stairs. As he ran he cursed himself. What had possessed him to go to bed early on this of all nights? The Evil had come back—his Evil, the thing he had named. And he had been brutishly asleep.

The paper gleamed, still damp from the press, impaled on the railings.

"Be careful of my lobelias, Mr. Ferris."

It was the landlady's voice behind him. She stood, with a shawl over her flannel nightgown, at the top of the garden path.

Ferris read eagerly the single sheet by the light of the street lamp, heedless of the tardy wind which fluttered his pyjamas.

The news which the *Eastrepps and District Gazette* placed before its readers was brief and startling:

"It is with the utmost regret and horror that we hasten to inform our readers of the appalling crime perpetrated scarcely two hours before this appears in print. Captain Porter, R.N., the energetic and popular secretary of the Eastrepps Golf Club, was discovered murdered about 10:30 this evening in the

Overstrand Road, outside the garden door of Tamarisk House.

"It is presumed that the unfortunate gentleman was on the way home from the Union Club, where he is accustomed to spend the evening at the bridge table.

"But this is not all.

"Over his body, with hideous wounds in her skull, lay the senseless form of Mrs. Dampier, whose brilliant services to the town have so often been referred to in these columns. Mrs. Dampier has been conveyed to the Cottage Hospital, and we are informed as we go to press that her condition is regarded as desperate.

"The discovery of the crime was made by Police-Constable Birchington, who was returning to his home after late duty."

Ferris looked at his wrist watch. Twelve-thirty, and the London edition of the *Daily Wire* was put to bed at three. Caught napping, by George! but there was still time to retrieve the position.

"Mrs. Snell," he said sharply, moving to the door as he spoke, "where is the Overstrand Road?"

The landlady began to explain.

"I see," said Ferris. "Then I must have a bicycle. Your eldest son has one," he continued accusingly.

"Good gracious, sir, you can never be going out tonight."

"The bicycle . . . the bicycle," repeated Ferris.

He dashed upstairs, put on trousers and a coat, and hurried down again, to find Mrs. Snell wheeling her son's bicycle from the kitchen.

"Thank you, Mrs. Snell."

He vaulted upon the machine, forgetting in his excitement to light his lamps.

The quiet road, with the neat trees on each side and the neater houses beyond, seemed never to end. At last, however, he turned to the right, and, crossing the Norwich Road, entered a broader way. The houses were larger here and stood in their own grounds. Tamarisk House, on the right hand, was one of those. Ferris pedalled towards it.

He saw a group of men standing by an open door in an oaken paling, and as he drew near there came a blinding flash, which dazzled him so completely that he ran the bicycle into the group and was knocked off it. He got to his feet with an oath. There came another flash.

"You had better take another one from the other side," a voice was saying.

Ferris perceived that the words were addressed to the local photographer, who was struggling with an unwieldy tripod. He was photographing something on the ground —the body of a man lying on his back, his pointed grey beard jutting at the sky. The head was turned a little to the left, and above the right ear was a deep gash, from which a dark smear of blood ran down. "The mark of the Evil," whispered Ferris, and made a note of the phrase which he would use later in his article.

There came a third flash. Ferris stepped hastily forward, as the photographer began to fold up his camera and to unscrew the tripod.

"You shall have these first thing to-morrow morning, Inspector," he said.

"Thank you, Atkinson."

"Inspector," said Ferris, eagerly approaching Protheroe, "may I have a word with you?"

The Inspector flashed a torch on him.

"No, you can't," said Inspector Protheroe, with an air of curt finality.

"Get that chalk, Birchington," he continued. "Run a line round the body. Then we can lift it and send it to the mortuary."

Ferris stepped back. Should this, in justice, be his

reward? Had not the *Daily Wire* stood alone in England
in the support of the local police? But this, of course,
was Inspector Protheroe, who was naturally inclined to
be sore. There had been no particular mention of him
in the *Daily Wire*. On the contrary, Sergeant Ruddock
had been the prime cut.

Ferris, hurt but unabashed, stood a moment on the
outskirts of the official group. His time would come.

Even as he took up his position he heard beyond a
woman's voice:

"I won't stay here, Sergeant, and that's a fact. You
had better take me to the station and lock me up. You
can't expect a person to sleep in the house with them
dreadful bodies lying in the gate."

"The bodies are being removed," came a quiet voice
in answer. "You will be quite all right, and in no danger whatever. There will be an officer on duty in the
hall till to-morrow morning."

Ferris knew that voice. It was Sergeant Ruddock,
and he was comforting the cook or housemaid of Tamarisk House.

Ferris moved in the direction of the voices, but at
that instant he was thrust violently aside. A man had
jumped from a car newly come to the spot, and was
moving rapidly towards Inspector Protheroe.

"Here, I say," began Ferris resentfully, but stopped
suddenly on seeing that the man who had pushed him
in the back was the Chief Constable, Sir Jefferson Cobb.

"Good God, Inspector! this can't be true."

Sir Jefferson was down on his knees by the body.

"Dead . . . cold," he was heard to mutter.

"Why the devil wasn't I informed of this before, Inspector?" he added in a burst of anger. "They are
crying it in the streets already, a special edition."

"You were away from home, sir," said the Inspector.
"We telephoned as soon as the crime was discovered.

That was at 10:57 P.M., by Constable Birchington here.
Your butler said you had gone out and had omitted to
state where you were dining."

But Sir Jefferson Cobb was not listening. He had
bent over the dead man. An officious constable stepped
forward and flashed a light on the group. A white face,
bristling with a grey beard, gleamed up at them. The
blood from the wound was black. The dead eyes stared
into the face of Sir Jefferson with a questioning, a fear-
ful look in them. The light was equally pitiless to the
living. The Chief Constable's mouth was working under
his moustache, and, if Ferris was not mistaken, there
was something rather like tears in his eyes.

Ferris saw him swallow in his throat. He jerked his
head back.

"Turn out that damned light," he called.

There was a click, and then it was dark.

Ferris, however, had no time to lose. He had seen
enough, but decided before leaving that he would try to
have a word with Sergeant Ruddock. He slipped away
from the group, and following the oaken paling, soon
found himself at the main entrance to Tamarisk House.
Entering the drive, he turned again to the left, and
passed by way of a small kitchen garden to a lawn with
banked roses. Two persons were crossing it, the stouter
of whom cried out upon sight of him.

"Who's that?"

The voice rose to a shriek.

"Sergeant, save me."

Ferris moved quickly forward.

"It's all right, Sergeant," he said, "it's Ferris of the
Daily Wire."

"There, ma'am, what did I say? I know this gentleman."

"Good evening, Sergeant," continued Ferris. "Can
you spare me a moment?"

"Come with me," said Ruddock quietly. "I am just going to see Mrs. Simpson to the house."

He turned to the woman beside him.

"Come, Mrs. Simpson," he said, "Mason will be with you for the rest of the night. He will not move 'from the house, and he will take your evidence in the morning."

Sergeant Ruddock led his charge to the back door and handed her over to the monumental care of Police-Constable Mason. Then he turned and walked back across the lawn.

"Well, Mr. Ferris," he said, speaking in a low tone, "I'm afraid I can't tell you anything much at present. But the facts are simple. Birchington found them both, Mrs. Dampier lying beside Captain Porter, half in and half out of the door there"—he pointed across the lawn. "There can hardly be a doubt of what happened. The murderer, who must have known Captain Porter's habits, lay in wait for him there as he was walking home from his club and struck him as he passed. Captain Porter fell against the door in the garden paling. The door was not locked, for we found that the catch was broken. Mrs. Dampier must have been standing just the other side of it. She probably heard something and looked out. Almost certainly she saw the murderer. He had not time to stab her, but hit her on the head, smashing the skull."

"Is she dead?" asked Ferris.

"She died half an hour ago in the Cottage Hospital without recovering consciousness."

"You say that he struck her on the head," said Ferris. "Isn't that rather strange? All the other victims were killed with a knife."

Sergeant Ruddock looked at Ferris a moment.

"You might perhaps make a point of that," he replied.

They were now approaching the gate, and could hear the voices of Protheroe and Sir Jefferson Cobb in the road outside.

"Another thing," said Ferris urgently. "This cannot, of course, be the work of Rockingham. I suppose he is still under detention."

"He was taken to Norwich this morning," replied the Sergeant. "This will be a crushing blow for the Yard. They have obviously arrested the wrong man."

He fell silent a moment, then laid a hand on the journalist's arm.

"Listen," he continued, "I have one or two ideas on this business, and I believe you can help me."

"Yes?" said Ferris eagerly.

Ruddock stood still beside Ferris, gripping his arm lightly.

"Come to the station to-morrow," he continued. "Would half-past ten suit you?"

"Certainly," said Ferris.

"Thank you," said Ruddock.

"Nothing more for me to-night?"

The Sergeant shook his head.

"Then I'll be getting my story off to London," said Ferris.

Ten minutes later Ferris stood in the telephone box at the Church Street Post Office. A voice spoke sharply in his ear.

"*Daily Wire*, London."

"Ferris speaking. Put me through to Miss Cavell, please." The telephone clicked.

"Is that you, Miss Cavell? William Ferris speaking. . . . Dictation please:

"To-night the Eastrepps Evil has stalked again. That is the appalling message which the special correspondent of the *Daily Wire* is enabled to place exclusively before its readers this morning . . ."

II

Mr. Thomas Ackersley, M.P. for East Norfolk, was walking briskly down Whitehall from Trafalgar Square. The session, he was glad to remember, was drawing to an end. He would be in Yorkshire on the 12th, with two solid months of recreation in front of him. He hoped Lawson's grouse were better than last season. This should be an excellent year—young birds in plenty, and a mild spring. Coveys were plentiful and strong on the wing.

Thick block letters on a newspaper bill switched him from pleasant anticipations to the immediate present.

THE EVIL AT EASTREPPS.
RELEASE OF ROCKINGHAM.

There was a whole row of placards at the corner of Whitehall and Westminster Bridge. His eye ran over the headlines.

INQUEST ON THE EASTREPPS VICTIMS. CORONER SPEAKS OUT. EASTREPPS ENIGMA UNSOLVED. QUESTIONS TO BE ASKED IN THE HOUSE.

Mr. Ackersley paused on the kerb. A policeman raised his hand, and he hastened to cross the road towards Palace Yard.

Questions to be asked in the House—it was no joke being Member for Eastrepps. The hand of his constituency was heavy upon him, and his correspondence was becoming a nightmare. A force of special constables had, it seemed, been organized in the town, led by prominent members of the Golf Club. It called itself the Eastrepps Vigilance Association, and half the male population, turn and turn about, was patrolling the streets. Phrases remembered from the letters he had received that morning slipped through his brain like the advertisements that ran in letters of fire across the big building at Charing Cross.

"We gave you our votes. Can you do nothing for us? *(Signed)* Marian Sibley."

"It is time the troops were summoned and martial law proclaimed. *(Signed)* R. Hewitt, Lt.-Col. (retired)."

Mr. Ackersley deliberately fanned his indignation. He must convince his constituents that afternoon that he really did feel very strongly on the subject. Hitherto he had counselled patience and moderation. This was a local matter, and the needs of Empire must necessarily have pride of place. But the time for patience was past. It was really a scandal that the Government had, so far, failed to take any direct interest in the matter. That afternoon he would press his question home. Somehow he must shake the complacency of the Treasury Bench.

Mr. Ackersley acknowledged the salute of the policeman at the entrance of Palace Yard, crossed it with dignity and passed into the lobby.

"Good afternoon, Ackersley. I should like a word with you before the next division."

"Sorry, Thwaites," he answered, "but I've got a question down."

Mr. Ackersley passed into the house. Thwaites always wanted a word with somebody—forever lobbying on behalf of some private bill for a Gas Company or Building Society. Mr. Ackersley had no time for Thwaites.

He moved towards his seat on one of the back benches just opposite the Treasury Bench. The House was cheering as he arrived, but not, alas! for him. In the early days, as a young Member, he had dreamed of the sudden hush as he rose to speak, of the cheers as each measured and telling phrase fell from his lips, of the excitement in the lobbies when he had sat down, after driving yet another nail into the coffin of the Government. But that had been twenty years ago. He had since spoken but four times, and even his impassioned oration on the price of herrings in Yarmouth had failed to create any

real sensation. And he knew something about herrings.
The cheering was for the Prime Minister, who had apparently just disposed successfully of an awkward question about safeguarding tariffs. The Treasury Bench, Mr. Ackersley perceived, was looking even more smug than usual. The sight of it was a spur to his climbing passion.

Meanwhile, young Slingsby was on his feet, performing as usual. Slingsby, since he had been complimented by the Prime Minister on his maiden speech at the start of the session, had been many sizes too big for his boots.

"Will the Right Honourable the Secretary of State for Home Affairs inform the House whether he considers the conduct of the two police officers who arrested Mrs. Amy Gaskett for loitering in Trafalgar Square to be in conformity with the police regulations, and, if not, what action he proposes to take?"

The Home Secretary had risen.

"The conduct of the police officers in question is at present under investigation. Until that investigation is concluded I would ask the Honourable Member for West Orpington to be content with an assurance that all the relevant papers will be laid upon the table in due course."

Slingsby was up again.

"Is it a fact that the Right Honourable Member is considering a proposal to despatch the two police officers in question to Eastrepps, where their zeal in effecting arrests may be more serviceably employed?"

Slingsby resumed his seat amid the laughter of the House.

"Jackanapes!" said Mr. Ackersley to himself.

Such impertinence was really not to be borne. What had the murders in Eastrepps to do with Slingsby? He rose to his feet.

"Will the Right Honourable the Secretary of State for Home Affairs inform the House what steps have been taken by the police to deal with the recent outbreak of crime in Eastrepps?"

The laughter had died away. Mr. Ackersley felt that he had quite definitely raised the tone of the proceedings. The House was silently awaiting the answer of the Home Secretary.

"The matter is engaging the full attention of Scotland Yard."

There was a movement of protest from the Opposition benches. Mr. Ackersley felt emboldened to continue. He rose again:

"Is the Right Honourable Gentleman aware that a series of atrocious crimes has been committed, and that all that Scotland Yard have yet done is to arrest the wrong man?"

An indignant murmuring came from the back benches on the other side of the House.

"Order! . . . Order!"

"I have nothing to add to my previous answer," said the Home Secretary.

Mr. Ackersley felt, for the first time in his life, that he had the attention and respect of the House. Strange to say, however, he did not greatly care. He saw as at a distance the familiar benches, the oaken galleries, the Speaker in his chair, the mace upon the table. Nearer to his inward vision was the little town, one of a half-dozen he represented, with its red-brick houses, its grey sea, its sandstone cliffs, its happy visitors fleeing as from the plague.

"Has the Right Honourable Gentleman or his Department taken any steps whatever to allay public apprehension in regard to these crimes?"

"Every possible step is being taken," said the Home Secretary.

"Will the Secretary of State for Home Affairs," continued Mr. Ackersley, conscious now that the House was with him, "state whether the police hold out any prospects of an early arrest, or whether the authorities intend at all costs to maintain their present attitude of indifference?"

"Order!"

This time it was Mr. Speaker who intervened. All eyes were turned to the Chair.

"There would seem to be an imputation in that question," said Mr. Speaker, "but I will give the Honourable Member the benefit of the doubt."

The Home Secretary had hardly waited for the ruling of the Chair.

"I cannot accept the Honourable Member's suggestion," he warmly declared, "that the authorities are indifferent. They are doing their best in very difficult circumstances."

Mr. Ackersley rose again.

"Will the Right Honourable Gentleman inform the House," he said slowly, "how many more murders will have to be committed in Eastrepps before he abandons his present callous attitude and condescends to give the matter his serious attention?"

Cries of "Withdraw" came from the Government benches, followed by Opposition cheers.

The Home Secretary jumped up. His pale face was faintly flushed.

"I have said all that I can say on the matter at the moment. My personal attitude does not arise."

"Will the Right Honourable Gentleman . . ." began Mr. Ackersley.

But Mr. Speaker was already on his feet.

"The last question was one which I would not have allowed if I had known its character beforehand. The Honourable Member for East Norfolk is well aware that a question making or implying a charge of a personal character is out of order, and I must ask him to withdraw it."

"On the point of order . . ." began Mr. Ackersley.

"No point of order arises. I must ask the Honourable Member to withdraw the imputation he has made."

"I refuse to withdraw, Mr. Speaker," said Mr. Ackersley. "The matter had gone too far. The present attitude of the authorities . . ."

It was inferred from the Press Gallery that Mr. Ackersley was making the speech of his life, but anything he may have said was lost to posterity amid cries of "Order," "Withdraw," "Sit down," "Name," "Name," and a storm of cheering from the Opposition benches.

Mr. Speaker took advantage of a lull.

"Once more, and for the last time, I call upon the Honourable Member to withdraw."

There was now tense silence in the House.

"It is impossible for me to do so."

"Then I have no alternative. I must name the Honourable Member for East Norfolk as disregarding the authority of the Chair."

"It is my duty . . ." began Mr. Ackersley.

The leader of the House rose from the benches opposite.

"I move," he said, "that the Honourable Member for East Norfolk be suspended from the service of the House."

The question was put.

A confused roaring of "Ayes," with here and there a splutter of "Noes," greeted the motion. Mr. Speaker declared that the Ayes had it, but a few challenging Noes were heard. Mr. Speaker paused a moment, and then directed a division to be taken.

Mr. Ackersley stood looking blindly about him, and then, as the members began to stream past him on their way to the lobbies, he turned with resolution and passed heroically from the House to vote against his own suspension.

"The Ayes have it."

Mr. Speaker a few minutes later was announcing the

result. Mr. Ackersley, his mouth set in a thin line, rose from his seat.

"Sir," he began, "in the interest of the constituency which I have the honour to represent, I must continue . . ."

It was then that he became aware of a quiet, implacable figure beside him. The Serjeant-at-Arms touched him lightly on the shoulder.

Mr. Ackersley paused, looked round upon the rows of faces, all suddenly rather blank and unsympathetic. Then he turned a vivid pink, moved slowly down the bench, bowed stiffly to Mr. Speaker and left the House.

III

Colonel Hewitt's beat extended for some three hundred yards from the entrance of the concrete passage leading to West Cliff to a point opposite and slightly beyond Tamarisk House, where he was met every fifteen minutes by Major Hinckson. Both were members of the Union Club, and both had volunteered for patrol duty. When public authority failed of its purpose it was time that appeal should be made to the old English habit of local initiative and self-help. It was said that fifty constables had been drafted from Norwich for special duty in Eastrepps; but Colonel Hewitt had seen precious little of them. It was said, too, that Chief Inspector Wilkins had returned to London for a special conference with the Home Secretary and the heads of Scotland Yard. But the murderer was still at large, and was hardly like to be caught by conferences in London. All the police had done so far was to shut up a poor fool like Rockingham, for no better reason, apparently, than that somebody had heard a dog bark. It was high time, as Colonel Hewitt had said at the Club three days ago, that the local residents took the law into their own hands; and all the members had agreed with him—Hinckson and Jefferson and old Bickley, even that ass Tomlinson, the secretary.

They had all, in fact, been rather decent about it, voted him into the chair and carried all the resolutions he had proposed. And they had been very good resolutions—calling on every able-bodied man to volunteer for patrol work until an arrest had been made.

Colonel Hewitt, President of the Eastrepps Vigilance Association, straightened his back, and marched along the pavement, looking warily to right and left. It was just dark. He had only come on duty half an hour before; and, truth to tell, these four-hour shifts—as he had arranged them—were rather tiring for a man of his age. Still, it would not do for the president of the Association himself to admit it. The Colonel braced himself and, swinging his niblick, strode forward. The patrols were armed, of course, to their fancy. Some carried sticks, one or two had come by a truncheon. Personally, he preferred a niblick. It was the heaviest club in his bag. He could hit the ball, sometimes, with a niblick, and he felt no kind of doubt that he could hit a murderer with it.

He glanced to the right. The black ribbon of road was empty under the first pale stars. A quarter moon hung in the sky. The trees overshadowing the path were dark and massive, twisting above his head—oak, with here and there a spacious elm or sombre fir. These were goodly trees, in their prime of life, not like those contorted specimens in Coatt's Spinney, where poor Mary had met her death.

He heard a soft footstep behind him, and wheeled round instantly, grasping the niblick He crept close to the wooden paling and waited. The step came again—light and fairly frequent, probably a woman. There, indeed, was someone—a horrible figure in long skirts. And why was the head round, dark and of inhuman shape?

"I don't believe it's a woman at all," said the Colonel to himself. "It's a man disguised."

He lifted the niblick and fell into a posture of attack. "Halt!" he cried.

The figure came to a stand, not three yards away.

"Who are you?"

A thin voice, shaking with terror, came through the darkness.

Colonel Hewitt lowered the niblick. He had recognised the voice.

"My dear Mrs. Cappell, this is most unwise. What are you doing out at this time of night?"

"Is that you, Colonel Hewitt? How you startled me!"

Mrs. Cappell put out her arm for support, resting it on the fence.

The Colonel put a hand on her sleeve. She was trembling like a frightened horse.

"I'm on patrol," he said—"President of the Vigilance Association."

The Colonel looked curiously at Mrs. Cappell. He could see her clearly now, and the curious contraption on her head.

"You are looking at my hat, Colonel," she said. "It's a crash helmet. I borrowed it from Bertie, my nephew, who wears it on his motor-cycle—lined with steel, you know, and I thought that it might be just as well . . ."

She paused.

"Exactly," said the Colonel. "But wouldn't it have been even better to stay at home?"

"I have been to see old Mr. Taplow," Mrs. Cappell explained. "He is naturally very low—very low indeed. I went down to see if he would like a game of bridge, but he did not seem to feel up to it."

"You should not take such risks," said the Colonel severely. "Now, however, that you are here, I must insist on seeing you home. That is to say, I will see you to the end of my beat. I will then hand you over to Hinckson, and he will pass you along to—er—Tomlinson. Not much good, I'm afraid, is Tomlinson. But he will see you through."

Already they were walking down the empty road.

"I think it's simply splendid the way you have organised your service, Colonel," said Mrs. Cappell.

She peered, as she spoke, in the direction of Tamarisk House, which stood dark and blank, with lowered blinds. Her thoughts turned to its mistress lying dead upstairs, white and sheeted.

"Perhaps," she said in a low voice, "if you had done all this before you might have saved the life of my dead friend."

Footsteps were approaching, and a stocky little man appeared in the roadway.

"Is that you, Hinckson?" asked the Colonel.

"Hinckson it is," said the other.

"This is Mrs. Cappell. She had been visiting the Taplows. Perhaps you would see her off your beat and hand her over to—er—Tomlinson."

"I'm sure it's very good of you," said Mrs. Cappell.

"Not at all, madam, not at all." It was Hinckson speaking.

"Carry on, Hinckson," said the Colonel. "Let me impress on you that Mrs. Cappell is not to be out of sight of your patrols till she reaches her home. Is that clear?"

"Perfectly, Colonel."

The Colonel raised his niblick in a vague gesture and turned away.

Another three hours to go. . . . Not a doubt of it, this patrol work was fatiguing, especially when one could not sleep in the day-time. It was really too preposterous. One paid rates to be protected in life and limb, and then had to do the work oneself.

A figure moved into view. That would be Eldridge. He was patrolling the next section down to the corner of Church Road.

"Seen anything?" asked the Colonel as he approached.

"Not a mouse stirring."

The Colonel turned on his heel.

"One moment." It was Eldridge speaking.

The Colonel swung around.

"I'm sorry," said Eldridge, "but I have to go to London to-morrow on urgent business. So I'm afraid I shall not be available for patrol during the next two days."

The Colonel drew himself up.

"Not available?" he said.

Then, remembering that he was no longer an officer commanding troops, he added in a less military tone:

"You should have mentioned it before, Eldridge. This upsets all my reliefs."

"Sorry, Colonel," said Eldridge drily. "But everybody knows that I go up to London on Tuesdays."

"Well," said the Colonel, "if it is really necessary . . ."

"Unavoidable," said Eldridge.

"Then there is no more to be said," observed the Colonel.

"Good night," said Eldridge.

"Good night."

The two men turned and walked away in opposite directions.

IV

Ferris paused on the threshold of the Post Office. The clock staring at him from the flint-faced tower of the church that soared into the night fifty yards away informed him that it was a quarter-past ten. The moon was sailing clear upon a field of stars. The wind from the sea had fallen; a fine mist ran softly over the waters.

"A lovely night," he thought.

Church Street was deserted, though this was no time for a seaside town at the height of the season to have gone to bed.

"Truly," thought Ferris, "a city of the dead."

He felt the silence of it like a physical thing. He was tired, and his nerves, after nearly an hour spent in the telephone-box, were raw.

Not far away, where the shops ended and the houses began, he would find the patrols—men with white hair, clubs in their hands. But there were none of them to be seen in Church Street, where the shopkeepers and their wives, behind shutters, whispered of the Evil, and dared not venture abroad.

Ferris moved down the road in the direction of "The Three Fishermen." Then, turning to the left, he paused and looked up the street. It was there that the East Coast Revellers had their quarters, usually gay with lights, playbills, photographs, and a commissionaire in his cap of office. But this evening the brighter lights were out, and there was no one at the door. One or two lamps burned dimly behind the glass-fronted entrance.

Ferris approached, and as he did so the doors opened with a sharp click. Ferris winced. Undoubtedly to-night his nerves were raw. He looked uneasily over his shoulder. The road stretched behind him, bright under the lamps. He looked hastily back again. Two or three figures came through the glass doors, carrying shapeless things in their hands—two girls, two men, and then a third, who paused to lock the door behind them. They came down the steps to the pavement. One of the girls, seeing Ferris, caught at the arm of her companion.

"You are early to-night," said Ferris, advancing to meet them.

The group looked at him with startled eyes.

A thin man with a drooping mouth slowly approached him.

"Are you the *Daily Wire?*" he asked.

"I am," said Ferris.

The melancholy comedian looked at him with mournful appreciation.

"Then you can say in your next, Mr. Special Correspondent, that we are shutting up shop. Tell your readers that there isn't a soul in Eastrepps who has the pluck to come to a show after nine P.M."

"And I don't blame them," a thin voice broke out. "It would be asking for trouble."

Ferris looked sympathetically at the girl who spoke. Her wide mouth, liberally made up, looked as though at any moment it might fall at the corners.

"Yes, Mr. Special Correspondent—not one single person in the audience to-night, and we had a fortnight's contract here at the height of the season."

The melancholy comedian was again speaking.

"But one man's meat . . . as they say. This must mean a pretty good business for you. Murders twice nightly, so to speak."

"It keeps me going," said Ferris.

They stood awkwardly a moment.

"Well, good night," continued Ferris. "And don't be downhearted. They are bound to make an arrest soon, and then the place will be crawling with visitors."

The girl with the wide mouth laughed.

"Another Rockingham, I suppose."

"Come on, Maggie," said the comedian. "Better get to bed, old girl."

The little group moved up the road through the chequered patches of light and darkness.

Ferris was alone again. He paused for a moment before resuming his walk. These poor devils were hard hit, of course. Panic held the town. It was strange that people should be so easily scared, but nobody would now leave his house after nine at night except on duty. Ferris went always to the Post Office at half-past nine to send off his nightly message. He was getting used to the empty streets, the silence. Panic was not for him. He could not afford it. It was his job to describe it. Once he had been caught napping. . . . Not again.

Ferris looked at his watch. Nearly half-past ten. The murders always happened at half-past ten—almost to the minute, as though the monster committing them had consulted a stop-watch.

He wandered slowly down the street, taking the middle of the road and swinging his heavy stick. Why were people so easily scared? Five persons in all had been murdered in three weeks, and there were fifty million people in the British Isles. But somehow folk were easily stirred by the morbid and the rare. Murder, without cause, by a madman with his wits astray, monstrous, terrible, fascinated and filled them with an irrational and panic fear. It let loose the Devil among them, and people still believed in the Devil. He struck only here and there, but threatened all alike, for once he got the upper hand of law, order and all good things, he might regain the world, and use it for his ancient purposes.

Ferris, obscurely meditating these things, felt suddenly a strange humility. He stood alone in this little town, facing the grey sea—not as satisfying an ignoble curiosity, but as one who had been set apart to record one small chapter in a chronicle of life and death, of courage and unbecoming fear . . . the eagle and the serpent. The absurd old men, with their white moustaches, their stiffening limbs, their waving clubs and travesty of discipline, assumed the mien and port of heroes, representatives of the great succession, inadequate but unafraid, who from the beginning of time had faced the Evil, who now were stalking the Evil through the streets by night.

Ferris, shaken but exalted, stood now before "The Three Fishermen." The door was shut, but there was a light shining through the window, and, on coming closer, he saw faintly through the thick glass the figures of half a dozen of the regular customers gathered round the bar in earnest conversation with the landlord. He decided not to enter. He knew too well what the talk would be. These were fishermen, slow of speech and action, sturdy, with salt sense, but full of superstition. They would be talking again of Eric, the red-haired ghost of the Danish wanderer, shipwrecked on that shore a thousand years and more ago. He had come from under the sea where the ancient town lay engulfed long since by the waves, to the cliff where the modern city stood, to prowl through its streets, a thin wraith brandishing a phantom axe in the name of Odin and Thor. That was how they saw the Evil. The old pirate, slipping through a gap in eternity, had found his way back into time, to wander over the tarred streets, past the cringing houses, looking for a sacrifice.

"Nonsense!" said Ferris to himself, and looked fearfully around.

It was time he went home, though, strange to say, he was not tired, though his nerves . . .

"All keyed up," he said to himself.

Here was the sea. He had come by narrow streets to the short esplanade that stretched broadly away under the lamps to the limit of East Cliff and the common that separated Eastrepps from West Runton. The sea was dark, save where the moon caught a moving ripple. On the esplanade, however, all was light—light and solitude. The crowd that should have been streaming from the pier to the lodging-houses or hotels was absent, and there was no patrol, for it was assumed that the Evil was unlikely to venture within the glare of the sea front.

Light and solitude. Fear and Evil, they said, were of the dark. But there was something unnatural in the bright expectancy of the staring lamps. Did they not in a sense proclaim their own defeat? The Evil had won for itself all that gleaming stretch where men feared to walk.

Ferris looked round uneasily. He scorned the thin ghosts of the churchyard or spirits that rapped in a darkened room. But this was different. He could understand this terror of the lamplight—of his own time and world. He walked on a few paces, stopped again, startled by the sound of his own footsteps. Shadows of the kiosks and seats on the parade showed black and angular at his feet. He turned in a sudden anguish.

William Ferris was afraid.

He was walking fast through the streets of the town. Fifty million people in the British Isles . . . he must try to remember that.

The speed of his walk increased. But he would not go directly home. It was his custom, before making for the eighth house in the little row of semi-detached villas facing the sea which was his goal, to stroll a while at random and pass a word with the patrols. He was not going to be driven from the exercise of his profession.

Fifty million people in the British Isles. . . . He glanced at his watch . . . past half-past ten . . . scarcely ten minutes since he had left the esplanade.

Odd that his footsteps should echo like that. He stopped abruptly, and the echo ceased. He tried, as he went on again, to think of connected, significant things. . . . He had crossed several streets, and was now in a road bordered by small houses, cottages almost. An inscription swinging from a lamp-post caught his eye . . . "Sheffield Park." That set him thinking as he wished to think. He had seen that man Eldridge in Sheffield Park on the night of the third murder, though he had pretended to be in London. It was a matter worth investigating—such, at least, had been the view of Sergeant Ruddock. Ruddock had been distinctly interested, had even asked him to sign a deposition; and presumably the police were now making inquiries. Where had Eldridge been on the other nights when the Evil had struck?

Ferris smiled . . . Eldridge, in his city clothes, was hardly his idea of the Evil. . . . The Evil . . . he was beginning to be haunted by his own phrase—only a newspaper headline which he had invented to impress the public.

There was that echo again. Or was it his fancy? He

had been growing fanciful of late. More particularly he
had that childish sense of someone behind him. He
wanted continually to turn round in order to make sure.
He always resisted it on principle as long as he could,
and he would resist it now. . . . He would not turn
round.

Almost he had reached the end of the street. Soon he
would have to yield. His nerves would give him no rest
until he did. He could hear things, almost feel things,
stealing upon him from behind.

Suddenly he pulled up short.

The Evil, he knew, was upon him.

He turned round.

It was.

V

The Right Honourable the Viscount Pilkington,
Secretary of State for Home Affairs, removed his pince-
nez, wiped them, replaced them on his nose and sat back
in his chair.

"Well," he said, "that is the position, and something
has to be done. An arrest . . ."

"Presumably the right man," came a soft interpola-
tion to his right.

The Home Secretary turned impatiently.

"This is a serious matter, Sir Geoffrey," he said.

Sir Geoffrey Robinson, High Commissioner at Scotland Yard, was unabashed. He regretted that Pilkington
should be so consistently Pilkington. It sometimes made
their relations difficult. But he had outlived many Home
Secretaries. He looked as gravely as possible at this
one, which was difficult, for though Sir Geoffrey lived on
Apollinaris and water biscuits, and was serious by nature,
he had the red face and twinkling eyes of one to whom
the good things of the world were precious.

"I have been taking this matter very seriously for
several weeks past," he said.

There were five men at the table. Chief Inspector Wilkins, Inspector Protheroe, and Sir Jefferson Cobb were sitting side by side opposite the other two. This was the High Commissioner's office at Scotland Yard, a pleasant room, adorned with portraits of Sir Geoffrey's predecessors in office.

"We are accused," said the Home Secretary, "of being callous and indifferent. The public must be made to realise that everything possible is being done."

Sir Geoffrey Robinson stiffened.

"I would submit," he said, "that it is hardly the object of this conference to reassure the public. For that purpose a conference of newspaper editors would be more appropriate."

"It may seem childish to suggest that these crimes should have a political significance," continued the Home Secretary, "but such is the case. Public confidence in the present administration is being seriously undermined. Yesterday, as you are aware, the Member for East Norfolk was suspended from the service of the House, after a scene—a really disgraceful scene—in the course of which it was suggested that I, as Home Secretary, was failing to realise my responsibilities. The Member for East Norfolk is now regarded in his own constituency, if not throughout the country, as more or less of a martyr."

The High Commissioner nodded.

"Not a doubt of that," he said. "You have only to look at the Press this morning."

"I come back to my original point," said the Home Secretary. "What is to be done?"

Sir Geoffrey looked across at Chief Inspector Wilkins.

"So far as the police are concerned," he said, "everything possible is being done. To suggest that we could do more is a serious reflection on my Department."

The Home Secretary had risen from the table, and was walking up and down the room.

"Five murders in three weeks," he exclaimed, "all committed in the same way, in the same town, at the same hour. And the murderer is still at large. . . . The thing is preposterous!"

He came down the room and looked peevishly across at Chief Inspector Wilkins.

"I make no criticism," he added, "but I feel bound to point out, in justification of the public feeling aroused by these incidents, that all you have done so far . . ."

He broke off. Wilkins, perceptibly flushed, was looking him very straight in the face.

"All we have done so far, sir, is to make a very serious mistake," said Wilkins. "I do not think, however, that any other course was possible. You have seen the evidence against Rockingham, and I think you will admit that in the circumstances it was more than adequate."

"If I might venture . . ." began Sir Jefferson Cobb.

The Home Secretary turned to him hopefully.

"Yes, what is it, Jefferson?"

"Is it not perhaps a case for the military?" asked Sir Jefferson.

Chief Inspector Wilkins moved impatiently.

"What do you mean?" asked the Home Secretary.

"The whole town might be patrolled by troops and, if necessary, a house-to-house search conducted."

"And what do you expect to find?" asked the High Commissioner.

"Your suggestion," said the Home Secretary, after a pause, "is impracticable. It would be equivalent to proclaiming martial law. Things have not yet reached that stage."

There was a pause.

The Home Secretary looked in turn at the three men.

"Have none of you anything to suggest?" he asked.

Sir Geoffrey looked at Chief Inspector Wilkins.

"For the moment," said Wilkins, "we are frankly at a loss. We had a strong case against Rockingham. The last two murders, however, committed when Rockingham was shut up, have destroyed it entirely. It is just possible that some unbalanced person took it into his head to carry on the murders in exactly the same way after Rockingham's arrest, but that is hardly a theory I should care to have put before a jury."

The respectful silence in which these observations were received was broken by the buzzing of the telephone on the table of the High Commissioner. Sir Geoffrey Robinson rose, crossed the room and picked up the receiver.

"Yes," he said, "this is the High Commissioner speaking. . . . What's that? . . . trunk call. . . . Eastrepps. . . . Yes . . . who is that speaking?"

The High Commissioner listened a moment, then turned to Wilkins.

"A man of the name of Ruddock," he said gravely. "Perhaps he had better speak to you."

Wilkins began to cross the room.

"Anything special?" he inquired.

The High Commissioner handed over the receiver.

"Sounds interesting," he observed. "He says that another murder was committed at half-past ten this evening and that he has made an arrest."

VI

"Then it is understood, Sir Jefferson. We start at seven o'clock. I will telephone again to Ruddock instructing him to meet us at your house at noon. He can then report upon his action in detail. Good night, Sir Jefferson; good night, Protheroe."

"Good night, Sir Geoffrey," said Jefferson.

"Good night, sir," said Protheroe.

The door closed behind them, and Sir Geoffrey turned back to where Chief Inspector Wilkins was leaning against the mantelpiece. Big Ben was booming his twelve strokes at midnight.

"Well, Wilkins," he said, coming to the mantelpiece, "now we can talk. I hope you don't mind me coming down to-morrow. This is your show, but I should like to hear this man Ruddock for myself."

Wilkins smiled.

"I'm not anxious to lay claim to the case," he said. "I shot my bolt over Rockingham."

Sir Geoffrey looked at Wilkins over the edge of the pipe he was lighting.

"This affair," he said, "remains sensational to the end. The last of the victims is a journalist murdered in the exercise of his profession, and the murderer is brought to justice by the local Sergeant."

"You believe that Ruddock will be able to prove his case?"

"He was pretty convincing on the telephone."

"Meanwhile," said Wilkins with a smile, "I suppose we take our orders from him."

"You made a note of those requests?"

"I did. We are to bring with us to Eastrepps a copy of the finger-prints of James Selby of Anaconda Ltd., and obtain from the manager of the Goodwood Hotel, Bloomsbury Square, a calendar of the arrivals and departures of Robert Eldridge as from July 16th."

"And so to bed," said the High Commissioner.

VII

Sergeant Ruddock stood a little awkwardly in the library of Sir Jefferson Cobb. The walls, relieved with books that mounted to the ceiling, glowed in the noon sunshine. Through the tall windows he could see the level lawns stretching to the park, with a ribbon of white road leading to the gate a mile away. A puff of dust and the winking of the chromium-plated steel radiator and headlamps of a large limousine caught his eye. It was moving along the white road towards the house.

He looked at his watch—noon within the minute. He slipped his hands into his belt and out again, smoothing his uniform and glancing at himself in an old Venetian mirror hanging above the mantelshelf. He must make a good impression. This was the vital moment, a turning-point in his career. But he was ready for them—the facts all safe in his brain. None the less, his hands strayed nervously to the official note-book in his hip-pocket.

There came the soft whine of tyres, the crunch of gravel, the sound of footsteps and voices. The mahogany door of the library swung open noiselessly and a number of men entered.

"Come in, Sir Geoffrey."

Sir Jefferson Cobb was speaking over his shoulder to a large man with a red nose and a pair of shrewd blue eyes, who was followed by Chief Inspector Wilkins and Inspector Protheroe.

Sergeant Ruddock came to attention. That was Sir Geoffrey Robinson himself, the High Commissioner of Scotland Yard.

Ruddock stepped forward a pace or two and clicked his heels.

"You are Sergeant Ruddock, I suppose," said the High Commissioner.

"Yes, sir," answered Ruddock quietly.

"Well, Sergeant, we will take your report at once."

Sir Jefferson was waving his chief guest to a chair. Protheroe and Wilkins nodded to Ruddock.

"By all means," said Sir Geoffrey, "let us sit down and be comfortable. You, too, Sergeant."

There was a slight scraping of chairs. Sir Jefferson Cobb glanced at the High Commissioner, who gave a gesture of assent. Sir Jefferson, thus encouraged, broke the silence.

"Ruddock," he said, "last night you arrested Robert Eldridge as the result of certain evidence which you obtained at his house. You communicated the main facts to Chief Inspector Wilkins on the telephone, but we have still to review the case in detail. I think the best thing for you to do now is to acquaint us with the facts as they presented themselves to you in the course of your investigation."

"You wish me to make a complete statement?"

"Yes, Sergeant." It was the High Commissioner who spoke. "Assume that we know nothing beyond what is in the newspapers this morning—namely, that last night another murder was committed and that Robert Eldridge has been arrested."

Ruddock laid his note-book on the table in front of him. Chief Inspector Wilkins nodded at him encouragingly.

"Carry on, Sergeant," he said.

"Last night, sir," began Sergeant Ruddock, "a little after ten thirty, I was in Sheffield Park, being on my round, according to official instructions. I had reached a point about two hundred yards short of Heath Road when I perceived a man in front of me. He was too far off for me to see who he was, but I quickened my pace at sight of him, for, as you know, anyone out after dark in Eastrepps is kept more or less under observation. Constable Birchington's beat was not far away—in fact, I expected to meet that officer at the corner of Sheffield Park and Heath Road. I reached the corner about three minutes later, but my man had disappeared down Heath Road. It is a narrow thoroughfare, well shaded by trees. I walked down the road about fifty yards, expecting to meet Constable Birchington, when I heard a noise. It might have been that of a man falling. I broke into a run, pulling out my torch as I did so. About twenty yards from the corner I saw by the light of the torch a man lying on the ground. I bent down, and realised at once that I had all but seen him struck. The blood was still trickling from the wound in his right temple.

"I blew my whistle. There were half a dozen men within call, and I gave instructions that they were to go for Dr. Simms and to detain anybody found near the spot, with a view, if necessary, to inquiries at the station.

"Meanwhile, I stayed by the body, which I identified at once as that of William Ferris, Special Correspondent of the *Daily Wire*. I had seen Ferris only that morning, and he had made to me a certain statement to which I shall shortly allude."

The High Commissioner looked approvingly at Ruddock.

"Continue, Sergeant," he said.

"Beside the body," Ruddock went on, "I found the weapon with which the murder had been committed—a stout club, such as was used in trench raids during the late war, with a knife blade thrust into the end of it at right angles.

"I had hardly finished my examination of the body when I heard voices at the end of Heath Road, and I saw Constable Birchington talking to a man who appeared to be giving trouble."

"Trouble?" said Wilkins.

"I could see that he was excited, and I imagined that he was refusing to accompany Birchington. So I went to the assistance of my colleague."

Ruddock paused.

"It was Mr. Robert Eldridge, of 14, Oakfield Terrace," he continued, "and I saw that he was in a somewhat abnormal condition—agitated and inclined to be violent. 'What's this, Sergeant?' he said as I came up. 'I know nothing of what has happened—nothing at all. You have no right to detain me.' "

"One moment," Wilkins interrupted. "Had Birchington told him of the crime?"

"Birchington had told him of the crime and asked him to come to the station. I repeated that request, saying that I had no alternative but to insist on taking a deposition."

"You were exceeding your powers, Sergeant," said the High Commissioner.

"I had special reasons for detaining him," said Ruddock quietly. "This was not my first encounter with Robert Eldridge, and to justify my action I must now relate how my attention had first been drawn to him.

"I first visited Eldridge on the afternoon of July 24th, the day after the murder of Miss Taplow. I was then, in accordance with instructions, making a house-to-house visit in the neighbourhood of the second crime. Eldridge was interviewing a visitor when I arrived, and I could not avoid hearing through the window something of what was passing. The visitor was a person of the name of Coldfoot, and the two men were quarrelling violently. The word blackmail was used."

"Why was not this reported to me?"

Inspector Protheroe, very red and breathing heavily, hands spread upon his ponderous knees, stared resentfully at his subordinate.

"I attached no importance to the incident at the time," said Ruddock smoothly.

He continued:

"I asked Mr. Eldridge on that occasion whether he had heard or seen anything at all unusual on the preceding evening at the time of the murder. He told me he had been in London, and had only arrived home that morning. When I was being shown out a telegram arrived, and I heard him tell his housekeeper, after reading it, that he would have to go to London again next day and that he would stay in town for the night. I paid little or no attention to this incident at the time, but remembered it later.

"On Friday night, July 25th, John Masters was murdered on the West Cliff, and on the following morning Ferris of the *Daily Wire* happened to be talking to Colonel Hewitt near Eastrepps station shortly after the first train had arrived from London. Eldridge, coming from the station as though he had just left the train, ran into them, and some conversation took place, in the course of which Eldridge gave them both to understand that he had in fact only that moment arrived. It happened, however, that Ferris on the evening before—the evening of the murder of John Masters—had seen Eldridge in Sheffield Park. Eldridge, moreover, realised that he had been seen and that Ferris knew he was lying."

"How did you come to know of this meeting?" asked Wilkins.

"Why was I not informed?" inquired Inspector Protheroe.

"Ferris came to me yesterday. He wrote and signed the statement to which I have already alluded. It struck him as singular and worthy of inquiry that Eldridge should have pretended to be in London when he was really in Eastrepps. There was no reason, of course, to connect him with the murders, but it had been impressed upon me"—here Ruddock glanced at Chief Inspector Wilkins—"that any circumstance at all unusual should at once be investigated. I had intended this morning, on the return of Inspector Protheroe from London, to acquaint him with the statement of Ferris, but the events of last night compelled me to act entirely on my own responsibility."

"Of course," said the High Commissioner.

"You will now appreciate my situation when I saw Eldridge last night near the scene of the crime. I knew that Eldridge had created a false alibi on the night of one of the murders. I knew that Ferris had seen Eldridge in Eastrepps on that occasion, and was therefore in a position to destroy that alibi. Rightly or wrongly, I decided that Eldridge must be detained, and that I must pay a surprise visit to his house."

"What did you expect to find?" asked Chief Inspector Wilkins.

"First, I wanted to ascertain whether Eldridge had framed a false alibi for yesterday evening, and possibly for the other evenings on which the murders had been committed. Secondly, there was the weapon . . ."

Sergeant Ruddock paused.

"Go on," said the High Commissioner.

"I had noticed on my previous visit to his house a trophy of war weapons on the wall of his study, and I seemed to remember seeing among them a club not unlike the one I had just found beside the body of Ferris. I could not have sworn to such a weapon being there, but my memory was sufficiently definite to make me want to settle the matter at once, one way or the other.

"I accordingly told Birchington to take Eldridge to the station."

"Did he resist detention?" asked the High Commissioner.

"No. He ceased even to protest when I said I was determined that he should go. Meanwhile Dr. Simms had arrived. I left him with Constable Mason in charge of the body. I myself went straight to Eldridge's house in Oakfield Terrace. It was dark and shuttered, and I had some difficulty in obtaining admission. The door was opened to me at last by his housekeeper, Mrs. Brandon. She told me that her master had gone up to town on the morning of the day before and would not be back until lunch-time on the day following. I am afraid that my next step was . . . irregular. I insisted, in fact, on being shown into the study.

"Mrs. Brandon refused at first, but I told her that if she persisted I should apply for a search warrant, which would certainly be executed before her master's return. On that, very reluctantly, she admitted me.

"I went at once to the study and looked at the wall where I remembered seeing the trophy. It consisted of two German automatic pistols, a German stick bomb, a gas-mask, and a trench knife. In the centre there appeared to be something missing. I examined the wallpaper, and found a patch where it had been covered and had kept its colour. The patch corresponded in size and shape to the trench club with which Ferris had been killed.

"That was sufficient. I informed Mrs. Brandon that I must search the room, but that I would do so in her presence and take nothing without her knowledge. It was then that I found the list of which I spoke to you last night over the telephone. I discovered it wedged behind a drawer of the roll-top desk between the windows. I also found a rubber date-stamp of the adjustable pattern on one of the trays."

"You have the list?" Sir Goeffrey inquired.

Sergeant Ruddock pulled from his pocket a buff envelope. From this he extracted a sheet of typewritten paper, which he passed to the High Commissioner.

"A list of names," said Geoffrey Robinson slowly.

He passed the paper to Chief Inspector Wilkins.

"Several of the names I recognised as being those of residents in Eastrepps," Ruddock continued. "You will observe that some of them are underlined in red ink, and that there is a date against each of them stamped with a rubber stamp."

"These are the names underlined and dated," said Wilkins. "Miss Mary Hewitt, July 16th; Miss H. Taplow, July 23rd; Mr. John Masters, July 25th. There are other names underlined in red ink, but undated, including that of Sir Jefferson Cobb."

"What's that?" said Sir Jefferson.

"You will observe," said Ruddock, "that all the persons underlined are living in Eastrepps or in the neighbourhood, and that the paper is headed: 'List of shareholders in Anaconda Ltd.' "

"Anaconda Ltd.," said Sir Jefferson Cobb. "That was one of Selby's companies. I lost a couple of thousand when Selby bolted."

"I also remembered Anaconda Ltd.," said Ruddock,

"though I was very young at the time. A relative of mine had invested money in the company, and used to talk about it a good deal. It occurred to me on finding the list that Robert Eldridge might very well be the missing Selby, and that there would probably be some means of identifying him at Scotland Yard. I knew there had been a hue and cry after him, and I wondered whether his finger-prints might not have been taken. So I ventured to ask for them when I telephoned last night."

Sir Geoffrey Robinson signed to Chief Inspector Wilkins, who opened a dispatch case on his knee.

"Here are Selby's prints," he said. "They were taken from some deed boxes which he left behind him in his office when he bolted in May 1914."

Ruddock produced an envelope from his pocket.

"I took Eldridge's prints on getting back to the station and formally arresting him," he said.

Chief Inspector Wilkins took from Ruddock a sheet of paper and examined the ink impressions, comparing them with the photographs of Selby's prints.

"Not a doubt of it," he said at length. "They are identical in every respect. This was a long shot, Ruddock, but it hit the mark."

He passed the records to the High Commissioner, who looked at them, and handed them in turn to Sir Jefferson Cobb.

"So Robert Eldridge is James Selby," he said, "and he had me down for slaughter."

"I think we can assume that, without undue stretching of the facts," said the High Commissioner. "Proceed, Sergeant."

"I found nothing else of importance in Eldridge's house, but I next questioned the housekeeper. She informed me that Mr. Eldridge invariably went to London every Tuesday morning and returned every Thursday at noon. He was accustomed to sleep at the Goodwood Hotel, Bloomsbury Square. There, again, was a clue which I thought should be followed up. Hence my further request that inquiries should be made of the manager."

"We discovered that Eldridge keeps a permanent room there," said Wilkins. "The manager states, however, that he never sleeps there more than one night a week. He arrives on Tuesday, and always leaves on Wednesday."

"In other words," said Ruddock, "the murders in Eastrepps were committed invariably on a day when Eldridge was supposed by his housekeeper to be in London, but when he was really here in Eastrepps."

Chief Inspector Wilkins studied the list again.

"But John Masters was killed on July 25th, which was a Friday."

"Yes, sir," said Ruddock. "But you will remember that Eldridge received a telegram on the 24th calling him to London on urgent business. I was, as I have said, present at his house when he received it. He went to London as he had arranged, and the next night John Masters was murdered. That same evening Ferris, as I have already mentioned, saw him in Sheffield Park, and the next morning near the railway station when he maintained that he had just arrived from London. You will have noticed that Ferris is the only name not down on the list. He was murdered, not as a shareholder of Anaconda Ltd., but as the only witness able to destroy Eldridge's elaborate alibi. The murder of Ferris is, to my mind, the most conclusive point of all."

"It's pretty damning," said Sir Geoffrey Robinson, looking up from the list which he was examining, and handing it back to Ruddock.

"One other point, sir," said Ruddock. "Mrs. Dampier was murdered out of turn so to speak. I think she must have heard the attack on Captain Porter. He was killed first outside her garden. She must have seen Eldridge.

and he had to kill her then and there in order to escape detection."

There was a pause.

"Just one thing more," added Sergeant Ruddock. "All the persons murdered were killed when they were fulfilling a regular habit. Miss Hewitt was murdered on her return from church, where she went every Wednesday evening to leave flowers. Miss Taplow was killed coming back from the fortnightly meeting of the Literary Society. John Masters was returning from the girl he is courting, who lives out at Overstrand, and Captain Porter on his way back from the Union Club, where he spends every evening of his life. It can, I think, be shown that Eldridge was well aware of the habits of all these people."

"There is one point that appears to have dropped out," observed Wilkins. "How do you fit in the blackmailing of Eldridge by Coldfoot?"

"That," said the High Commissioner, "will have to be investigated. It may or may not be material. Meanwhile I will get into touch with the Director of Public Prosecutions. The case is good enough. I congratulate you, Sergeant Ruddock, on a very efficient piece of work, and not least on the clearness and precision of your statement."

Ruddock flushed a deep red.

"Thank you, sir," he said. "I will make a report from my notes and let Inspector Protheroe have it this afternoon." He met the eye of Protheroe as he rose from the table, and noted without surprise that his superior officer seemed less pleased than he should have been at the success of the local police.

CHAPTER EIGHT

I

Robert Eldridge stood by the door of his cell in the Old Bailey which the warder had just closed behind him. It was not more than ten or twelve feet long, and half as wide, very clean, bare and hygienic. The walls were lined with reddish-brown tiles halfway up and white tiles to the ceiling. A small high window opposite the door allowed the due quantity of light and air to enter. There was no furniture save for a deal table and a wooden stool.

Eldridge sat down.

So this was No. 1 cell. He had heard the warders refer to it as they led him from the Black Maria by which he had arrived that autumn morning from Brixton. No. 1 cell was reserved for the big cases, being just under the dock, which was only a few feet away, above his head. On the stool now supporting him Seddon had sat, and Dr. Crippen and the infamous Smith, who had drowned his wives. Warders showing people round the Old Bailey might point to it in days to come as the stool on which Eldridge had sat—the murderer of Eastrepps, known in his time as the Evil.

He started to his feet.

"What would you like for your lunch?" they had asked him. He could have what he wanted, of course, provided he paid for it. His solicitor had told him that. So had the prison authorities. Not that he felt much like choosing his lunch; but he had ordered something. Margaret had urged him to keep up his courage.

How hot and airless the room was! Even the tiles were warm to the touch. He would spend what most remained of his life between walls such as these. For, even if he were proved innocent of murder, he would, he supposed, hardly get less than seven or perhaps ten years' penal servitude as Selby, the defaulting chairman of Anaconda Ltd.

He had not wanted to fight, but Margaret had insisted. He must prove, for her sake, that he was not guilty of the murders, and his defence was terribly simple—neither more nor less than Margaret herself. She would come forward in open court and swear from the witness-box, before judge and jury, public and Press, that on every one of those fatal nights when a man or woman had been struck down in Eastrepps he had been lying in her arms. How he had cried out at her, commanded and implored, in his efforts to dissuade her! She had said but one thing at the end of all his pleadings; that she would have done as much even if he had committed the murders, so how could she do otherwise when she knew that he was innocent?

She had thus become the principal witness for the defence, and from that moment he had not been allowed to see her again.

In another few minutes now he would be facing the court, and in due course he would himself go into the witness-box. That might not be to-day or even to-morrow, for the mills of the law ground exceeding small. Hundreds of questions would first be asked of the witnesses for the prosecution, so that the jury might be acquainted not only with the facts of the case, but be able —so clever these lawyers were—to look into every private corner of his life, appreciate the man he was or, rather, the man they would make him out to be. Then his moment would come, and Sir Henry Grey, his counsel, would take him through the main points of his defence once more—this time with judge and jury noting every word, marking down this or that against him.

Let him for the last time get it clear.

There were three fatal points to be met—the list found in his drawer, the weapon missing from his wall and the alibi. Margaret would deal with the alibi. As to the list and the weapon, he must simply deny the whole thing, swear he had never seen such a list, swear that to the best of his knowledge the weapon with which the crimes had apparently been committed had never left his study. Then it would be for Sir Henry to suggest that he was the victim of a conspiracy. They had to make the jury believe that some enemy had planted these crimes upon an innocent man in sheer hatred or to divert suspicion from himself. Inevitably his thoughts returned to the insoluble question. Who was this secret enemy? Who had planned this monstrous thing? Somewhere in England, perhaps even in the court room itself to which he would soon be taken, that enemy was waiting to watch the working of his scheme. He sat down again.

What did Sir Henry make of it all? Did he even believe that his client was innocent? Of course he pretended to believe—had listened with respect to that desperate suggestion of a conspiracy. But Sir Henry had made no secret of the fact that it would be difficult, in the absence of any obvious conspirator, to shake the prosecution with such a theory. Clearly he was relying chiefly on Margaret, and was concentrating on getting all the support he could for her evidence. So much was obvious from his decision to call Coldfoot as a witness—the only person who would testify that he (Robert Eldridge) was usually at her house on Wednesday evening. The decision to call Coldfoot alone showed how treacherous was the ground. Margaret would have nothing to support her but the evidence of a man who must begin by confessing to blackmail, and who, likely as not, believed him to be guilty.

If only some means could be found of dealing with the fatal list. . . . Sir Henry had urgently pressed him to suggest anyone in the world who might have planted it. But he could think of no one, except possibly Withers himself. Had Withers discovered his intrigue with Margaret and planned this horrible revenge? But that was too fantastic. As well believe that Coldfoot himself . . .

There was no issue along those lines. Sir Henry was right. The jury must believe Margaret. Otherwise . . .

There came a click from the door. A warder was looking through the observation window, and an instant later the door opened and he entered the cell.

"The court is waiting," he said.

Eldridge rose, staggering a moment.

The man put out a hand with a kindly gesture, but Eldridge drew himself up.

"It is nothing," he said. "I am only a bit stiff from sitting down."

"This way," said the warder.

Eldridge passed from the cell into the passage. Two other warders were standing outside.

For a moment he looked down a long corridor, tiled like his cell, with its row of doors like his own. Then, obeying a slight pressure on his arm, he turned to the left, and found himself near the top of a staircase that wound about a well down to a couple of stories similar to the one he had just left.

Turning to the right, he ascended a short flight, and came out abruptly into a small enclosed space, boarded with yellow oak.

This was the dock.

He had not expected to arrive so soon.

Puzzled by the light that filled the court and the sudden presence of many people, he recoiled upon the warder behind him. Again came that steady pressure on his arm, and he walked forward.

To his immediate front, as he turned on the top stair, was a wooden chair, and to the left of it, a few paces away, a table at which was seated a warder. The two warders who had brought him up the stairs took up positions behind him. He walked to the front of the dock and stood waiting by the wooden chair.

This was different from what he had expected. He had thought to emerge into the stir and rumour of an assembly. Instead, there was an almost complete silence in the court, broken only by someone coughing in the gallery. Confronting him from the long dais opposite sat a figure in crimson robes trimmed with ermine, and a white wig falling stiffly on each side of his face. That was the judge, in his heavy chair, with the City arms stamped in gold on black leather on the back of it, and the motto "Domine dirige nos." The man who was to try him sat framed by two carved pillars of light oak. Below him, from a table in the well of the court, rose a man in wig and gown:

"Robert Eldridge, *alias* John Selby,

"You stand charge upon his indictment:

"With having on the sixteenth day of July of this year, at Eastrepps, in the County of Norfolk, murdered Mary Hewitt;

"With having on the twenty-third day of July of this year murdered Helen Taplow;

"With having on the twenty-fifth day of July of this year murdered John Masters;

"With having on the thirtieth day of July of this year murdered Thomas Porter and Winifred Dampier;

"With having on the sixth day of August of this year murdered William Ferris.

"Are you guilty or not guilty?"

"Not guilty," said Eldridge steadily.

There was a slight rustle as he heard his own voice break the silence. A man with a book in his hand was moving towards the oaken benches to his left, on which were sitting a number of men and women. The man was speaking as he tendered the book to the person nearest the judge.

"*You shall well and truly try and true deliverance make*

between our sovereign lord the King and prisoner at the bar."

That, then, was the jury, and it was being sworn.

Eldridge, still gripping the front of the dock, looked about him. His uppermost feeling for the moment was one of curiosity. Just below him on his right was his counsel, so close that he could easily hand a note down to him if he wished. To the right of his counsel sat Sir Robert Lorimer, the Attorney-General, giving a final glance to his papers, for he would be speaking in a moment.

Eldridge looked with interest at the face he knew so well from newspaper photographs and cartoons—kind and handsome, but somehow conveying that he would be ruthless in pursuit of evil.

Then, suddenly, he found that Trenchard, his solicitor, was standing just beneath him in the well of the court. Trenchard thrust a folded document towards him. He bent to take it.

"In case," Trenchard was saying. "Sign it under your real name—the name you were born under."

Eldridge unfolded the document.

"I, James Selby, being of sound mind and body," he read, "hereby revoke all former wills and testaments . . ."

For a moment the court was turning about him. Then he threw back his head and read steadily to the end. Yes . . . he must sign this document while yet there was time—while, technically, he was still a free man. Such was the law.

He looked up from the sheets. His solicitor, waiting below him as he read, handed up to him a green enamelled fountain-pen. Eldridge took it and signed: James Selby.

The solicitor beckoned to the two warders in the dock, who came forward and signed as witnesses. Trenchard then rejoined his colleagues at the big table in the centre of the court.

"And true deliverance make . . ."

They were still swearing in the jury. Eldridge looked again at the Attorney-General, the man who must do his professional best to hang the accused . . . kind but ruthless. He had risen to speak to one of the Juniors behind him, and stood, a tall, lean figure, with wig slightly awry and ascetic face. But for his wig he might have been some young member of the Society of Jesus, bent upon converting the heathen.

"And true deliverance make . . ."

Eldridge's eyes next went to the judge. Again the face was mild with a pair of steady blue eyes, but the mildness stopped short at the mouth, which was firm, with twin furrows running up to the nose . . . Mr. Justice Burrows. Next him was the Mayor—who had come down to the court himself that morning, this being the first day of the session, and the man next to him, also in antique dress, must be the Sheriff. . . . And above the judge's chair was a great sword.

"And true deliverance make . . ."

The eyes of Eldridge travelled to a corner near the jury-box, where two men sat at a table sharpening pencils. They were the court stenographers. And presumably the stand immediately above them, with a flat canopy and general air of being a pulpit in a cubist nightmare, was the witness-box.

The court was no longer silent. There was whispering and a low hum of voices. Away to the right, high up, was the public gallery—very full. There was a fair sprinkling of women there, from whom came all that sighing and fluttering. They had come to see the show. There were more of them sitting on the benches behind the Juniors. Those, he understood, were privileged spectators, who, on the pretext of having some special interest in the case, had secured a seat in the court through the City Fathers.

"And true deliverance make . . ."

Eldridge turned from the public benches with a sudden sense of revolt, only to perceive the Press upon the left of the dock, keen-faced young men for the most part. They would not miss a word, trust them—not a word, not the flicker of an eyelid. Well, it was their job, and he wished them joy of it. Come to think of it, they owed him something, the pressmen of England. He had been their daily bread for many days past, and there was not a paper in the land that had not fought to get its special correspondent a place in the court room.

"And true deliverance make . . ."

He wondered.

The Clerk of the Assizes was speaking, repeating once more the indictment now that the jury had been sworn:

"To this indictment he has pleaded 'not guilty.' Your charge is to say whether he is guilty or not and to hearken to the evidence."

The warder touched him on the shoulder, indicating that he might sit down.

There was a moment's pause. Then, amid an abrupt silence, the tall form of the Attorney-General rose in his place. He bowed slightly in the direction of the splendid figure in the high chair.

"My lord and members of the jury," he began, "I do not think I am wrong in saying that the case which I am about to open to you is one of the most terrible and most extraordinary in the annals of crime. The prisoner at the bar stands accused of no less than six brutal murders. It will be my duty to lay before you . . ."

II

The great hall in which the witnesses for the four courts composing the Old Bailey awaited their turn was thronged on this opening day of the session. Margaret stood apart from the crowd, beside the severely gracious statue of Elizabeth Fry, watching the ushers as they moved about their business, the solicitors who passed

this way and that, the men and women who would sooner
or later be called upon to bear a part in one or other
of the dramas then in progress. Mr. Trenchard had
warned her to be in attendance, though it was almost
certain that she would not be wanted for some time to
come—probably not that day.

She felt calmer than she had expected. She had her
work to do, and would not, for the moment, look beyond it. Nothing mattered at this stage but that she
should tell her story without fear, and that the jury
should believe it. She would make them believe it. Sir
Henry had warned her very kindly, concealing nothing
of what she would have to face, that it would be the aim
and duty of the prosecution to destroy her credit, and
that within the limits of the law she would be called
upon to answer in public any questions which were intended to help the court to decide whether she was a
person whose evidence might reasonably be believed.

Never mind, he had said, the shame of it; and upon
that she had laughed. Her relations with Robert had
never struck her in the least degree as shameful. Nor
did it seem to matter that she must confess to loving,
not Mr. Robert Eldridge—the only man who had ever
shown her kindness—but the man she now knew to be
James Selby, the swindler of Anaconda Ltd. The crimes
of Selby were lost for her in the chivalry with which
Eldridge had implored her to leave him to his fate. He
had had, in peril of his life, only one thought—to save
her from the ordeal of bearing witness. To that man
she would be faithful. He was innocent, and she would
save him.

High upon the wall at the northern end of the great
hall a group of maidens danced about the golden apples
of the Hesperides, beneath a sky of perpetual blue, with
flowers at their feet—a frescoe of the golden age when
the law had run its course and there was no more need
of justice. Meanwhile, beyond the low door through

which she would shortly pass, in a bleak room of white
stone and oaken panels, her lover was being tried for his
life according to the cold, antique ceremony of the law.
He was standing now, a still figure, in the dock, confronting that other still figure in his robes of scarlet.

She became aware that an usher was approaching.
She took a nervous pace to meet him. Was it to be so
soon? But the man looked at her, and shook his head.

"Not yet," he said. "You are witness for the defence
—aren't you?—No. 1 Court. I'm looking for Dr.
Simms."

A tall figure in a morning coat, with striped trousers,
fastidiously groomed, stepped forward.

"I am Dr. Simms."

"The Attorney-General is just finishing," said the
usher. "You will be wanted in about five minutes. Will
you please to step this way?"

Margaret watched the tall figure move in the wake
of the usher towards the door through which, in due
course, she, too, would be invited to pass.

III

"It is no part of the duty of the Crown to prove motive,
but I feel that in this case the facts as presented, being
circumstantial, cannot be appreciated in their full significance unless you can be enabled to answer the question
which I am sure is in the minds of you all: what man in
his sane mind would seek to commit in cold blood—for,
as I hope I have made clear to you, these crimes were
minutely premeditated and planned—this series of brutal
murders? Obviously no ordinary person could have done
so. Nevertheless, you have before you a man outwardly
as other men."

Here the Attorney-General paused, and directed the
briefest of glances at the accused.

"It is true that on his own confession he is abnormally
unscrupulous and unfeeling—a man who has ruined with-

out compassion hundreds of investors who were rash enough to entrust their worldly possessions into his care. But it is a far cry from the common swindler, who appears too often in these courts, to the murderer six times over, who was responsible for the crimes committed at Eastrepps.

"You will be shown the facts of the career of James Selby up to the moment when he returned to England under the name of Robert Eldridge. I would ask you to look with me through the list of those who were struck down between the sixteenth day of July and the sixth day of August of this year. Mary Hewitt was a spinster living with her brother, and wholly dependent upon him. She had put every penny that she possessed into Anaconda Ltd., the fraudulent company of which that man, under his true name of James Selby, was the Chairman and Managing Director. Helen Taplow was the sole legatee of her uncle, Sir Benjamin Taplow, whose entire fortune had, unfortunately for her and for him, also been invested in the same fraudulent concern. John Masters, the gallant seaman, of whom the town of Eastrepps was justly proud, and whose memory will be green in the hearts of men long after you and I are dust and ashes —he, too, had handed over his small savings, wrested from the deep, unwilling sea, to Anaconda Ltd., seduced, as hundreds of others had been seduced, by prospects of easy gold from that Eldorado, which, since Raleigh sailed the seas, has drawn men to destruction. Thomas Porter and Winifred Dampier were killed together. Thomas Porter—and evidence will be brought to prove it—lost over £1700 from the failure of Anaconda Ltd.; while Winifred Dampier herself lost an even larger sum. Moreover, Winifred Dampier, as I shall in due course suggest to you, had the misfortune, fatal and terrible, to be a witness of the murder of Thomas Porter and suffered the horrible and inevitable consequence.

"Finally there is the journalist, William Ferris. Here

the motive is blindingly clear. It will be proved to you in evidence that Ferris was in a position, and the only man in that position, to testify that Robert Eldridge on the night when John Masters had met his death was not, as he had given it to be understood, in London, but in Eastrepps, not far distant from the scene of the crime. Ferris was the only man in Eastrepps who could confidently and plainly say that the prisoner, who all the time was relying on his alibi to divert suspicion from himself, was in fact walking the streets of the little town. His deposition to that effect will be read to you in due course.

"The reason, then, why William Ferris was murdered on August the sixth is clear, if the case for the Crown is substantiated. All the other victims, as the list found in James Selby's desk will show, were shareholders in Anaconda Ltd. Why were they marked down for murder on that list? I have explained to you already how James Selby fled, in May 1914, from this country and found refuge in Montevideo. I have told you how he wandered over the vast continent of South America till he encountered Robert Eldridge—the real Robert Eldridge—a dying man in a Uruguayan swamp, and how, when he was dead (and how he came by his end it is neither your purpose nor mine to inquire), James Selby, with the papers and the identity of the dead man, came back to England and to the life he had always desired. He settled down, as we saw, in Eastrepps. And what did he find? That there, even in that small town of five thousand inhabitants, there were several victims of Anaconda Ltd. still alive—persons who might recognise him as Selby and denounce him at any moment. The presence of these persons, whom he was meeting every day, so that he knew all their daily habits, preyed upon his mind till at every turn of the street, at every wave of the hand, he saw a hidden enemy—someone who might strip him of his disguise. And he knew—none better—that, should he be thus unmasked, the result must inevitably be many years in close confinement and penal servitude. So he set himself deliberately, with the mind of a skilled and unscrupulous financier, who had lived all his life through by getting the better of his fellow-men, to eliminate those persons in Eastrepps who might have been expected to reveal his identity.

"You will feel that for a normal man the motive was inadequate. You will wonder why he did not leave the town and seek some other place of residence. You will find it difficult to believe that any man could plan a series of atrocious crimes merely that he should be able to live on securely in the place which he had elected for his domicile. But it must be remembered that we are not looking for a normal person. Those crimes have been committed, and the murderer, wherever he may be found, if he be not a complete madman, will be a man with all the enormous vanity of the criminal who is prepared to take life for his own ends and purposes. There must needs be this dreadful disproportion between the small motive and the monstrous crime. That such a man is abnormal I do not question; but that for the purposes of the law he must be regarded as being equally sane as you and I—of that I am just as firmly convinced. There is a great gulf, members of the jury, between madness as the law defines it, and as my lord will describe it, and abnormality, even though that abnormality drives a man to commit murder for his own security and comfort.

"Robert Eldridge, *alias* James Selby, is not mad. He is a man who came quietly to the conclusion that he could not continue to live in constant fear of exposure, and in continual contact with the evidence of his criminal past. And he now stands upon his trial for six of the most callous and brutal murders that have ever been brought before a court of justice.

"It is for you to weigh the evidence that I shall put before you, and I submit, finally and for the last time, that, when you have heard that evidence in all its details, you can come to but one conclusion—which is that James Selby, *alias* Robert Eldridge, killed those six persons fully aware of what he was doing, fully cognizant of the significance of his act. It will then be your duty, however painful it may seem, to pronounce him guilty, and thereafter it will be for the law to take its course."

The Attorney-General had ceased. A stir ran round the court. He sat down for a moment and sipped a glass of water.

Mr. Douglas Sanderson, his Junior, rose from the seat behind him.

"Call Dr. Simms," he said.

IV

Mr. Douglas Sanderson, the Attorney-General's Junior, was speaking.

"And in your opinion, doctor, could the wounds on any or all of the six bodies you examined have been caused by this weapon?"

Warder Edwardes, sitting at his small table to the left of the prisoner, followed with some interest the passage of Exhibit No. 7 from the hands of the police-constable on duty in the well of the court to those of the doctor in the witness-box. It was a hearty sort of weapon— about two feet of stout bamboo with some twine wrapped about one end of it to form the handle. The other end terminated in a small round knob covered with leather, and from this knob there projected at right angles from the shaft a steel blade some three inches long, pointed and ever so slightly curved.

Warder Edwardes had no difficulty in recognising it. He had used one himself that never to be forgotten night on May 21st, 1915, when he had taken part in a trench raid with the Canadians. He had been seconded to a battalion of Western Ontarios, hefty lumbermen, and he, with fifteen of them, had slipped across the German line one hundred and fifty yards away. Just south of the salient they had been. Half of them had been armed with clubs similar to the one which was now in the hands of the doctor—the blade of a jack-knife inserted in a lump of lead at the end of the club, a product of the trenches. And they had blacked their faces, he remembered, so that they should not be seen, and had crawled silently, like a party of nigger minstrels, through the gaps in the German wire and fallen upon a machine-gun post and scuppered its crew. He was never likely to forget how Sergeant Oliphant had swung his weapon and neatly punctured with it the skulls of three of the enemy. That, of course, had been before the days of steel helmets. And each one had died the same death, struck on the temple, and falling dead as door-nails, on the bottom of the slimy trench. "Woodpecker Oliphant" he had ever afterwards been called, till he had been killed on the Somme.

"And you would not expect to find much bleeding from the victims?"

"Not as the blow was delivered. There was a good deal of blood in the case of William Ferris," answered the doctor. "But that blow must, I imagine, have miscarried. The blade of the club entered at right angles to the bone, whereas in the case of all the other victims it had taken a backward trend and pierced the rear portion of the brain."

That was right, reflected Warder Edwardes, for it was just what had happened in the case of those Germans. They had hardly bled at all . . . just gone down like ninepins at the blow of the Woodpecker's beak. He glanced covertly at the prisoner seated by his side.

Robert Eldridge seemed at first sight to be paying no attention. His expression might almost have been that of a bored spectator. Only the slight flush on his cheek-bones and an occasional glimpse of the tip of his tongue as he passed it across his lips showed the strain to which he was put.

"Poor devil!" thought Warder Edwardes. "Not a hope."

"And in the case of Mrs. Dampier," continued Counsel, "the wounds, you say, were of a different nature."

"Yes," said the doctor. "Mrs. Dampier had been struck five or six times—I am not prepared to say exactly how many—with some blunt instrument. Her skull had been broken in three places."

"Could the wounds from which Mrs. Dampier met her death have been caused by the same weapon as those which you have already described?"

"Yes," answered the doctor without hesitation. "It was only necessary to turn the weapon round and use the back of the leaden knob."

"Thank you, doctor," said Counsel for the Crown.

Sir Henry Grey rose.

"I have no questions to put to the witness," he said quietly and sat down.

A low buzz of excitement, instantly suppressed, sounded in the crowded court.

Dr. Simms bowed stiffly to the judge and left the box.

v

Mr. Justice Burrows looked with interest at the young police officer in the witness-box. This Sergeant Ruddock made an excellent witness—clear, concise and admirably straightforward. The learned judge could not, in his long experience, recall any police witness who had created a more favourable impression. And now, under cross-examination by the defence, he was civil and unflustered. Sir Henry Grey would have his work cut out to impair in any way the effect of his testimony.

"Where exactly in the desk did you find this list of the shareholders of Anaconda Ltd.?"

"Behind one of the drawers, sir—the third drawer on the left as I faced it."

"Behind the drawer?"

"Yes."

"Not in the drawer?"

"No."

"Please describe to the jury the exact position in which you found it."

The pen of Mr. Justice Burrows moved steadily across the paper. Behind the drawer—that was rather an odd place for it to be, but he could not yet see the object of Sir Henry's questions. Would the defence endeavour to suggest conspiracy?

"Were the rest of the papers that you examined in that desk in order?"

"In order?" said Sergeant Ruddock.

"Answer the question, please," said Sir Henry Grey.

"I would, sir, if I understood it," replied the Sergeant quietly.

"I am sorry that it should appear so complicated," continued Sir Henry. "Let me explain. You have told my learned friend that you examined the desk and its contents with the greatest care."

"Yes."

"Then you can tell me whether the various papers contained in the desk were arranged neatly in the drawers or whether they were scattered and disordered."

"The papers were all neatly arranged," answered Sergeant Ruddock.

"So the list of shareholders was the only paper out of place. You found it wedged behind a drawer, in fact?"

"Yes."

"Did it strike you as curious at the time that of all the papers in that desk this was the only one which was out of place?"

"It did not strike me in that way," replied Sergeant Ruddock.

"Now that I put it to you, are you at all disposed to think it curious?"

"Perhaps," answered the Sergeant. "But, having regard to the nature of the list, I cannot say that I am surprised."

"We are not concerned with the nature of the list for the moment," said Sir Henry. "Was the drawer behind which you found the list empty or full?"

"The drawer was full."

"To the top?"

"No. It was about half full."

"Of papers neatly and smoothly arranged?"

"Yes."

"So that the list could not, in your opinion, have been caught by accident at the back of the drawer?"

The Attorney-General rose.

"Is this necessary, my lord?"

Mr. Justice Burrows leaned forward.

"It seems to me, Sir Henry, that you are leading. The witness need not answer that question."

Sir Henry bowed to the judge.

"It will be part of the defence, my lord, that my client had no knowledge of the list, and that he had never had such a list in his house. I am trying to elicit whether the list could have been lying among his papers in the ordinary way, and have been pushed by accident to the back of the drawer, or whether . . ."

"That is a speech, Sir Henry. Please put your question."

Sir Henry turned to the witness.

"Was the list crumpled or damaged in any way when you found it?"

"The list was crumpled. It had caused the drawer to stick, and I had some difficulty in pulling it out."

"But the drawer was by no means full of papers?"

"No."

"You are sure of that?"

"Yes."

"We come now to the rubber stamp . . ."

The questions continued, relevant and seemingly ir-relevant, probing this way and that for a flaw, but all they really succeeded in showing was that Sergeant Rud-dock had been very careful in his search and remembered it in every detail. Mr. Justice Burrows doubted whether Sir Henry was wise to go on.

Sir Henry Grey continued:

"Now as to Mrs. Brandon, Sergeant, the housekeeper of the accused. You have said that you conducted the search in her presence?"

"I did."

"Did you put any questions to her?"

"Yes."

"What did you say?"

"I asked her whether the accused went to London regularly," replied the Sergeant.

"Nothing else?"

"I put to her quite a number of questions on that point," said Sergeant Ruddock. "She informed me . . ."

The judge again leaned forward, but Sir Henry Grey was too quick for him.

"You must not tell me what she replied," he said. "She will herself inform the jury. I want to know whether you asked her any questions as to the people who came to the house."

"No."

"Did she strike you as normal in every way?"

"Perfectly."

"No peculiarities?"

"None."

"You are ranging rather wide, aren't you, Sir Henry?" said Mr. Justice Burrows.

"My object will be apparent in a moment, my lord."

He turned back to the witness.

"Did she hear you quite well when you spoke to her?"

Ruddock hesitated.

"No," he answered. "She struck me as being a little deaf."

"And you had some difficulty in gaining admittance when you came round to the house?"

"Yes. I knocked and rang for some time."

"How long?"

"I couldn't say for certain. Some five or ten minutes, perhaps."

"And how was Mrs. Brandon dressed when she opened the door?"

"She was fully dressed, as far as I could see."

"Was she wearing an apron?"

"Yes."

"She did not strike you as having just got out of bed to answer the door?"

"No."

"But, owing to her being a little deaf, it took her some time to realise that you were knocking on the door."

"I suppose so."

"Thank you, Sergeant."

Sir Henry sat down.

"The court will now adjourn," said Mr. Justice Burrows.

VI

Mr. Alfred Bickersteth was bored. He had been a faithful reader of prosecutions for many years, and had once waited vainly in the street for hours on the chance of getting into that very court to hear Rex *v.* Brown & Kennedy. But there it was. He was foreman of the jury in the most sensational trial of the times, and for three days he had held a front seat such as anyone of his less fortunate friends would have paid dearly to occupy for half an hour. But this was the third day, and he was bored.

There was so much of it that seemed unnecessary.

The Crown had not yet concluded its case, which, on the face of it, was simple as could be. There was the list and the weapon and the alibi. Surely these were enough, and, anyway, it was time that the other side had an innings. The defence had done precious little so far— just a bit of mild cross-examination here and there, mostly on trivial points. Yet this was the famous Sir Henry Grey, whose reputation in these cases was second to none. Bricks without straw, he supposed.

Mr. Smithson was now in the witness-box, the Manager of the Goodwood Hotel, Bloomsbury Square. That was where Eldridge had stayed in London during his weekly visits. It was, again, very simple to follow. Eldridge had slept in the hotel every Tuesday night, but had never appeared at his house in Eastrepps till the following Thursday at noon. His housekeeper had always supposed him to be in London on Wednesday, but that was only a blind. This was the famous alibi, of which more than enough had already been heard.

But Sir Henry was on his feet.

"When did Mr. Robert Eldridge first book a room in your hotel, Mr. Smithson?"

The Manager paused a moment before answering.

"I should have to consult the books," he said, "but I fancy it was at the end of January or the beginning of February of this year."

"Please hand the witness Exhibit No. 26," said Sir Henry.

A ledger was handed up to the Manager.

"You recognise that as the register of the Goodwood Hotel?"

"Yes."

"Would you please consult it and answer my question?"

Mr. Smithson opened the book and glanced down the pages.

"I see from our records," he said, "that Mr. Eldridge first booked a room in the hotel on January 21st."

"Has Mr. Eldridge occupied that room regularly as from that date?"

"I see that he engaged it permanently on the 27th of January."

"Are you prepared to swear that the accused occupied that room on the Tuesday night of every week since January 21st until his arrest?"

"I find that to be the case."

"And during the whole of that period he never occupied the room on a Wednesday night?"

"Never. Only on Tuesday."

"Thank you."

Mr. Bickersteth scratched the back of his neck. What was the meaning of that? But, of course, he saw it now —quite a good point. The prisoner had been creating this famous alibi since January, but the murders had only started in July. Therefore it was not necessarily connected with the murders, but with something that had been going on before the murders had started.

Sir Henry was looking pleased, and here was Mrs. Brandon in the box.

Mr. Bickersteth glanced at the other members of the jury. They were all beginning to look a little worn—especially the stout woman at the end of the second row. But Mrs. Brandon was saying her piece, and he must pay attention. It was the old story, of course. Eldridge had never returned to Eastrepps on Wednesday evening, to her knowledge, but only on Thursday morning. And the Attorney-General was needlessly emphatic about it —almost shouting at the poor old lady.

She was describing now what had happened on the night when Sergeant Ruddock had searched the house. . . . No flies on that Sergeant fellow.

But Sir Henry was up again.

"Are you Mrs. Brandon, the housekeeper of the accused?"

That, if you like, was a silly question. She had told them quite plainly all about herself once already. Perhaps it was the heat. . . . Sir Henry seemed out of spirits. . . . He had put his question in a low tone, quite unlike the ringing accents of the Attorney-General.

Mrs. Brandon shook her head.

"Never on a Wednesday," she said.

"I do not think you understood my question," continued Sir Henry, in a somewhat louder voice. "I am asking whether you are Mrs. Brandon, the housekeeper of Mr. Robert Eldridge."

"Never on a Wednesday," repeated the witness firmly.

The Attorney-General rose.

"I would ask my learned friend to speak up. The witness is rather hard of hearing."

"Thank you," said Sir Henry. "That is the fact I was trying to elicit."

"Are there any other servants in the house?" he continued, turning to the witness.

"No. There's a girl that comes in the day."

"When does she leave the house?"

"About eight o'clock in the evening."

"Do you ever, when alone in the house, answer the front door after eight o'clock?"

"I answer anyone that comes."

"Can you hear anyone who knocks or rings from your quarters in the kitchen?"

"It's like this," said Mrs. Brandon earnestly. "It is one of them hanging bells, and I keep my eye on it pretty close."

"Is the front door usually bolted or kept on the chain?"

"Not till I go to bed."

"That would be at about what time?"

"Usually at about eleven o'clock."

"Not before?"

"No. I don't like to go to bed too early. I wake up too soon next morning."

"Thank you, Mrs. Brandon."

Mr. Bickersteth sat back on the bench. . . . So Mrs. Brandon was deaf, and the Counsel for the defence appeared to attach some importance to the fact. It was all rather puzzling, and it was quite impossible to think. However, he would make a note of the circumstance. Mrs. Brandon was deaf, and when the bell rang she must see it before she believed it.

VII

"With reference once again to this list, Mr. Eldridge. Will you tell the jury in your own words how you account for its being discovered in your possession?"

Sir Henry Grey looked across at his client in the witness-box. It was the fourth day of the trial. Eldridge was wearing well—surprisingly well, considering what he had been through, and his evidence had so far been effectually given—quietly and with a certain hopeless dignity.

"I cannot account for it."

The voice of the witness was still clear and steady.

"You have no explanation as to how it came to be found in your desk?"

"None whatever."

"It purports to be a list of the shareholders in Anaconda Ltd."

"Yes."

"Have you examined the list?"

"I have."

"Is it to your knowledge a genuine list? Are the names upon it, in fact, those of former shareholders in the company?"

"I do not know."

"What do you mean by that?"

It was Mr. Justice Burrows who spoke, leaning forward from his seat.

"Do you really mean to say that you do not know?"

"I could not answer whether it is or whether it is not a list of the shareholders, my lord," said Eldridge, turning his head in the direction of the judge. "I destroyed all records of Anaconda Ltd. many years ago."

The judge nodded.

"So that you have no means of knowing whether that list is genuine or not," continued Sir Henry.

"I have no means of knowing."

"And you cannot in the least account for its presence in your desk?"

"It is a complete mystery to me."

"Is there anyone who, in your knowledge, could have put it there?"

Eldridge hesitated a moment.

"It would be quite easy for anyone to do so."

"You mean that there may be someone?"

"Yes."

"Do you wish to add anything to that reply?"

"I have many enemies," said Eldridge. "Many persons who knew my antecedents might have been glad of the chance to bring suspicion upon me."

"Is it a fact that your housekeeper is deaf?"

"It is."

"Would it, in your opinion, have been easy for anyone to enter your house during your absence for that or any other purpose without her being aware of the fact?"

"I am sure it would."

"Now with reference to the weapon. It formed part of a war trophy?"

"Yes."

"Belonging to yourself?"

"The trophies were part of the property of the real Robert Eldridge."

"The man whose identity you confess to assuming. How did you obtain possession of his effects?"

"Robert Eldridge, when he died, left me his papers. Among them was a receipt for certain furniture stored by the firm of Harrington in Harrow Road. That furniture is now in the house in Eastrepps. It included a number of war trophies."

"Robert Eldridge served in the war."

"Yes."

"Have we his records, Sir Henry?"

Again Mr. Justice Burrows had intervened.

"Yes, my lord. I have handed the relevant papers to the clerk of the court. He could perhaps acquaint the jury with them."

"That will come later," said the judge.

"As your lordship pleases. I am merely trying to elicit that Robert Eldridge, the real Robert Eldridge, served in the war and left those trophies behind him."

Sir Henry turned again to his client.

"You hung these trophies upon the wall of your study?"

"I did."

"Did you ever take them down?"

"They were taken down occasionally and dusted, and I was in the habit of showing them to my friends, especially the trench club."

"You did occasionally handle it?"

"Frequently."

"So that it has your finger-prints upon it?"

"I suppose so."

"How is it secured to the wall?"

"By a loop of wire."

"Do you recognise the weapon?"

A constable handed the exhibit to Eldridge, who looked at it long and closely.

"That is the weapon."

"When do you last remember handling it?"

Eldridge paused, and thought a moment.

"I cannot say for certain," he answered at length, "but I remember showing it to Mrs. Brandon's nephew one day when he came to tea with his aunt."

"When would that be?"

"Somewhere about the end of June. I can't remember the exact date."

"You cannot account for the fact that this weapon was found by the body of William Ferris."

"I can only assume that someone removed it for the purpose of killing Ferris and did not replace it."

"Did you fight in the war?"

"No."

"Have you ever used a weapon such as the one produced in court?"

"Never."

Sir Henry folded back his billowing silk gown. He looked Eldridge straight in the face.

"Have you committed any of the crimes laid to your charge?"

Eldridge was gripping the rail of the witness-box in front of him.

"No," he said.

"You swear it?"

"I swear it, by Almighty God."

"Thank you."

Sir Henry Grey, Counsel for the defence, sat down. The Attorney-General rose.

"You have not denied," he said, "that your real name is not Robert Eldridge at all, but James Selby?"

"I admit it."

"You were formerly the chairman of Anaconda Ltd.?"

Eldridge felt the sweat breaking out across his forehead. He took a grip of himself. This was the cross-examination—the thing he had lived through in dread a hundred times already. He must keep cool and calm at all costs. It was his only chance.

"I was."

"And you absconded on May 16th, 1914, with a considerable portion of the Company's funds."

"I did."

"The amount was over one hundred and ninety thousand pounds, was it not?"

"Yes."

"Had you ever any intention of repaying that money?"

"Yes," said Eldridge.

"You did intend, Mr. Eldridge"—the voice of the Attorney-General was silky smooth—"to pay back the persons from whom you stole this very large sum?"

"If circumstances permitted."

"That perhaps was one of your motives in returning to England many years later under an assumed name?"

"One of the motives."

"How is it, therefore"—the Attorney-General consulted his notes—"that you destroyed all records of Anaconda Ltd. many years ago?"

"I don't understand," said the witness in so low a tone that the official court stenographer raised his head sharply in an effort to catch the reply.

"Come, Mr. Eldridge"—the Attorney-General's voice was still smooth, but there was a latent rasp in it—"you told my lord here that you destroyed all records of Anaconda Ltd. many years ago. I am quoting your own words."

"That is so."

"How could you have hoped to repay the shareholders if you did not keep a list of their names?"

"I . . . I should have advertised," said Eldridge.

"I see. You were going to put advertisements in the Press, asking the shareholders of Anaconda Ltd. to come forward."

"Yes," said Eldridge.

"Have you in fact inserted any such advertisement?"

"No."

"How long have you been in England?"

"Two years and three months."

"Is it not a fact that there is at present a credit balance in the London County and Midland Bank standing in your name of £281,129 16s. 4d.?"

"Yes," said Eldridge.

"And is it not a fact that according to the books of your present business—the Furnish-out-of-Income Society—your net profits for the last four weeks have averaged £851 a week?"

"If you say so, I suppose it is correct."

"You may take it from me, Mr. Eldridge, that those figures are quite correct," said the Attorney-General quietly. "Nevertheless, you have not yet advertised for any shareholders in Anaconda Ltd. with the object of repaying them?"

"No."

"Thank you."

"Now with reference to your alibi. You informed my learned friend here that you were accustomed on the Tuesday of every week . . ."

VIII

Robert Eldridge glanced at the watch on his wrist. . . . Half-past five. Perhaps the court would now adjourn. Sir Henry had just sat down, and Margaret, free for an instant from the need to answer the questions whereby he had enabled her to tell her story, had flashed him a look across the court full of love and compassion. Did she know—could she imagine—what was about to happen? His own cross-examination had been bad enough. Answering the questions of that terrible man, with the wig ever so slightly awry, who had always so politely addressed him as "Mr. Eldridge," he had been thinking that it would soon be her turn, perhaps within an hour. She, too, would have to face that unending torment, feel the ground slipping from beneath her, sense the hostility of the court, its curiosity and unbelief, its pleasure, even, in her slow discomfiture or sudden anguish. He longed to cry out, to tell her to go away. And then she had smiled at him; he had caught the gleam of her courage; and he knew that they must fight to a finish.

But perhaps the court would adjourn.

There was a drumming in his ears. He could not hear properly what was being said. Then he saw that the Attorney-General had risen.

"With reference to the visits of the accused. . . . You say that he arrived every Wednesday evening between nine and half-past?"

"Yes," said Margaret.

"You fully realise the importance of being able to fix the exact hour."

"Of course."

"How was it that the moment of his arrival came to be so precisely fixed in your memory?"

"I was waiting for him to come."

"With your eyes on the clock?"

"I should have noticed at once if he had been late."

"He was never either early or late?"

"It depended on the train. The train was occasionally late, but never more than a few minutes either way."

"Mr. Eldridge invariably remained with you until the following morning?"

"Yes. He was accustomed to leave the house at about half-past eleven."

"Why at half-past eleven?"

"So that he might reach the station in time for him to join the passengers arriving from London by the midday train."

"You are prepared to swear that on each of the occasions when murder was committed the accused was with you at White Cottage?"

"Yes. He was with me the whole time."

"Have you accepted anything from Mr. Eldridge?"

"He has been in the habit of helping me now and then."

"You live apart from your husband, do you not?"

"Yes."

"But you are not divorced from him?"

"No."

"Are you seeking a divorce?"

"Yes."

"What steps have you taken?"

"I don't quite understand."

"Is it not a fact that during the period of his visits to you the accused was employing a private detective to watch your husband?"

"Yes."

"You were a party to that arrangement?"

"Yes."

"What was your object?"

"I wanted to obtain evidence which would enable me to divorce him."

"Does that strike you as a fair proceeding?"

"I had no reason to consider my husband. He had treated me abominably."

"Are you fond of Mr. Eldridge?"

"I am."

"Did you expect to marry him if you obtained your divorce?"

"I did."

"Were you aware of his real identity?"

"Not at the time."

"Now that you know who he is, has your determination to marry him been changed on that account?"

"Certainly not."

"Nor on account of the charges under which he at present lies?"

"He is innocent."

"You are, in fact, in love with Mr. Eldridge?"

"Heart and soul."

Eldridge gripped his knees. That she should say such things before the whole world.

"You would do anything for this man?"

"Yes."

"You were prepared to live with him while seeking to obtain evidence against your husband in order to secure a divorce?"

The blood ran to Margaret's cheeks, then back to the heart again, leaving her face very white.

"I was prepared," she said, in almost a whisper.

"Do you realise that had your project been successful you would have come before the courts of this realm as an innocent and wronged woman?"

"I should have applied for a divorce in the ordinary way."

"I will repeat my question in a different form. Do you realise that you would have had no right to a divorce under the laws of the land, and that to obtain that divorce you would, in effect, have been obliged to bear false witness?"

Sir Henry Grey rose.

"That, my lord, is a purely hypothetical question, and I submit that it has nothing to do with the present case."

Mr. Justice Burrows leaned forward.

"The learned Counsel," he said, "is presumably attacking the credibility of the witness. Perhaps he will put the question rather differently."

The Attorney-General bowed.

"Certainly, my lord."

He turned back to the witness.

"Is it a fact that you were prepared to obtain this divorce in a manner which I have discribed?"

"It did not occur to me quite in that light."

"Answer my question, please. You were prepared to deceive the judge in the divorce court in order to gain your private ends?"

"It is a very usual proceeding, is it not?"

"Is it a proceeding which you would expect this court to recognise?"

"The proceeding was forced upon me. I wished to keep my daughter. I could not let her go to my husband."

"You preferred that your daughter should be associated with a man like Eldridge than with her own father?"

"Yes."

"You are still of that opinion?"

"Yes."

"Even though you now know that Eldridge, on his own confession, is a swindler."

"Yes."

"You are so infatuated with this man that you would let any ordinary considerations go by the wall in order to marry him?"

"I am prepared to marry him whatever happens."

The Attorney-General paused a moment.

Then the questions began again.

"How long have you been living in Eastrepps?"

"Nearly three years."

"And it was there that you first met the prisoner?"

"Yes."

"Have you always lived . . ."

IX

Mr. Bembridge, author of *The Stolen Casket* and other plays, looked with interest at the sharp, handsome face of the man in the box. One could hardly help rather admiring the fellow. Already, under the considerate promptings of Sir Henry, he had confessed to blackmail, and he was quite obviously in for a bad time when the prosecution got to work upon him. But he carried it off with a certain rather attractive insolence. "Vanity," said Mr. Bembridge to himself. All these criminals are alike.

One day he would write a book about it—crime and conceit . . . by that sin the angels fell.

He sat back in his seat. The benches of the City Fathers were hard, and this was the fifth day of the trial. It would, he supposed, be one of the really famous ones, but frankly it had been rather disappointing. For a man of the theatre these trials at the old Bailey lacked form and finish. There were effective moments. One could pick up a useful thing or two. The cross-examination of the man's mistress had been not so bad—not, of course, good enough, as it stood, for the stage, but with a little polishing and a good deal of compression it would pass muster.

The worst defect of the present trial, of course, from the dramatic point of view, apart from its length—how these lawyers did talk!—was the appalling weakness of the defence. Sir Henry was doing his best, but the poor devil in the dock simply had not the beginnings of a case. Not that he was himself at all sure that the man was guilty. The evidence was all against him, and yet, somehow, he did not look the part; and there had been an extraordinary air of candour and conviction about that woman in the box. She did really believe her lover to be innocent. So, apparently, did Sir Henry, though he, of course, could always make himself believe anything he pleased.

But Sir Henry was speaking:

"I am anxious to get this quite clear, Mr. Coldfoot. You were aware—were you not?—when you called on Mr. Eldridge on July 24th that he had been in the habit of visiting Mrs. Withers for some time?"

"Yes. The visits began in January last."

"You threatened to reveal the fact of these visits to her husband unless she could induce Mr. Eldridge to pay you a certain sum of money."

"Yes."

"You are prepared to swear that the sole ground on

which you were seeking to obtain money was that you knew of these visits and that you also knew that it was vital for her to keep all knowledge of them from her husband."

"Yes."

"You had no other grounds whatever?"

"No."

"It had never, for example, struck you that the dates on which these visits took place coincided with the dates on which the two previous murders had been committed?"

"No."

"You did not connect my client in any way with these appalling crimes?"

"No."

"Thank you, Mr. Coldfoot."

Sir Henry Grey sat down. The Attorney-General came to his feet.

"You told my learned friend here that Robert Eldridge *alias* James Selby was accustomed to visit Mrs. Withers every Wednesday night and remain in her house until the following morning?"

"Yes."

"You communicated your knowledge of this fact to the prisoner, and asked him what he was going to do about it —I am quoting your own words."

"Yes."

"The prisoner gave you a sum of money in return for your silence?"

"Yes."

"He was purchasing your silence concerning his visits to Mrs. Withers? There was nothing else in your mind in demanding money from the prisoner?"

"Nothing at all."

"You knew of no other reason why the prisoner should be anxious to conceal his movements on those nights?"

"No."

"You swear to that?"

"Yes."

"You informed my learned friend that at the time you were blackmailing the prisoner you never connected him in any way with the murders?"

"That is true."

"Do you realise that, had you connected him with the murders and had you then acted in the way you did, you would now be in a very serious position?"

"I don't quite follow."

"I will repeat the question differently. Are you aware that, if you had suspected the prisoner of murder and if you had then extorted money from him in return for your silence, you would now be liable to arrest as an accessory after the fact?"

"It sounds pretty bad."

"Not the sort of thing to which you would care to confess in open court?"

"I did not say so."

"Have you ever appeared in court in any other capacity than that of a witness?"

The witness paused. Mr. Bembridge could see that he was ill at ease.

"I have appeared in court," he said at last.

"It was in 1926, was it not?"

"It may have been."

"On the occasion of the Guildford Autumn Assizes, was it not?"

"I believe so."

"And were you on that occasion convicted of a certain offence?"

"I was wrongly convicted."

"That is as it may be," said the Attorney-General quietly. "But you were convicted?"

"Yes."

"Of perjury, was it not?"

"I was not guilty."

"Were you not on that occasion sentenced to twelve months' hard labour?"

"I was not guilty."

"Did not the judge on that occasion describe your evidence as a tissue of falsehood from beginning to end?"

"I do not remember what he said."

The Attorney-General turned a moment to his Junior, who handed him a file. The Attorney-General fluttered the pages. Then he clipped a pair of pince-nez to his nose.

"This is what Mr. Justice Harrowbin said before sentencing you. 'You have been convicted of the very serious crime of perjury, and in my view rightly convicted. Your evidence in the case of Rex *v.* Justin was a tissue of falsehood from beginning to end. In the circumstances the least sentence this court can impose is twelve months' with hard labour.'"

"What has all this to do with the present case?" burst out the witness.

"You are here to answer questions, not to put them," said the judge severely.

The Attorney-General had laid down the file.

"You live by your wits, don't you?"

"Like you or anyone else."

There ran a little ripple of laughter round the court.

"Silence!" came the voice of the usher.

"What I meant was," pursued the Attorney-General, quite unruffled, "that you have no regular profession?"

"Not at the moment."

"You held for some time a commission in His Majesty's army?"

"Yes."

"In the 15th Loamshire Foot?"

"Yes, but I sent in my papers."

"Was not a court of inquiry held into your conduct just before you did so?"

"Yes."

"The court had been asked to inquire into the manner in which the mess funds had been kept?"

"I believe so."

"Were you not Mess Secretary at the time?"

"I was."

"Thank you, Mr. Coldfoot."

x

Margaret Withers was facing Mr. Justice Burrows from the back of the court. She sat on the first of the benches reserved for witnesses who had given their evidence and who desired to remain through the subsequent proceedings. It was the morning of the sixth day, but she was aware of nothing except that she was tired—too tired to feel or think or listen. And it was rather important that she should listen for Sir Henry Grey was making his last appeal for the prisoner. He was talking, it appeared, about her.

"If you believe Margaret Withers—and I submit to that whatever my learned friend put to her in his cross-examination was quite irrelevant to the issue which is before us—you are bound to find Robert Eldridge not guilty of the crimes laid to his charge. It will not have escaped you that the sole object of the cross-examination of my learned friend was to discredit the character of this witness, so that in weighing the evidence before you her statements should be, in fact, disregarded. It is part of the case for the Crown, that Mrs. Withers, when she told us that Robert Eldridge was with her on those fatal evenings, was deliberately lying in order to save a man whom she knew to be a murderer six times over. You have heard and seen the witness. You have doubtless realised what the consequences of her evidence will be to her personally. She had everything to lose by coming here. She knew that she must part with her child and submit to an ordeal such as few would be ready to face.

"My learned friend has made much of the fact that

Mrs. Withers was prepared to obtain a divorce from her husband in spite of the fact that she had no right to that divorce under the laws of this country. I can understand the indignation of my learned friend that she should have had that intention, and it is far from me to defend it. She pleaded, rashly perhaps, that such a procedure is not unusual. My learned friend must admit that here, at least, she was speaking the truth. I am not asking you in any way to condone such practices, but I must remind you that you are not here to try the moral issue, and that you must not allow your judgment to be in any way distorted by your distrust, however profound and justifiable it may be, of those who disregard the moral law. The sole issue before you in regard to Mrs. Withers is whether she has wilfully lied to this court, and is thus an accessory to the dreadful crimes of which the prisoner stands accused. My own deeply felt conviction is that she has witnessed to the truth, and that she is ready even to lose her child rather than hide the truth."

Margaret was watching as at a great distance the gestures of Sir Henry. It was as though a gauze curtain had been drawn between her and the little man in his billowy gown. Nothing was real. She felt in the bag between her fingers the divorce papers which had that morning been served upon her. But nothing seemed to matter very much. She looked at her watch. Sir Henry had been speaking for over an hour, but she had scarcely heard a word.

"I come now to the circumstantial evidence against the prisoner. For I would emphasise that all the evidence against him is a matter of inference and probability. His presence near the scene of the crime on August 6th is easily explained. He was paying his customary visit to Mrs. Withers on that fatal Wednesday evening, and he would in that event naturally be where he was, in fact, discovered by Police-Constable Birchington. The sole evidence of any weight against the prisoner is his alleged possession of the fatal list and the fact that the weapon with which the last of the murders was committed was one which had been taken from his study wall. The prisoner has denied all knowledge of the list, and has informed us that he cannot account for the removal of the weapon. Our inference must be that he has been the victim of a conspiracy, and I would submit to you that the enemy who did this thing is far from being the shadowy and hypothetical individual my learned friend has suggested to you. I have shown conclusively how easy it would have been for anyone in the world to enter 14, Oakfield Terrace, and there to plant the evidence which he confidently hoped would secure the conviction of Robert Eldridge. Two expert locksmiths have testified before you—and their evidence was unshaken in cross-examination—that both the front and the back doors of the house in Oakfield Terrace could be opened with ease by anyone with the most elementary knowledge of house-breaking. You yourselves have noted that Mrs. Brandon has the misfortune to be deaf—doubtless the only defect in an otherwise admirable housekeeper.

"My learned friend has dwelt at length on the improbabilities implicit in the theory—the only theory that explains the facts as I perceive them—that the murders were committed by a person unknown who successfully planted them upon the prisoner. I would ask you, however, to consider for a moment the improbabilities implicit in the case for the prosecution. You are asked to believe that the prisoner, who, according to my learned friend, is a criminal of superhuman cunning and resource, kept in his house, accessible to the first policeman who might enter it, a list of his crimes, carefully kept up to date, recording them day by day, and fastening upon himself clearly and unmistakably the evidence of his guilt. You are further asked to believe that he committed the murders with a weapon that was notoriously in his possession—which he even exhibited from time to time to his friends and neighbours—and that he threw down this weapon and left it beside the body of his victim when he realised on the last fatal evening that the police were at hand.

"I submit that such conduct is utterly incompatible with the picture offered us by my learned friend of the cool and cunning criminal who was responsible for these crimes. I submit, indeed, that the finding of the list and the weapon, on which the case for the Crown ultimately rests, far from being an argument in favour of the prose-cution, is the strongest possible argument for the defence. The person who committed the murders would never have kept such a list and would never have advertised his possession of such a weapon. No better devices could, on the contrary, have been invented by a person who was seeking to manufacture evidence against the prisoner.

"Let me, if I may, for one moment reconstruct what in my view, and in that of my client, in all certainty hap-pened."

Sir Henry Grey paused. Even Margaret was stirred. She leaned forward the better to observe him.

"You are to imagine this enemy—one among the many bitter enemies whom the prisoner has on his own con-fession made for himself—coming after dark, every Wednesday, to that small house in Oakfield Terrace. He knew that Robert Eldridge was safe in London, and he knew that Robert Eldridge's housekeeper, Mrs. Bran-don, would hear nothing, shut safely away, as her custom was, in the kitchen parlour. With one turn of a skeleton key"—here Counsel for the defence thrust out his right hand and twisted it in the air—"this unknown man un-locked the front door, which was never chained, crept silently into the sitting-room, took down the weapon from where it hung upon the wall and stole forth again, to return it half an hour later when he had committed his crime. One evening, when he had already perpetrated the last of them, he took from his pocket the typewritten list and thrust it into the drawer, where he knew it would be found. It was then that he hit upon a device which should fix suspicion quite irrevocably upon the prisoner. He took the date-stamp which lay on the table ready to his hand. He twisted the dies, and he stamped the date of each murder against the name of each victim. Why did he use the date-stamp? Surely, members of the jury, the reason is clear. Had he written the dates with the same red ink which he used to underline the names, his handwriting would have betrayed him. It would have been apparent that the dates had been written not by Robert Eldridge, but by some unknown man. He used the stamp to overcome the difficulty—to him the only real difficulty—of adequately forging the handwriting of my client."

Margaret felt a sudden glow of relief.

Sir Henry, describing the imaginary progress of the secret enemy, each gesture bringing to life the scene which he was endeavouring to stamp on the imaginations of the jury, had all but carried her away. Surely this was what had really happened? Surely the picture he drew was the true one? How could anyone disbelieve it?

She looked towards the Attorney-General. He was sitting quite unmoved; he was even whispering to one of his juniors. And there, too, was the judge, impassive as a rock, his head resting sidelong upon his hand and a look on his face that might have been one of faint disapproval.

The play-acting of Sir Henry was notoriously unpopular with the bench.

XI

From the point of view of Mr. Blatchett, court stenographer, Mr. Justice Burrows was a good judge. He spoke slowly, with fairly frequent pauses—not like Sir

Henry Grew, who, when he really got going, became excited and voluble and very difficult to punctuate.

Mr. Blatchett was tired. He was never at his best at the beginning of the session, and the strain of a continuous big trial was always severe. He had not had much energy to spare, and he had not yet troubled to form his own opinion on the merits of the case. It was odd how you could think of all kinds of things and still take down quite mechanically what someone was saying a few feet away from you.

"The defence has relied chiefly on the testimony of two witnesses, Margaret Withers and Richards Coldfoot, to prove that at the time when these crimes were committed the accused was at the house and in the presence of the former. You have seen Margaret Withers in the witness-box. She does not deny her intimate relations with the prisoner. She has informed you that she is in love with him, heart and soul. It is not for you to pass judgment on the fact that this love of hers for the prisoner has led her into an irregular union with him. You have simply to make up your minds whether you are going to believe her evidence or not. Do not forget that she admitted in cross-examination that she was preparing, with the aid of the prisoner, to come before the courts of this realm and sue for a divorce from her husband, John Withers, though she herself, on her own admission, was living in circumstances which made any divorce or petition from her out of the question. Counsel for the Crown had laid special stress on this fact. He did so, an did so rightly, because in a defence such as that put forward by the prisoner—that of an alibi—the testimony of the witnesses to that alibi and the precise value to be attached to it are of cardinal importance. These remarks apply also to the testimony of Richard Coldfoot. For you must not forget that the evidence of Margaret Withers was not unsupported. Richard Coldfoot has come into the witness-box and testified that to his own proper knowledge the purpose of the accused in constructing his elaborate alibi was merely that he should visit Mrs. Withers without exciting the suspicion of her husband. You must ask yourselves whether Richard Coldfoot is a witness who should be believed. Were the relations between Margaret Withers and the prisoner all that Richard Coldfoot knew, or did his knowledge extend further? Was he telling the whole truth, or only part of the truth, or none at all? Richard Coldfoot has confessed to conduct which he has cynically admitted to be the blackmail of the accused. He admitted, too, in cross-examination that he has served a sentence of twelve months for perjury, and that he was forced to send in his papers from the Army under threat of exposure for misappropriation of Mess funds."

Mr. Justice Burrows paused and sipped from a glass of water. Mr. Blatchett glanced at the clock . . . midday. . . . With any luck the charge to the jury would be finished by the luncheon interval, and in that case the trial would not go on beyond the evening.

"Counsel for the defence has urged that the prisoner has many enemies. He has suggested to you that one of these enemies may have committed these crimes and planted evidence upon the prisoner with the object of securing his conviction. You have been shown very fully by the defence how in their view those crimes might have been committed. Much has been made of the deafness of Mrs. Brandon, the housekeeper, and of the fact that the locks upon the doors of 14, Oakfield Terrace, the residence of the prisoner, could easily have been opened by anyone desiring to do so.

"You must, however, bear in mind that no evidence has been put before you that those locks were in any way damaged or scratched; nor must you forget that, apart from this material evidence, nothing has been put before you which might enable you even so much as to conjecture the identity of this alleged enemy. The defence has contended that the dates set against the names of the victims in the list which, it is alleged, was concealed in the prisoner's desk to his undoing, were stamped upon the paper by the murderer to avoid the necessity of having to forge the prisoner's hand. That, again, is pure hypothesis. Do not forget that the list of which the accused denies all knowledge is a list containing the names of shareholders in a concern which was once under his control. . . ."

"The defence has urged that it is highly improbable that the resourceful criminal who committed these murders should have kept a list of his victims and used a weapon which was known to be in his possession. The improbability is manifest; but murder upon this scale and upon such motives as we have been asked to consider is in itself improbable. The murderer has a special and peculiar psychology of his own, and experience shows that the most resourceful criminal is liable to take risks and to commit blunders which would instinctively be avoided by the normal man."

Mr. Blatchett felt a hand on his shoulder. He looked round at his colleague, who had come in to relieve him, and nodded thankfully.

"Two minutes still to go," he said, and continued writing.

XII

Mr. Bickersteth, foreman of the jury, stifled a yawn. Two hours had passed in the narrow room, with the stiff chairs and its view of the prison yard, and he really did not see what there was for his colleagues to argue about. The case was as clear as daylight. If ever a man had been guilty, that man was Robert Eldridge, *alias* James Selby, and Mr. Primrose and Mr. Birkett, who sat one on each side of him at the long table, were clearly of the same opinion. It was the little man half-way down, with white spats, who was giving most of the trouble.

He was of the sort who would always vote contrary to general opinion just in order to be original.

"Well," said Mr. Bickersteth, "we must try again, I suppose. Is there any special point which any member of the jury still wishes to discuss?"

"It comes to the same thing every time, Mr. Foreman" —it was the man with the white spats who spoke. "Either you believe that Mrs. Withers was telling the truth or you don't, and nothing the prosecution was able to produce in evidence can make me believe that she knew of these awful murders."

"That, Mr. Bland, is not the point."

The stout lady at the end of the table leaned forward pugnaciously.

"It is not the point at all," she repeated. "I'm not saying that she knew of the murders. I do say that her evidence was false. She believes the man to be innocent, and she was trying to save him by swearing that he was in her company every Wednesday evening before ten o'clock."

"But consider what she stood to lose by coming forward," objected Mr. Bland.

"No woman in her state of mind would hesitate for a moment between losing the child and losing the man," said the stout lady. "If she had been as keen on the child as all that she would have waited decently for her divorce before . . . taking up with the prisoner."

"But Counsel for the defence," began Mr. Bland.

"Hadn't a leg to stand on," interrupted the stout lady. "And no one knew it better than he did. That is why he threw up all that dust about the child. That kind of thing doesn't deceive a woman."

A subdued snuffling came from a corner of the long table, where a frail lady in black was dabbing her eyes with a moist handkerchief.

"This is awful!" she said. "You none of you seem to realise that a man is going to he hanged."

The man sitting beside her, lean and cadaverous, laid a hand awkwardly upon her shoulder.

"Madam," he said, "that is the law. We are not responsible for the law. We have merely to answer certain questions, and there our responsibility is joint. We cannot escape it. You are yourself convinced that the prisoner is guilty. It is your duty to join with us in saying so."

"I am not convinced that Mrs. Withers was bearing false witness," persisted Mr. Bland, "and I do not think that the case is proven."

The Foreman looked towards an elderly gentleman at the far end of the table.

"And you, Major Hesketh," he said. "Do you still persist in believing the prisoner to be innocent?"

Major Hesketh was wearing a dark grey coat and striped trousers, with a monocle in the left eye. He had kind, intelligent eyes, and spoke with a quiet authority.

"I've already stated my views, Mr. Foreman. I admit that the evidence against the prisoner is overwhelming, but I can't somehow see that sort of man committing these appalling crimes."

"Someone committed them," said the stout lady.

"They were the work of a madman," rejoined the Major, "and the prisoner is obviously as sane as you or I. The motive suggested by the Crown was absurdly inadequate."

"We have to judge upon the evidence," said the Foreman.

"It is all very difficult," said the Major. "I cannot even be sure that Mrs. Withers was not telling the truth. There was something about her . . ."

"Exactly," said Mr. Bland. "That is just my point."

A young man sitting next to the Major, wearing a ready-made suit, looked up from scribbling idly on the back of an envelope.

"You don't any of you seem to see *my* point," he

complained. "There hasn't been a single murder since Eldridge was arrested. The prosecution didn't think of that. It clearly shows . . ."

"It shows nothing whatever," said Mr. Bland. "The criminal, whoever he was, would naturally stop his murders on the arrest of Eldridge."

"Still thinking of the secret enemy?" said Mr. Bickersteth. "Do consider once more the evidence of the list and the weapon. Who on earth could have used them except the prisoner? As the judge himself said, there is no evidence to prove that Eldridge ever had an enemy. It is all pure fancy from start to finish. Who would commit six murders simply in order to hang someone he didn't like? It isn't natural, to me."

"Nothing in this case is natural," said the Major. "That's why I can't make up my mind. I should like to return a verdict of non-proven."

"We can't do that," said Mr. Bickersteth peevishly.

There was a pause. The young man in the ready-made suit looked at his watch . . . already past two o'clock, and at Stamford Bridge they kicked off at 3:30. There came the sound of a rhythmic clicking. The stout lady had taken a sock from a large bag and was finishing off the heel.

"We are wasting time," she said, without looking up from her needles. "The man is guilty, and in any case he deserves to be hung."

"I don't think, if I may say so, that that is quite the proper spirit, Mrs. Arkwright," said the little woman in black.

"It is a clear case," said the stout lady. "The woman in the box was lying. Look at her record."

"It is no part of our duty," said the Major, "to pass judgment on the relations between the prisoner and Mrs. Withers."

"Perhaps not," said Mrs. Arkwright, "but one thing leads to another."

"Order, order," said Mr. Bickersteth. "This discussion must not be allowed to take a personal turn. We are here to consider facts. Our personal feelings must be set aside. Can you, Major Hesketh, on the facts, maintain that the prisoner is the innocent victim of a conspiracy?"

"Not on the facts," admitted the Major reluctantly.

"And you, Mr. Bland?"

"It's no use your trying to rush me, Mr. Foreman," returned Mr. Bland. "I am not yet convinced, and I am not going to pretend that I am. Perhaps we might go over the evidence together again while the rest of you wait. I am sorry, but I have my conscience to consider, like the rest of you."

The Foreman rose and retired to a corner of the room. A hum of talk broke out round the jury table. The young man in the ready-made suit looked again at his watch and shrugged his shoulders resignedly. He then produced from his pocket a folded newspaper, moistened the tip of a lead pencil with his tongue and bent over the sheet for some moments in silence.

Finally he nudged the Major on his left.

"Excuse me," he said, "but can you tell me the name of a pagan God in four letters beginning with L?"

XIII

Mr. Justice Burrows rose from his chair in the judge's room and began to pace slowly up and down. The clock on the wall showed that the jury had been out for just over two hours. His wig was lying on the table, and without it he looked mild and singularly unimpressive. His hair was sparse and grey, and had long since left his forehead.

He had not expected the jury to be so long. The case seemed to him to be clear enough. Still, there was always a minority on these occasions, and it was only right that the twelve good men and true—though there were women

now—should feel their responsibilities. His own seemed
no heavier than usual. He had tried, as always, to be
scrupulously fair, and on the whole he was well satisfied
with his charge to the jury. Naturally it had been
against the prisoner, but he was bound to present the
facts, and the facts were sufficiently conclusive.

You never could tell, of course, with juries, and Sir
Henry Grey's play-acting had in more than one hopeless
case won acquittal in the teeth of evidence almost as
strong as that of the Crown in the present instance.
Men and women were far more easily moved by their
emotions and prejudices than by facts. Henry Grey was
a dangerous fellow. He carried people away. He carried even himself away, and usually ended by really believing in the innocence of his clients. That perhaps was
the secret of his astonishing success. His pleading was
more than tricks of the trade. He became for the time
being a champion—the defender of his own fine faith in
a losing cause.

He should have been an actor, of course; for, though
he was earning big money at the Bar, he could never
expect to achieve the higher honours. He was notoriously ignorant of the law, and would never be cool enough
for the bench. On the stage the gifts which made him
so effective and popular as a pleader would have had full
scope.

Dear old Harry! Mr. Justice Burrows shook his head
a little sadly. He would look in at the Club that night.
Harry was always there after a big trial, usually in his
brightest mood, and when in form Harry was hard to
beat. It would be pleasant to sit for an hour after
supper in the members' corner of the Garrick listening to his stories. Harry Grey was a witty fellow—witty
and inexhaustible. Most men would slip away for a
week-end after such a strain, but not Harry. His vital-
ity was enormous.

There came a tap at the door.

"Come in," said the judge.

His clerk entered the room.

"The jury has sent a message to say that they are agreed, my lord."

Mr. Justice Burrows turned to the table and lifted his wig. He had been on the bench seven years, but this moment always caused a quickening of the pulses.

"I am ready," he said, and passed from the room.

As he made his way to the court three knocks upon the door announced his coming.

XIV

MR. WETHERBY, the judge's marshal, settled himself in his seat and looked expectantly towards the door by which the judge would enter. It had really been very decent of Burrows to give him the job—nothing much to do, of course, but he was keen to get on in his profession, and one learned a lot in court and made some pretty useful friends.

There at last was Burrows. This was the great moment. Very shortly now the verdict would be known. Not that there would be any doubt about it. Or had Sir Henry brought it off again? Personally, of course, he thought it was a mistake to appeal to the emotions in court. Mr. Wetherby decided that, when he was called upon to conduct a defence in a big murder case, he would eschew sentiment. Cold, clear, passionless argument—it got you further in the end.

The prisoner was standing in the front of the dock between two warders. He looked rather white, but very calm.

A voice spoke somewhere below. The wig of the Clerk of the Court was bobbing in its well.

"Members of the jury, are you agreed upon your verdict?"

"We are."

They were looking very solemn. The little Foreman

with the receding chin was staring straight in front of him.

"Do you find the prisoner guilty or not guilty?"

The little Foreman opened his mouth. There was a moment's pause. Then he burst into a paroxysm of coughing.

The court waited breathless as he strove to master himself.

Mr. Wetherby glanced at the prisoner. Robert Eldridge had gone very white, and was swaying slightly on his feet. The warder beside him put out a hand to support him, but he brushed it away.

My God! thought Mr. Wetherby, how horrible—to start coughing at a time like this!

He glanced again at the Foreman of the jury. The little man was still gasping, jerking his head about like a hooked fish.

"Guilty," he barked.

"And that is the verdict of you all?"

"Yes," said the Foreman.

"Robert Eldridge," the Clerk of the Court was speaking, "you stand convicted of wilful murder. Have you anything to say for yourself why the court should not give you judgment of death according to law?"

God! how white the prisoner looked. But he stood firm enough.

"Nothing, my lord," he said, "except that I am innocent."

From somewhere came the voice of an usher:

"*Oyez, oyez, oyez . . . my lords, the King's justices, do strictly charge and command all persons to keep silence while sentence of death is passing upon prisoner at the bar, upon pain of imprisonment. God save the King.*"

Mr. Justice Burrows was leaning forward. Two hands with something black between them were stretched out above his head.

"Prisoner at the bar," Mr. Justice Burrows was speaking, "you have been convicted by the jury of the most serious crime known to the law of this country. I can see no reason whatever to doubt the righteousness of that verdict. Knowing the position in which you now stand, all that I can do is to implore you most earnestly to make your peace with God Almighty. It remains for me only to pass sentence. The sentence of the court is that you be taken from this place to a lawful prison and thence to a place of execution; that you be there hanged by the neck until you be dead, and that your body be afterwards buried within the precincts of the prison wherein you shall have been confined before execution. And may the Lord have mercy on your soul."

"Amen," said the chaplain.

The warders put a hand each on the prisoner's arm. He seemed a little dazed. Then he was turned about abruptly, and disappeared below the level of the dock.

"Members of the jury, on behalf of the court," said the judge, "I thank you for the care and attention which you have devoted to these long and painful proceedings. You will be excused from service on a jury for ten years."

There was a rustling in the court. The judge had not moved.

"Silence, silence," said the usher.

"I should like to take this opportunity," said Mr. Justice Burrows, "to congratulate the police, particularly the local force at Eastrepps, for the zeal and ability which they have shown in connection with this case. Their action reflects the greatest credit on the persons concerned."

CHAPTER NINE

I

SUPERINTENDENT RUDDOCK of Scotland Yard paused on the threshold. So this was to be his room—not so large or fine as the room of Chief Inspector Wilkins, but a good room. His predecessor had liked to feel at home in his working hours. He had put down a carpet on the floor, unearthed from somewhere a collection of prints of Old Scotland Yard, and contrived to do himself pretty well in the way of office furniture. The desk was well placed and well appointed. There was nothing that suggested a sordid routine, no litter of papers on the mahogany trays, no thumbed, tattered files anywhere to be seen. Through the open window came the sun and the pleasant murmur of London.

Superintendent Ruddock closed the door and stood in awed content looking about him. His thoughts went back to the police station at Eastrepps—its worn and inky tables, the wooden chairs and walls hung with proclamations concerning foot-and-mouth disease or things lost, stolen or strayed. Wilkins had soon got him out of that. With all the newspapers crying his praise and that special pat on the back from the judge, his promotion—unprecedented and unexpected promotion—had come without question or delay.

Superintendent Ruddock—with infinite possibilities for good work and further distinction. Had not Sir Geoffrey Robinson himself called him only that morning to his room, welcomed him and bade him prosper?

He walked slowly to the big desk. Already there awaited him a neat pile of letters opened and arranged for his inspection. Beside it was a copy of *The Times*.

He felt in no hurry to begin. He was not yet even supposed to be in the office, but the habit of early hours was hard to break.

He unfolded the newspaper.

Sergeant Ruddock had bought the *East Anglian Gazette* every morning on his way to the station. Superintendent Ruddock of Scotland Yard would have *The Times* delivered at his office.

He turned to the Law Reports:

A MURDERER'S APPEAL DISMISSED

"The Court of Criminal Appeal," he read, "presided over by the Lord Chief Justice, yesterday dismissed the appeal of Robert Eldridge, convicted of the murders of Mary Hewitt, Helen Taplow, John Masters, Thomas Porter, Winifred Dampier and William Ferris, all of Eastrepps, Norfolk. The case was tried by Mr. Justice Burrows from the 18th to the 23rd October at the Old Bailey. Sir Henry Grey and Mr. Charles Cumberland appeared for the appellant, the Attorney-General, Mr. Sanderson and Mr. Richard Cripps for the Crown.

"Sir Henry Grey said that the grounds for the appeal were: (1) the Judge had shown a bias against the appellant in his charge to the Jury, and that (2) certain evidence had been improperly submitted to the jury.

"On the first count Sir Henry Grey represented that Mr. Justice Burrows had laid undue stress on the prisoner's past, and had emphasised the fact that he was wanted by the police on another and totally different charge. . . . Passing to the second ground for the appeal, Counsel urged that the evidence with regard to the list of shareholders found in the appellant's desk and containing the names of certain of the victims of the crimes had been improperly presented to the jury. The question of the date stamped against certain names had told in the favour of the appellant, and this fact had not been sufficiently emphasised. Counsel further submitted that the evidence of Margaret Withers who had sworn to the alibi produced by Eldridge for the nights of the crimes, had been almost wholly nullified by the severe strictures passed upon her character by the judge and counsel for the prosecution.

"Counsel for the Crown was not called upon to argue.

"The Lord Chief Justice, in dismissing the appeal, said that he had seldom been called upon to listen to more frivolous grounds for an appeal against a sentence. Had the case not been one of murder it would never have been brought. There was nothing to show that the jury had been in the least degree misdirected. On the contrary, the summing up by Mr. Justice Burrows had been scrupulously fair and, if anything, had erred upon the side of benefit to the prisoner."

Ruddock laid down the paper.

"So that," he said, "is the end. And now to work . . ."

II

The crowd at the entrance to Pentonville prison was not large. But it was early yet. Margaret shifted her position and stretched her limbs. She had been there for nearly two hours, and now, in five minutes, all would be over.

There were a dozen workmen who had stopped on the way to their jobs, and three or four women.

The sound of a motor horn came to her ears, and a taxi drew up beside the cold grey gates. Two young men stepped out and looked about them.

"Not much of a crowd, Jim," Margaret heard one of them say.

"Where's the flagstaff?" said the other.

Margaret could have told them where it was. She had seen little else since the first light of morning had thrown it into slender relief against the sky.

There was a stir in the crowd. She perceived that its numbers had increased.

There came a deep sigh from the people about her and the sound of a clock striking. A terrible line of poetry floated into her mind:

> "Strapped, noosed, nighing his hour,
> He stood."

"There she goes," said a voice.

"Look."

Margaret turned. The flagstaff had been bare, but, even as the sound of the clock ceased, something fluttered at its foot and floated slowly to its summit. It was a little flag and it waved black, brief and official in the sharp morning air.

Margaret wanted to think. But what on earth was that woman sobbing for? She had no cause to sob.

"Can't you stop it?" said Margaret aloud, and then realised that she was listening to the sound of her own tears.

CHAPTER TEN

I

RICHARD COLDFOOT came to a stand in Kensington High
Street and looked at his watch. . . . Six o'clock. The
little public-house in Abingdon Road, "The Three Tuns"
or "The Three Bells"—he could never remember which
—would be open now, and there was time for a drink—
and need for it too—before he went about the business
of the day.

Margaret would be far from pleased to see him. She
believed him to be at least two thousand miles away,
and his reappearance would not be the glad surprise it
should have been. She had given him that last fifty
pounds to buy himself a passage to Canada. She had
even offered him two hundred a year to stay there.
What on earth did she suppose he could do in Canada?
Besides, he had already spent the fifty pounds, or the
greater part of it.

He pushed his way into "The Three Bells"—or was
it "The Three Tuns"?—and ordered a double brandy.

Margaret was now alone in the world. Now, if ever,
was his chance. Margaret was rich, and she was unlikely
to remain alone for very long. Why couldn't she realise
that he was her natural friend and ally? Had he not
borne witness in her defence—been flayed in public by
the lawyers for her sake? Was he not also the only
person in the world who believed in her? He alone of
all men knew that she had told the truth and nothing
but the truth, in Rex v. Eldridge.

As for Eldridge—she would soon forget all about that
dreadful business. She had alms for oblivion. Nothing

like money to keep one from brooding on the past, and Eldridge had left her stacks of it.   The authorities had impounded sufficient to pay his debts, including all the shareholders of Anaconda Ltd., but there had remained over a very comfortable residuum.   Margaret had got it all.

And now she wanted to get rid of him—pack him off to Canada, while she queened it and made any number of new friends and champions.   Friends, indeed!   One knows how it ends—with friends.   He was going to stay in London and look after her.   He intended to keep her well in sight . . . well in sight.

At half-past six, after his third brandy—nothing else for him these days—he passed through the swing door of the public-house and started down the quiet road which led to the new block of flats in Burnham Court.   He was going straight to Margaret.   He would offer her friendship and alliance.   That would do to begin with.   And then . . .

Mrs. Bradenham, as she now called herself, lived, so the porter told him, on the fourth floor.   The lift was not working, and the porter eyed him curiously as he began walking up the stairs.   They were covered with a felt carpet, and were interminable, coiling sleekly round the lift shaft like a well-fed snake.   He felt, he told himself, like the climber on Fortune's wheel in the mediæval pictures of that lady.   He had been at the bottom, but he was now climbing up . . . up . . . up to Margaret. She would not be pleased to see him, but, after all, they must eventually come together. . . .   Friendship and alliance.

The door of the flat opened almost before his finger had finished pressing the bell, and a smart maid stood on the threshold.   He inquired for Mrs. Bradenham. The maid informed him, civilly enough, that she was out.

"When will she be back?" asked Coldfoot, controlling his voice with difficulty.

"At any moment, Sir," said the maid.

"Then I will wait, if you don't mind."

He walked very steadily behind the maid into the drawing-room. There were chintz-covered armchairs, ornaments on the mantelpiece, three or four good water-colours on the walls. But there was something lacking about it. He looked round. There were no photographs, nothing intimate. The room looked like a stage setting. Undoubtedly she was alone in the world, beginning her life all over again. Undoubtedly this was his chance . . . friendship and alliance.

He wandered restlessly round the room.

Here, at last, was a photograph—a child, aged about six, with eyes set wide apart and curly hair. That, of course, was Cynthia, whom she had lost.

He put the photograph down, and noticed a letter stuck behind it against the wall on the mantelpiece. He picked it up and squeezing it between fingers and thumb, looked curiously inside. *Very much at heart . . . deeply moved by your courage and loyalty.* . . . The phrases jumped at him from inside the envelope. He extracted the sheet and read:

> "28 *Hanbury Road,*
> "*Hampstead.*

"DEAR MRS. BRADENHAM,

"I shall be only too happy to do anything I can to help you. I have often had an uneasy tormented feeling that Robert Eldridge, whom I always believed to be innocent of the crimes for which he suffered, might have been saved if only I had found somewhere the flaw which I am sure exists in the evidence on which he was condemned. I have this case—more than any other case in the whole of my career—very much at heart, and I have thought about it a great deal. I never doubted that you were telling the truth, and I was deeply moved by your courage and loyalty in coming forward.

"I should not be at all surprised to hear that Chief Inspector Wilkins has also had his misgivings. He is always, in any case, most kind and sympathetic, and I am sure he would not refuse to hear anything you may have to say. I enclose a letter of introduction, and am writing to him independently telling him to expect your call.

"Be assured, my dear Mrs. Bradenham, that I will do my utmost to assist you in any possible way. Perhaps you would do me the honour of lunching with me one day this week, and we could talk things over. What about Tuesday or Wednesday? I will keep myself free on these days till I hear from you.

"Yours sincerely,

"HENRY GREY."

Coldfoot stood a moment with the letter in his hand; then with shaking fingers thrust it back into the envelope.

"I might have known it," he said to himself. "She has started her little games already . . . luncheon is it . . . with their heads together over the mystery of Robert Eldridge. . . . The famous Sir Henry Grey will bring his great mind to bear on the problem . . . has the case very much at heart . . . deeply moved and all the rest of it."

He paused a moment, and with the letter still in his hand began to pace up and down the room.

"I won't have it," he continued. "It's no concern of this blasted lawyer. This is between me and Margaret. I shall tell him to keep out of it. . . . That's what I shall do."

A footstep sounded in the corridor outside. Coldfoot

hastily restored the letter to its place behind the photo-graph and moved away. The door swung open.

How pretty Margaret looked in her black frock!—for she was still in mourning. She looked at him coolly, and then walked across the room, taking off her hat as she did so and laying it on the sofa.

"Well," she said, "what do you want?"

"Surprised to see me, aren't you?" he asked. "You wanted to get rid of me, didn't you? . . . thought I was in Canada."

"I did not think you would go," she replied. "Now I suppose you want another fifty pounds."

"Fifty pounds don't last forever," he replied.

Why were his hands trembling in this ridiculous way? He pushed them behind his back.

"Look here, Margy," he continued shakily. "What is the sense of going on like this? You are alone in the world, aren't you? So am I . . . and we've both had the hell of a time. Why not make it up and be . . . friends? You know that for me there has never been any woman in the world but you. . . . And didn't I go into the witness-box for your sake? . . . And they wouldn't believe us. . . . We must stand together, Margy . . . stand together."

He advanced upon her unsteadily as he spoke.

"Stay where you are," she said sternly.

He came to a halt by the mantelpiece.

"There's another thing," he said eagerly. "I know that Robert Eldridge was innocent. I know that you were telling the truth. I can help you to prove it."

"I want no more of your help," said Margaret. She was looking away from him towards the photograph on the mantelpiece.

"I have all the help I need," she added.

Coldfoot suddenly snatched Sir Henry's letter from behind the photograph and thrust it towards her.

"This is what you mean, isn't it?" he stormed. "Don't

be a fool, Margy. This lawyer fellow can't do you any good. He's like the rest of them—knows a pretty woman when he sees one."

"You've read that letter?"

"You want someone to take care of you, Margy, and it's going to be me henceforth; no one but me can help you find the murderer of Robert Eldridge."

"I don't want your help, or ever to see you again. Are you going, or must I have you put out?"

She crossed the room and put her hand on the bell.

"Stop!" said Coldfoot.

His face was contorted with passion, and there was something in his eyes which sent through her a tremor of keen fear.

"What are you going to do?" she asked.

"I . . . I won't have it," he said. "You shan't go to that fellow. . . . I'll see him dead first.

The room swam in a mist of red. Margaret pressed the bell. He felt suddenly weak.

The door opened behind him.

"Get the porter, Alice," said Margaret.

"I'll go . . . I'll go," said Coldfoot. "But I shall come back again, you know. I shall come back."

Turning suddenly, he pushed past the astonished maid and staggered from the room.

II

Margaret did not move for an appreciable moment after Coldfoot had gone. Presently, however, she crossed the room, opened the drawer of her bureau, and took from it an envelope on which was written the name of Chief Inspector Wilkins. It was her letter of introduction from Sir Henry Grey.

She glanced at the watch on her wrist. . . . Half-past six. It was too late, perhaps, to go to Scotland Yard that day, but she had come to the end of her tether. She must see someone, and it must be right soon.

She picked up the telephone, and after a certain amount of delay got through to the Yard. Then, with something of a shock, she found herself speaking to Chief Inspector Wilkins. Rapidly she explained on the telephone who she was. The Chief Inspector was courteous. He had received a letter from Sir Henry Grey and would, of course, do all he could, though he was clearly embarrassed when it came to saying what that "all" might be. He suggested, at last, that she should come to the Yard and discusss her . . . difficulties . . . with Superintendent Ruddock, who had all the details, and who would go carefully through the evidence with her if she so desired.

"If you wait one moment," he concluded, "I will ask whether Superintendent Ruddock is free."

There came a click and whirr of the telephone.

"And so, dear," came a thin, spidery voice, "I bought the blue georgette, after all, and the most divine hat you ever saw."

"Is that you, Mrs. Bradenham," the Chief Inspector was speaking again.

"Yes."

"Could you come along at once?"

"Certainly."

"Superintendent Ruddock has to go down to the country to-night on another case, and he may be away some time. He is, however, still in his office."

"It's very good of you, Chief Inspector," said Margaret. "Are you sure that I shall not be giving him too much trouble?"

"Not at all. I will ask him to have the papers ready. And you can talk the whole matter over with him."

It was seven o'clock by the time she reached the Yard. A lift carried her to the third floor, and a minute or two later she found herself shaking hands with a little man with sandy hair and a well-trimmed moustache. His voice, as he greeted her, sent a sharp thrill along her nerves. She had heard it last from her seat in the Old Bailey, when towards the end of the trial he had been recalled on an additional point of evidence. Then he had worn the uniform of a police-sergeant, but now he was wearing a well-cut suit of clothes, and looked not in the least like a policeman. . . . From Sergeant to Superintendent—he had done pretty well for himself out of Rex *v.* Eldridge, and here was she asking him to look for evidence that he had tragically blundered.

How could she even begin? There was so much she wanted to say, and yet how was she to plead that the man, sitting there at his desk, so courteous and ready to oblige, had wrongfully sent Robert Eldridge to death? Behind that undistinguished face lurked a keen brain, shrewd and calculating. He had put two and two together, like hundreds of men before him, and he had made it five.

"Superintendent," she began, "I beg of you not to be offended by anything I may say. I know that Robert Eldridge was innocent."

The face of Superintendent Ruddock was kind and non-committal.

"Please, madam," he said, "do not consider my personal feelings in the matter at all. I only did my duty, and I am sorry, dreadfully sorry, that it should have caused you so much pain and suffering. If there is anything that I can do to help you. . . ."

He broke off with a helpless gesture.

"My evidence was not believed. You naturally did not believe it yourself. But I was telling the truth, and I know that somewhere, hidden perhaps in the papers themselves, there must be a flaw."

Ruddock placed his hand on a number of files on the desk in front of him.

"What can I say to you?" he asked. "These papers were carefully examined by experts again and again even before the case for the prosecution was opened. They were re-examined at the trial and again during the appeal proceedings. Copies of them were throughout at the disposal of the defence."

"But I know that Robert Eldridge was innocent."

"What do you wish me to do?"

"Surely there must be something."

Ruddock looked at her less kindly than before.

"Are you suggesting," he asked, "that any point of evidence was suppressed?"

"Of course not," said Margaret hurriedly. "But I cannot help thinking that the truth must lie somewhere between the lines of the evidence, if only we could read it aright."

Ruddock leaned a little forward and touched the papers.

"Mrs. Bradenham," he said, "I will do anything I can to help you, but it would be wrong of me if I did not again insist that the evidence contained in these files is overwhelming. It is evidence which two courts of justice have accepted without misgiving. By all means let us go through these papers, and if you can find anything that points to any possibility of error in our conclusions, I need hardly assure you that I should be the very first to bring it to the light of day. This is not, believe me, a question of personal credit, though, if it should be shown that Robert Eldridge suffered unjustly, I should be haunted by that discovery to my dying day."

Margaret got impulsively to her feet.

"Thank you," she said. "I appreciate your position—really I do. But I *know* that Robert Eldridge was innocent."

Ruddock, also rising, glanced at his watch. He thought a moment.

"It is unfortunate," he said, "that I am going away to-night on a case for three or four days. I am afraid I cannot let you take the files away from the office. That is against the rules. But I could make arrangements for you to come and examine them here to-morrow, or whenever you wish to do so."

"That is very kind of you," said Margaret. "And perhaps, when you come back, we could go through them together."

Ruddock nodded.

"Of course," he said, "I should be happy to do anything to set your mind at rest. If you would just come round here, I could show you the main headings."

Margaret passed round the desk till she stood by the side of the Superintendent.

"You will see," he said, "that the main document on which the Director of Public Prosecutions based his case, was my own report—Document 17 of Series No. 1. I typed it myself. The other papers in this series are mainly in support of that document."

He had opened one of the files and laid it before Margaret. She found herself looking at a typed document: *The Murders at Eastrepps: Report of Sergeant Ruddock of the East Norfolk Constabulary to Superintendent Protheroe:*

> *"Sir,*
>
> *"In re murders of Mary Hewitt, Helen Taplow, John Masters . . ."*

The names swam before her eyes.

> *"I am to bring the following facts to your notice:*
> *"(1) On the morning of July 24th I called, in accordance with instructions received, at the house of Robert Eldridge in 14, Oakfield Terrace . . ."*

"I will read that to-morrow," said Margaret.

"Here," said Ruddock, lifting another file, "are the documents which were put in as exhibits and shown to the jury."

Margaret looked at the file.

"This then would contain the list of shareholders."

"The third paper from the top," said Ruddock.

He opened the second file and laid it on the desk beside the first.

"If Robert Eldridge were innocent," said Ruddock, "that list was forged by his secret enemy and placed behind the drawer of the desk where I found it on the night of August 6th. That was the theory of the defence as suggested by the prisoner himself. You will find my references to the list"—here he turned the pages of his report in the first file—"on pages 23 to 27. Here, again, are the depositions of Mrs. Brandon, Dr. Simms, Constable Birchington and other witnesses for the prosecution."

Margaret looked from the list to the relevant passages in the report and back again. She turned one or two sheets. . . . *In the case of Mrs. Dampier the wounds were different* . . . that was Dr. Simms. *I am prepared to swear that on the evening of Friday, July 25th, I saw Robert Eldridge in Sheffield Park.* . . . That was the deposition of William Ferris. Again she turned the sheets, then drew back so suddenly that her elbow struck Ruddock a glancing blow on the side.

Was it possible? She looked at the files again, trying to collect her thoughts.

"What is it, Mrs. Bradenham?"

It was Ruddock speaking. He was looking at her steadily, trying to read what was passing in her mind.

"Nothing," she said.

She looked uncertainly towards the door. She must get away, decide what to do.

"I will come to-morrow," she announced.

"There is nothing that strikes you at the moment?"

"Nothing."

He was still looking at her in that intent way.

"Then I will leave instructions," he added, "that these

files shall be put at your disposal to-morrow morning."

"Thank you, Superintendent."

He walked with her to the door.

"Good-evening, Mrs. Bradenham. If there is anything further I can do for you . . ."

Their voices were lost in the corridor outside. A moment later Ruddock returned.

He walked quickly back to his desk.

He picked up the files in turn and examined them carefully.

"Now I wonder what it could have been?" he asked himself.

III

Five minutes later Margaret stood at the entrance of Scotland Yard. She did not recollect very clearly how she came to be there. She had wandered down endless corridors, been handed from constable to constable, but the details of her passage were unregarded. Swiftly her tumbled thoughts had taken shape. How quickly everything assumed order and purpose now that she held the clue!

But what was she to do? It was not enough to suspect. She must be able to prove what she suspected. Her thoughts turned at once to Sir Henry Grey. He, with his trained mind, would be able to realise the full implications of her discovery. Quickly she came to her resolution, hailed a taximan and told him to drive her to 28, Hanbury Road, Hampstead.

If only she had seen those papers in time. Tears started to her eyes as the taxi swung round a corner and entered St. John's Road. But she must not allow herself to give way. She must be cool and calm, lay her case before the great advocate. She had found the secret enemy, and he should be brought to justice.

The drive seemed interminable. Dusk had fallen, and the October day was dying slowly over the Heath as she paid off the taxi outside the walled garden of the red-brick Georgian house.   London, at her feet, was slowly preparing for the night, as it had done for two thousand years.   Lights twinkled below her.

"Sir Henry has not yet returned."

The maid glanced at the grandfather clock.

"He is dining, madam, at a quarter past eight," she added.

Margaret decided to wait.   She was shown into a low room, containing many books and comfortable armchairs. The minutes dragged on.   To master her impatience and bring order to her thoughts she began to set down the main heads of the case which she had been constructing for herself in the light of her discovery.   There were writing materials on the big desk in the window.

She thought she heard a step in the garden outside. Laying down her pen, she moved to the window.   Was that really someone outside, or was it a shadow?   Sir Henry had returned perhaps, and was walking through the garden.   But that was impossible.   A man did not usually enter his house by the back door.   She glanced at her watch . . . nearly eight o'clock.   Somewhere in the quiet Georgian house a bell sounded faintly.   Foot-steps became audible.   The door opened, and the maid stood before her.

"I am sorry, madam, Sir Henry's chauffeur has just telephoned to say that there has been a slight accident to his car.   Sir Henry will not be returning to dinner."

"Do you know where he is dining?" asked Margaret.

"No, madam."

Margaret hesitated a moment, then crossed to the writing-table, folded what she had written, put it in an envelope, addressed it and handed it to the maid.

"Will you give this to Sir Henry as soon as he comes in," she said.

She walked down the flagged path towards the garden gate and pushed it open.   It was now quite dark, and the road seemed deserted. She moved a pace or two to the right and glanced over her shoulder. There was an indeterminate mass, which might or might not be a man, in the shadow of the old brick wall. She could just distinguish a vague outline. She turned her back upon it and walked resolutely forward, becoming aware, as she did so, of footsteps behind her. Who could it be? She held in her hands the life of a criminal. But how was he to know that she had discovered his identity? Nevertheless, she was alone, and the road was deserted. She was as far from the company of men as if she had been on the South Downs or the Cotswolds.

She quickened her pace. The footsteps behind her also quickened. An instant later she was running down the road. Fifty yards away was a lamp-post. She made a final effort, but five yards from the light she slipped. Her ankle turned over, and she came down on her hands and knees.

A hand grasped her elbow.

"Steady, Miss," said a deep voice, "what's the hurry?"

She looked round. A policeman, seemingly gigantic, had her by the arm. For a moment she stood clinging to the man's shoulder.

"Come, Miss, what's the matter?" said the constable.

With a great effort Margaret mastered her terror.

"I am sorry, constable," she said, "but I thought someone was following me."

"I didn't see no one," said the policeman.

"It must have been my imagination," she said.

"It is a bit lonely up here," said the policeman kindly, "but we are always about, you know. All right now, Miss?"

"Yes, thank you. But do you think I could get a taxi?" she asked.

The policeman shook his head.

"Not hereabouts; but there will be one further down by the Tube Station."

He broke off as a taxi came running past.

"No luck, Miss," added. "That one has the flag down."

Margaret caught a swift glimpse of the passenger's face—a man with his head sunk forward between his shoulders.

"Is it far to the Tube?" Margaret asked.

"Straight on—about three hundred yards."

Some forty minutes later Margaret landed, after various changes, at High Street, Kensington, and, leaving the station, walked quickly home to her flat. She had already decided what to do. She might or might not have been pursued, but she would take no further risk.

She mounted swiftly to her flat, unlocked the door, shut it behind her and went straight to the telephone. Her maid was out, and she was quite alone, but that did not matter. She felt safe enough in these neat, familiar surroundings.

First she rang up the Garrick Club. But Sir Henry was not dining there. She then rang up Scotland Yard. Superintendent Ruddock had said that he was leaving the office at once. So she would ring up Chief Inspector Wilkins, if she could get him, and would put the whole matter before him. Perhaps by that time Sir Henry would have received her note.

"Is that Scotland Yard? I wish to speak to Chief Inspector Wilkins."

"Who is it, please?"

"Mrs. Bradenham."

"Can you tell me your business? Any particular case?"

"Rex v. Eldridge."

"Hold the line, please."

Margaret waited. Would the man never return? At last there was the voice again.

"The Chief Inspector is busy at the moment, madam. Can I take a message?"

"Would you ask him to be good enough to come round to my flat, 14b, Burnham Court, Kensington, as soon as convenient? Say it is urgent. I have made important discoveries about the case. I will hold on while you get the answer."

There was another pause, but the voice came this time rather sooner than before.

"Chief Inspector Wilkins presents his compliments and will call upon you in about half an hour."

"Thank you," said Margaret, and rang off.

It occurred to her as she waited that her stockings were torn and dirty from her fall. She went into her bedroom, changed them, slipped on another frock, bathed her hands, tidied her hair and went back into the drawing-room. She looked at her watch. It was less than twenty minutes since she had telephoned. She wandered again into her bedroom; thence into the bathroom to look for her nail polisher, which was missing from the dressing-table.

From the bathroom, as she entered it, she had a view of the staircase to be used in case of fire. A light streaming from a window two stories below picked out a shadowy figure that was climbing towards her.

She stood a moment with her hand on the bathroom door. She must lock that door on the outside. No, she could not do that. It shut on the inside with a catch, and there was no key. Then she must run from the flat, give the alarm. In another moment there would be nothing but a thin pane of glass between her and that climbing shadow.

At that instant came a sharp ring at the front door of the flat. With a quick gasping sigh she ran across the hall. Her hands trembled a moment on the latch. Then she slipped it back and flung the door wide open.

"Thank God you've come!" began Margaret, and broke off suddenly.

A figure, vaguely seen, had moved into the hall. The

light from the drawing-room was shining upon his face.
It was the murderer.

IV

"A lady called to see you at about half-past seven, Sir
Henry. She left a note."

Dora, the parlour-maid moved to the table in the hall,
and Sir Henry picked up the note from the salver. His
expression changed when he recognised the handwriting.
He slipped a forefinger under the flap of the envelope,
tore it open and read rapidly.

"Heavens!" thought Dora, the maid, "what has come
over the master?"

Sir Henry had brushed past her—most unlike him, for
he was always most polite—and had already unhooked
the receiver of the telephone.

"Give me Scotland Yard," he said, and then turning
to Dora:

"Leave me," he added curtly, "and shut the doors."

"Hullo! . . . I want to speak to Chief Inspector
Wilkins. . . . Left for home? Then please give me his
private number. . . . It's Sir Henry Grey speaking. . . .
Thanks."

He hung up the receiver, unhooked it again, and spoke
a number down the telephone.

"Hullo! . . . That you, Wilkins? . . . Yes, it's Sir
Henry Grey. . . . I want you to do something urgently.
. . . Mrs. Bradenham called at the Yard this evening.
. . . Yes. . . . Rex v. Eldridge. . . . Will you go
back to your office, ask for the papers in the case and
wait for me there? I am coming myself at once."

"Back to the office?"

The voice of the Chief Inspector was heavy with dis-
may.

"I'm afraid it won't wait till the morning. Mrs.
Bradenham called on me this evening; after her visit
to the Yard. She left me a note. I will read it to you."

Chief Inspector Wilkins listened. His face changed while the note was being read.

"So you see," concluded Sir Henry, "there is no time to lose. Since her visit to the Yard . . ."

But the Chief Inspector needed no further persuasion.

"Meet me at Scotland Yard in twenty minutes," he said and rang off.

During the drive Sir Henry Grey studied again the note which Margaret had left. If only he had seen this evidence at the trial. . . . But he had only had a carbon copy, such as is usually communicated to the defence. It was just as she said—once the small point was noticed everything fell into place. She had found the secret enemy.

The taxi drew up at the Yard. He got out, and began fumbling in his pocket for some money when he felt a hand on his arm.

"Don't pay him off," came a voice. "Take me on to Mrs. Bradenham."

It was Chief Inspector Wilkins who spoke. He was carrying a small dispatch case.

Sir Henry Grey turned to the chauffeur.

"Fourteen, Burnham Court, off Kensington High Street," he said.

"As fast as you can go," added Wilkins.

"And what about the perlice?" asked the man.

"We are the police," said Wilkins.

"Well?" said Sir Henry Grey. "Is it conclusive?"

"Conclusive enough," said Wilkins grimly. "And we may find something still more conclusive in a moment."

He thrust his head out of the window.

"Can't you do better than that?" he asked.

"I'm doing my best, sir," said the taximan.

"You believe he is after her?" inquired Sir Henry anxiously.

"There isn't a doubt of it," said Wilkins. "God grant he may not find her alone."

"What makes you think? . . ." Sir Henry began.

The voice of the Chief Inspector, as he began to explain, was drowned in the roar of a passing motorbus. He was still explaining as they sped into Knightsbridge.

Not yet at the Albert Memorial, thought Sir Henry. Yes, there it was at last. "Thank God!" he said. He had never thought to be thanking God for the Albert Memorial. Please heaven there would not be a jam in the High Street, but, of course, there had to be. Sir Henry fumed and fretted. The Inspector laid a hand on his arm.

"No good fussing, Sir Henry," he said.

The taxi moved on again with a jerk. It swung sharply to the left, then to the right, and drew up opposite a quiet block of mansions.

There was no porter in the hall, and the lift was out of order. Wilkins moved quickly up the stairs.

"Are you armed?" he said over his shoulder to Sir Henry.

"Good God, no!" said Sir Henry.

It was not his job to be armed. His acquaintance with criminals had always begun in the prison cell.

"Then keep behind me," said the Chief Inspector.

Already they had reached the fourth floor. A visiting card pinned to a door on the right of the lift bore the name of Mrs. Bradenham. Wilkins put his thumb on the bell, and they heard it ringing inside the flat.

Sir Henry pressed his ear to the panel. Wilkins was about to push the bell again when he paused. From behind the door came the sound of a scream abruptly stifled.

"Out of the way!" shouted Wilkins.

Sir Henry turned, and saw that the Chief Inspector had a service revolver in his hand. The muzzle was put to the lock and the trigger pulled. There was a loud report, and through a cloud of smoke the door swung open. The hall was empty, but at the further end of it a door stood ajar. They made for it together, and together they entered the room.

Sir Henry, as he followed the Chief Inspector, took in every detail. Two or three chairs were upside down; a small table lay in splinters, and on the floor beside it sprawled a man with a great streak of red across his white face; while at the far end of the room a pair of slim legs clad in silk stockings were thrust from the edge of a big sofa. Their convulsive movements were just dying away.

That was Margaret, and bending over her was another man. His right fist was buried in one of the sofa cushions which he was pressing brutally down upon her face.

He swung round as the Chief Inspector dashed across the room. His face was quite calm, but the eyes were blazing.

"Hands up, Ruddock!" said the Chief Inspector.

V

"Thank God!" came a voice.

It was still far off, and there was a funny smell in her nostrils. Then she tried to sit up, but found that a hand was on her shoulder. It was Sir Henry Grey, and she saw relief, perhaps something more, in his eyes.

"How are you feeling now, Mrs. Bradenham?"

"Better," she said. "But do you mind opening the window?"

He moved to do her bidding. She sat up and put her hands to her hair. She struggled to her feet, swaying a little.

"Don't get up," he insisted, and putting an arm about her, he made her sit back again on the sofa.

"Why?" she said, with a nervous laugh, "there are the files."

She pointed to a pair of buff-coloured envelopes which lay beside a despatch-case on the table in front of her.

Sir Henry smiled and bent to pick them up. She stretched out a hand and he put them on her lap. They looked at them together for a moment.

"It's pretty conclusive, isn't it?" she said. "Here is Ruddock's report typed in violet ink. The a's and the o's want cleaning, and the ribbon of the machine is worn. The tops of the l's, t's, h's and capital letters are badly marked."

He nodded.

"And here is the list of shareholders," she said, turning to the other folder. "It is perfectly obvious that both were typed on the same machine."

Sir Henry nodded.

"You seem to be something of an expert."

Margaret smiled.

"I used to do a fair amount of typing before . . . before I met Robert."

There was a moment's silence.

"When I saw the two documents it was as though someone had switched on a light. Ruddock found the list. Only he could have put it in the drawer. It was Ruddock, too, who found Masters, and he was right on the spot when Ferris was killed."

She paused a moment.

"How did Coldfoot come to be here?" asked Sir Henry.

"He was coming up the fire escape. He must have been following me about all the evening. He is not quite . . . quite . . ."

Sir Henry nodded.

"I thought it was Ruddock, and just as I was wondering what to do the bell rang. I ran to the door. The two of them met when I dashed back into the drawing-room. Dick hadn't a chance."

She broke off suddenly.

"Where is Dick?" she asked. "Is he . . . all right?"

"Concussion," said Sir Henry.

"He saved my life," said Margaret.

The door opened, and Chief Inspector Wilkins came into the room.

"Coldfoot is all right," he announced.

"The doctor says that the skull isn't fractured. I'm glad to see you so well recovered, Mrs. Bradenham."

"You got my message at the Yard? It was good of you to come," said Margaret.

"No," said Wilkins. "I did not get your message. It was taken to Ruddock, who decided to come himself."

There was a sound of footsteps. A large constable emerged from the dining-room. Beside him was a little short man in a dark well-cut suit. Margaret looked at his hands, which he held together in front of him. The wrists were handcuffed.

Margaret stepped back, and Sir Henry put a hand on her arm.

The little man in the dark suit was speaking.

"I have a statement to make, Chief Inspector," said Ruddock quietly. "I suppose it would be more convenient if I made it at the Yard."

"Quite so," said the Chief Inspector.

VI

"I am making this statement of my own free will, fully realising the consequences. I realise the weight of evidence against me, and have no wish to complicate the proceedings."

Ruddock paused.

"Perhaps I might have a cigarette," he suggested.

Wilkins handed him his case. Ruddock was sitting with the Chief Inspector in his office at Scotland Yard. Sir Henry Grey and Sir Geoffrey Robinson were also present, with a stenographer to take a record of the statement which Ruddock had volunteered to make.

"I was born on October 12th, 1894," Ruddock continued. "My mother, Eliza Ruddock, was a housemaid at Eastrepps Hall. My father was the Hon. Richard Brackley, second son of Lord Seaham. I am a bastard."

He paused to light the cigarette, and blew out a cloud of smoke.

"Perhaps you don't realise what it means to be born a bastard in a country town. In a big city, where society is less particular, it may be different. In a small place like Eastrepps it is not amusing.

"My mother died when I was twenty-three, shortly after I had joined the Force. My father had died three years before. He had settled money on her—done what I suppose would be called the decent thing—for there was enough and to spare. Unfortunately, however, the money was all invested in Anaconda Ltd., and after the crash in the Spring of 1914 my mother was dependent on my earnings.

"I served in the war with a Norfolk County Regiment, and afterwards, on returning to the police, I was sent at my own request to Eastrepps, where I was promoted Sergeant in due course.

"You may wonder why I should have chosen to return to Eastrepps. The scandal of my birth was not forgotten, and I suppose most men would avoid a place which was full of bitter memories. But I am not like other men. It was essential for me to keep alive the old sense of humiliation. I realised that the only success or triumph that could ever mean anything to me must be witnessed by those who had avoided or pitied me.

"I had as yet no idea in my head of trying to succeed —as I meant to succeed—in anything but the lawful way. I was ambitious, and I knew I was better educated than most. I soon saw, however, that success must be long in coming, and that in the normal course of events I might have to waste some of the best years of my life, under the orders of a man like Protheroe. I accordingly decided that I must look for a more rapid means of promotion.

"It was then that I first saw Robert Eldridge. He came to the station one day to see Protheroe about some small question that had arisen in connection with the parking of cars outside the golf course. His face struck me as somehow familiar. My mother had often talked to me of Anaconda Ltd., and for the last three years of her life, when we were penniless, it had become an obsession with her. She had cut out every photograph of Selby that had appeared in the press and stuck them in an album, which I still have in my possession. I recognised him by the eyes and ears, which never change in a man. I had trained myself to recognise people like that, and I have a naturally photographic memory.

"The point to determine was how I should use my knowledge. The ordinary man would have used it for blackmail. But I am not an ordinary man, and I had no great desire for money. I wanted fame and success. At first I thought of unmasking Selby in my capacity as Sergeant of Police. That would have been a point to my credit, and might have helped me in my career. Selby had been wanted by Scotland Yard for fifteen years, and a certain amount of kudos would naturally have fallen to the man who had seen through his disguise. But I soon realised that such an achievement was not nearly big enough. I should merely get an official commendation from the Bench and a good mark in my personal file.

"Meanwhile, I was keeping a watchful eye upon James Selby or Robert Eldridge, as he called himself, and I soon discovered his liaison with Margaret Withers and the elaborate precautions he was taking to conceal it. I took a day's leave once, followed him to London, and found that he stayed at the Goodwood Hotel every Tuesday and returned to Eastrepps on Wednesday night, which he spent invariably with Mrs. Withers."

Ruddock paused a moment and extinguished his cigarette.

"I had been thinking pretty closely over my problem that day on the way up to London. How could a sergeant of police in a provincial town hope to achieve sudden fame and quick promotion? I imagine every young recruit in the force has his dreams of the big case which will some day make his reputation, preferably a case of murder; it must have excited considerable attention in the Press; the experts must be baffled; perhaps they have gone so far as to arrest the wrong man. Such cases, however, are rare, and never come the way of the dreamers. I am not a dreamer."

Ruddock waited as though for applause. None came. The faces of his audience were fixed as stone. After a moment Ruddock resumed:

"Inevitably I asked myself the question: Why not create both the case and its solution? Would it not be possible to commit a series of crimes, arrange that there should be sufficient evidence to convict a third party, and produce this evidence myself at a favourable moment? Naturally my thoughts turned to Eldridge. He was an unconvicted criminal, and he was conducting an intrigue which had led him to create an elaborate and regular alibi. I felt that it should not be difficult to manufacture sufficient circumstantial evidence which, supplemented with what I knew already, would suffice to prove him guilty of the crimes I had in mind.

"I realised, of course, that only murder would create a sufficient interest, and that to work up a really big case a series would be necessary. It was obvious, however, that only by means of a series could the regular alibi of Eldridge be used with effect. The murders would have to coincide with his visits to Mrs. Withers. One such coincidence would be weak as evidence, whereas several might be damning. I regretted the necessity of having to look for several victims. But you will perceive that at every stage the nature of the solution which I adopted for my problem was defined for me in advance.

"Why should Eldridge commit murder?   That was my next question.   There was only one possible motive— namely, his wish to avoid detection as James Selby of Anaconda Ltd.   He had settled down in Eastrepps. There were several persons in the town who had suffered from his defalcations.   He would have a bad conscience, and fear at any moment to be recognised.   I admit that the motive would be normally inadequate, but these were not to be the crimes of an ordinary man.   Was I not my-self proposing to commit murder four or five times over in order to obtain promotion?   I felt, all things con-sidered, that the motive would pass muster when read in connection with Eldridge's antecedents.   James Selby had made callously away with large sums to a continent where the sanctity of human life is not respected to the same extent as it is in England.   He was potentially a mur-derer, and I should never find anyone more suitable for the purpose.   There was also this added advantage that outwardly Robert Eldridge was a most respectable citizen —a member of the Golf Club and the Union Club, and in the running, I found, for election to the Town Council. No one would suspect him of the crimes, a fact which could not fail to increase the sensation of my discovery and the credit I should thereby acquire.

"It remained only to work out the details.   More particularly I wanted to be clear as to the nature of the evidence I intended to produce at the trial.   There again the problem offered its own solution.   On going through my mother's papers I discovered an old and tattered list which she had compiled in her own handwriting from various sources of the shareholders of Anaconda Ltd. at the time of the crash.   This list I copied out on my type-writer.   It was my first definite move, and I suppose I was at that stage excited and thoughtless.   Anyhow, I made the mistake which has brought me to this confes-sion.   It was an elementary blunder, for had I stayed to think, I should have realised that the script of an old type-writer is as individual as the plainest of handwriting.

"Might I have another cigarette?"

The Chief Inspector again offered his case without a word. Ruddock took a cigarette and resumed:

"The next thing was to choose the victims, and it took me rather longer than I expected. I had not only to study their habits for myself, but to be sure that Eldridge was also acquainted with them. In every case my problem was definite and precise. I had to be certain that at a given time I should know where to find them, and that this knowledge should also be accessible to Eldridge. I had, moreover, to commit the crimes when Eldridge was with Mrs. Withers. Thus the victims virtually designated themselves. They had to be persons who had held shares in Anaconda Ltd.; their habits must be known to the town; and I must know where to find them of a Wednesday evening.

"By the 10th July I had collected the following facts:"

Ruddock turned his head.

"You can tabulate this," he said to the stenographer.

"(1) That Miss Hewitt went every Wednesday evening to the church to take a gift of flowers and do a little cleaning work in the chancel. She was a member of the Guild of Church Helpers.

"(2) That Miss Helen Taplow went every alternate Wednesday evening to the meeting of the Literary Society, which took place in the houses of its various members in turn, and returned on foot to her parents' house in East Cliff Road.

"(3) That John Masters was courting Peggy Brightside, living over at Overstrand. He went to see her whenever he could, and returned always by the same road to his cottage at the foot of the cliffs.

"(4) That Captain Porter went every evening of his life except Sundays to the Union Club, returning to the Golf Club between ten and eleven.

"(5) That Mrs. Dampier was accustomed in the summer months to spend a great part of her time before she went to bed in her rose-garden.

"(6) That Sir Jefferson Cobb dined every alternate Wednesday with Major Skidding, an old friend of his, and further, that his doctor had ordered him to take more exercise, so that the probabilities were that he would walk home.

"Perhaps I might mention in passing that I included Mrs. Dampier and Sir Jefferson Cobb in my list only provisionally. Had the necessary effect been created before their turn had come they were to have been spared. As things happened, Mrs. Dampier blundered into my scheme when I was dealing with Captain Porter, and had therefore to be taken out of turn, so to speak."

Ruddock waited while the stenographer completed his notes, and then continued:

"I come now to the first of the murders committed on the evening of Wednesday, July 16th. You are to imagine Eldridge slipping from the train at the junction of the Sheringham and the main Eastrepps–Norwich line to the house of Margaret Withers. I saw him safely to 'White Cottage,' and then hastened away on my bicycle to Coatt's Spinney, where I lay in wait for Miss Hewitt. She passed at about 9:45. I killed her according to programme, and went home to bed. I had expected to feel a bit nervous on this first occasion, but I was never for a moment flustered or shaken. On the contrary, after killing Miss Hewitt I thought it would be as well to take a walk along the cliff in order to ascertain more precisely the route followed by John Masters on his evening visits to Overstrand. I accordingly walked up to the lighthouse. I may mention here that I wore a black beard when committing the murders, in case I might be seen and recognised. The evidence of Masters at the inquest was therefore quite correct. He had seen the murderer.

"On the following Wednesday, again making sure that Eldridge had gone to Mrs. Withers, I waited for Miss Taplow and killed her, again according to plan, as she crossed the heath on her way home. On that occasion I, too, heard the barking of a dog, but attached less importance to the incident than some of my colleagues."

Here Ruddock glanced at the Chief Inspector and smiled slightly.

"My next victim," he continued, "was John Masters. You will remember that, acting on instructions"—here he smiled again at Chief Inspector Wilkins—"I called on Robert Eldridge the morning after the murder of Miss Taplow, and that during that visit I learned from his receipt of a telegram that he was going to London on the following day. I felt sure that he would take this opportunity to see Mrs. Withers on the Friday evening of that week. I accordingly waited for him at the junction and followed him to 'White Cottage.' I then made my way to the zigzag path by the lighthouse, and killed Masters as he was returning from Overstrand.

"You will have noted that in the execution of my plan, perfect in itself, I was at several stages helped by unforeseen circumstances. I have been extraordinarily lucky. I suppose, however, that quickness in seizing such opportunities is as important a gift as the ability to plan in advance. I had three unexpected strokes of fortune, and I took full advantage of them all. One was the presence in Eastrepps of the Hon. Alistair Rockingham, who was to be wrongfully arrested by the experts, thus increasing the sensation of my own discovery; the second was my visit to Eldridge's house at the very moment the telegram arrived from London; the third was the recognition by Ferris of Eldridge in Sheffield Park on the night of the murder of John Masters. The third was particularly helpful, as it enabled me to complete my case.

"On the Wednesday following I killed Captain Porter. No sooner had I struck the blow than Mrs. Dampier appeared at the garden gate of Tamarisk House, and I had no alternative but to strike again. By that time, of course, you, sir"—Ruddock turned to the Chief Inspector—"had arrested Rockingham, and it thus became apparent that one of the Big Five, if you will excuse the phrase, had blundered."

He paused, but the face of the Chief Inspector was expressionless.

"I now felt," continued Ruddock, "that a sufficient number of crimes had been committed to make the reputation of any man who discovered their perpetrator. I am not a bloodthirsty man.

"I had, however, one more thing to do. Ferris, the newspaper correspondent, had come to me two or three days previously with the information that he had seen Eldridge in Sheffield Park. It occurred to me, as I went home after killing Captain Porter and Mrs. Dampier, that if I killed Ferris the case against Eldridge would be overwhelming. It would appear quite obviously that he had murdered Ferris in order to remove the one person who was able to destroy his alibi. I knew that Ferris went every night to the Post Office to telephone his 'story' to London, and that he usually wandered about the streets on his way home in order, I presume, to get atmosphere for his next despatch. I therefore decided to follow him on the coming Wednesday, and to strike when, and if, the opportunity offered.

"Here again the luck was with me, for he wandered into Sheffield Park in the direction of 'White Cottage.' Perhaps that was not altogether by chance. He would be thinking of Eldridge and his false alibi, and it was in Sheffield Park that he had seen Eldridge on the night of the third murder.

"The road was well shaded, and I struck him down within a short distance of the house, knowing that Eldridge would pass that way. Everything went according to programme, and a few minutes later I 'found' the body. I gave the alarm and Eldridge was arrested."

"I at once went to Eldridge's house with the list in my pocket, stamped it with the rubber date-stamp, and pretended to find it behind the drawer in the desk. I also took note of the missing weapon."

Ruddock paused a moment.

"I had almost," he continued, "forgotten the weapon. I had seen it, of course, on the wall of Eldridge's study months previously, and it occurred to me that it was very suitable for my purpose. I accordingly made a similar club, with which all the murders except the last one were committed. For Ferris, however, I used the original, taking it from Eldridge's house earlier in the evening. That, as you showed so conclusively at the trial, Sir Henry, was quite an easy thing to do. The locks on the doors were easily turned by anyone with an elementary knowledge of skeleton keys, and I knew that, being deaf, Mrs. Brandon would not hear me. On that night I wore rubber gloves, which I subsequently destroyed, so that the only fingerprints found on the club should be those of Eldridge, who, as I knew, handled it fairly frequently when showing it to visitors."

Ruddock paused again.

"I think that is about all I have to say," he added, "unless there is anything else you would like me to add?"

There was a silence.

"I should like to get clear as to the position of Richard Coldfoot," said the Chief Inspector at last.

"He never had any knowledge of the murders," said Ruddock.

"Why did he go to Burnham Court this evening?"

"Is it necessary to inquire? He was drunk, and he was always very constant in his attentions to Mrs. Withers. He probably wanted something out of her—money or affection, perhaps both."

There was another silence.

"This is all you have to say?"

"Yes, Chief Inspector."

"Read his statement to the accused, Jackson," said Chief Inspector Wilkins in dry official tones.

The stenographer began to read.

"An admirable summary," said Ruddock, when, half an hour later, the typed sheets of his statement were laid before him. "I sign here, do I not?"

Wilkins nodded.

"And do I initial every page?" said Ruddock, as he wrote his name firmly at the foot of the last.

"If you please," said the Chief Inspector.

Ruddock bent over the sheets.

VII

Miss Scarlett was hurrying home to her tea along West Parade. The sea was grey, but no greyer than the sky, and a cold wind was blowing from the East. Autumn was fading only too swiftly into winter, and the town was derelict.

In her sitting-room at home, however, the prospect was brighter. The pot was on the hob, and there were, she was glad to note, buttered scones. Her new help was distinctly better than the last.

Miss Scarlett sat down and opened the evening edition of the *Eastrepps Gazette,* which she always read with her tea. Her attention was caught at once by the headline:

EXECUTION AT PENTONVILLE

"At eight o'clock this morning at Pentonville the Eastrepps Evil paid the penalty for the series of horrible crimes which he committed in our town. It is unnecessary to recapitulate the details on an historic case which will still be present in the minds of our readers. It will be remembered that it was the *Eastrepps Gazette* which first reported the terrible murder of Miss Mary Hewitt on July 16th of the present year. . . ."

Miss Scarlett read to the end, and then sat in silence a moment.

"And such a gentlemanly man," she said.

THE END

A CATALOGUE OF
SELECTED DOVER BOOKS
IN ALL FIELDS OF INTEREST

A CATALOGUE OF SELECTED DOVER
BOOKS IN ALL FIELDS OF INTEREST

RACKHAM'S COLOR ILLUSTRATIONS FOR WAGNER'S RING. Rackham's finest mature work—all 64 full-color watercolors in a faithful and lush interpretation of the *Ring*. Full-sized plates on coated stock of the paintings used by opera companies for authentic staging of Wagner. Captions aid in following complete Ring cycle. Introduction. 64 illustrations plus vignettes. 72pp. 8⅝ x 11¼.
23779-6 Pa. $6.00

CONTEMPORARY POLISH POSTERS IN FULL COLOR, edited by Joseph Czestochowski. 46 full-color examples of brilliant school of Polish graphic design, selected from world's first museum (near Warsaw) dedicated to poster art. Posters on circuses, films, plays, concerts all show cosmopolitan influences, free imagination. Introduction. 48pp. 9⅜ x 12¼.
23780-X Pa. $6.00

GRAPHIC WORKS OF EDVARD MUNCH, Edvard Munch. 90 haunting, evocative prints by first major Expressionist artist and one of the greatest graphic artists of his time: *The Scream, Anxiety, Death Chamber, The Kiss, Madonna,* etc. Introduction by Alfred Werner. 90pp. 9 x 12.
23765-6 Pa. $5.00

THE GOLDEN AGE OF THE POSTER, Hayward and Blanche Cirker. 70 extraordinary posters in full colors, from Maitres de l'Affiche, Mucha, Lautrec, Bradley, Cheret, Beardsley, many others. Total of 78pp. 9⅜ x 12¼.
22753-7 Pa. $5.95

THE NOTEBOOKS OF LEONARDO DA VINCI, edited by J. P. Richter. Extracts from manuscripts reveal great genius; on painting, sculpture, anatomy, sciences, geography, etc. Both Italian and English. 186 ms. pages reproduced, plus 500 additional drawings, including studies for *Last Supper*, Sforza monument, etc. 860pp. 7⅞ x 10¾. (Available in U.S. only)
22572-0, 22573-9 Pa., Two-vol. set $15.90

THE CODEX NUTTALL, as first edited by Zelia Nuttall. Only inexpensive edition, in full color, of a pre-Columbian Mexican (Mixtec) book. 88 color plates show kings, gods, heroes, temples, sacrifices. New explanatory, historical introduction by Arthur G. Miller. 96pp. 11⅜ x 8½. (Available in U.S. only)
23168-2 Pa. $7.95

UNE SEMAINE DE BONTÉ, A SURREALISTIC NOVEL IN COLLAGE, Max Ernst. Masterpiece created out of 19th-century periodical illustrations, explores worlds of terror and surprise. Some consider this Ernst's greatest work. 208pp. 8⅛ x 11.
23252-2 Pa. $5.00

HOLLYWOOD GLAMOUR PORTRAITS, edited by John Kobal. 145 photos capture the stars from 1926-49, the high point in portrait photography. Gable, Harlow, Bogart, Bacall, Hedy Lamarr, Marlene Dietrich, Robert Montgomery, Marlon Brando, Veronica Lake; 94 stars in all. Full background on photographers, technical aspects, much more. Total of 160pp. 8⅜ x 11¼. 23352-9 Pa. $6.00

THE NEW YORK STAGE: FAMOUS PRODUCTIONS IN PHOTO-GRAPHS, edited by Stanley Appelbaum. 148 photographs from Museum of City of New York show 142 plays, 1883-1939. *Peter Pan, The Front Page, Dead End, Our Town,* O'Neill, hundreds of actors and actresses, etc. Full indexes. 154pp. 9½ x 10. 23241-7 Pa. $6.00

MASTERS OF THE DRAMA, John Gassner. Most comprehensive history of the drama, every tradition from Greeks to modern Europe and America, including Orient. Covers 800 dramatists, 2000 plays; biography, plot summaries, criticism, theatre history, etc. 77 illustrations. 890pp. 5⅜ x 8½. 20100-7 Clothbd. $10.00

THE GREAT OPERA STARS IN HISTORIC PHOTOGRAPHS, edited by James Camner. 343 portraits from the 1850s to the 1940s: Tamburini, Mario, Caliapin, Jeritza, Melchior, Melba, Patti, Pinza, Schipa, Caruso, Farrar, Steber, Gobbi, and many more—270 performers in all. Index. 199pp. 8⅜ x 11¼. 23575-0 Pa. $6.50

J. S. BACH, Albert Schweitzer. Great full-length study of Bach, life, background to music, music, by foremost modern scholar. Ernest Newman translation. 650 musical examples. Total of 928pp. 5⅜ x 8½. (Available in U.S. only) 21631-4, 21632-2 Pa., Two-vol. set $10.00

COMPLETE PIANO SONATAS, Ludwig van Beethoven. All sonatas in the fine Schenker edition, with fingering, analytical material. One of best modern editions. Total of 615pp. 9 x 12. (Available in U.S. only) 23134-8, 23135-6 Pa., Two-vol. set $15.00

KEYBOARD MUSIC, J. S. Bach. Bach-Gesellschaft edition. For harpsichord, piano, other keyboard instruments. English Suites, French Suites, Six Partitas, Goldberg Variations, Two-Part Inventions, Three-Part Sinfonias. 312pp. 8⅛ x 11. (Available in U.S. only) 22360-4 Pa. $6.95

FOUR SYMPHONIES IN FULL SCORE, Franz Schubert. Schubert's four most popular symphonies: No. 4 in C Minor ("Tragic"); No. 5 in B-flat Major; No. 8 in B Minor ("Unfinished"); No. 9 in C Major ("Great"). Breitkopf & Hartel edition. Study score. 261pp. 9⅜ x 12¼. 23681-1 Pa. $6.50

THE AUTHENTIC GILBERT & SULLIVAN SONGBOOK, W. S. Gilbert, A. S. Sullivan. Largest selection available; 92 songs, uncut, original keys, in piano rendering approved by Sullivan. Favorites and lesser-known fine numbers. Edited with plot synopses by James Spero. 3 illustrations. 399pp. 9 x 12. 23482-7 Pa. $7.95

THE AMERICAN SENATOR, Anthony Trollope. Little known, long unavailable Trollope novel on a grand scale. Here are humorous comment on American vs. English culture, and stunning portrayal of a heroine/villainess. Superb evocation of Victorian village life. 561pp. 5⅜ x 8½.
23801-6 Pa. $6.00

WAS IT MURDER? James Hilton. The author of *Lost Horizon* and *Goodbye, Mr. Chips* wrote one detective novel (under a pen-name) which was quickly forgotten and virtually lost, even at the height of Hilton's fame. This edition brings it back—a finely crafted public school puzzle resplendent with Hilton's stylish atmosphere. A thoroughly English thriller by the creator of Shangri-la. 252pp. 5⅜ x 8. (Available in U.S. only)
23774-5 Pa. $3.00

CENTRAL PARK: A PHOTOGRAPHIC GUIDE, Victor Laredo and Henry Hope Reed. 121 superb photographs show dramatic views of Central Park: Bethesda Fountain, Cleopatra's Needle, Sheep Meadow, the Blockhouse, plus people engaged in many park activities: ice skating, bike riding, etc. Captions by former Curator of Central Park, Henry Hope Reed, provide historical view, changes, etc. Also photos of N.Y. landmarks on park's periphery. 96pp. 8½ x 11.
23750-8 Pa. $4.50

NANTUCKET IN THE NINETEENTH CENTURY, Clay Lancaster. 180 rare photographs, stereographs, maps, drawings and floor plans recreate unique American island society. Authentic scenes of shipwreck, lighthouses, streets, homes are arranged in geographic sequence to provide walking-tour guide to old Nantucket existing today. Introduction, captions. 160pp. 8⅞ x 11¾.
23747-8 Pa. $6.95

STONE AND MAN: A PHOTOGRAPHIC EXPLORATION, Andreas Feininger. 106 photographs by *Life* photographer Feininger portray man's deep passion for stone through the ages. Stonehenge-like megaliths, fortified towns, sculpted marble and crumbling tenements show textures, beauties, fascination. 128pp. 9¼ x 10¾.
23756-7 Pa. $5.95

CIRCLES, A MATHEMATICAL VIEW, D. Pedoe. Fundamental aspects of college geometry, non-Euclidean geometry, and other branches of mathematics: representing circle by point. Poincare model, isoperimetric property, etc. Stimulating recreational reading. 66 figures. 96pp. 5⅝ x 8¼.
63698-4 Pa. $2.75

THE DISCOVERY OF NEPTUNE, Morton Grosser. Dramatic scientific history of the investigations leading up to the actual discovery of the eighth planet of our solar system. Lucid, well-researched book by well-known historian of science. 172pp. 5⅜ x 8½.
23726-5 Pa. $3.00

THE DEVIL'S DICTIONARY. Ambrose Bierce. Barbed, bitter, brilliant witticisms in the form of a dictionary. Best, most ferocious satire America has produced. 145pp. 5⅜ x 8½.
20487-1 Pa. $2.00

THE PHILOSOPHY OF HISTORY, Georg W. Hegel. Great classic of Western thought develops concept that history is not chance but a rational process, the evolution of freedom. 457pp. 5⅜ x 8½. 20112-0 Pa. $4.50

LANGUAGE, TRUTH AND LOGIC, Alfred J. Ayer. Famous, clear introduction to Vienna, Cambridge schools of Logical Positivism. Role of philosophy, elimination of metaphysics, nature of analysis, etc. 160pp. 5⅜ x 8½. (Available in U.S. only) 20010-8 Pa. $2.00

A PREFACE TO LOGIC, Morris R. Cohen. Great City College teacher in renowned, easily followed exposition of formal logic, probability, values, logic and world order and similar topics; no previous background needed. 209pp. 5⅜ x 8½. 23517-3 Pa. $3.50

REASON AND NATURE, Morris R. Cohen. Brilliant analysis of reason and its multitudinous ramifications by charismatic teacher. Interdisciplinary, synthesizing work widely praised when it first appeared in 1931. Second (1953) edition. Indexes. 496pp. 5⅜ x 8½. 23633-1 Pa. $6.50

AN ESSAY CONCERNING HUMAN UNDERSTANDING, John Locke. The only complete edition of enormously important classic, with authoritative editorial material by A. C. Fraser. Total of 1176pp. 5⅜ x 8½.
20530-4, 20531-2 Pa., Two-vol. set $14.00

HANDBOOK OF MATHEMATICAL FUNCTIONS WITH FORMULAS, GRAPHS, AND MATHEMATICAL TABLES, edited by Milton Abramowitz and Irene A. Stegun. Vast compendium: 29 sets of tables, some to as high as 20 places. 1,046pp. 8 x 10½. 61272-4 Pa. $14.95

MATHEMATICS FOR THE PHYSICAL SCIENCES, Herbert S. Wilf. Highly acclaimed work offers clear presentations of vector spaces and matrices, orthogonal functions, roots of polynomial equations, conformal mapping, calculus of variations, etc. Knowledge of theory of functions of real and complex variables is assumed. Exercises and solutions. Index. 284pp. 5⅝ x 8¼. 63635-6 Pa. $5.00

THE PRINCIPLE OF RELATIVITY, Albert Einstein et al. Eleven most important original papers on special and general theories. Seven by Einstein, two by Lorentz, one each by Minkowski and Weyl. All translated, unabridged. 216pp. 5⅜ x 8½. 60081-5 Pa. $3.00

THERMODYNAMICS, Enrico Fermi. A classic of modern science. Clear, organized treatment of systems, first and second laws, entropy, thermodynamic potentials, gaseous reactions, dilute solutions, entropy constant. No math beyond calculus required. Problems. 160pp. 5⅜ x 8½.
60361-X Pa. $3.00

ELEMENTARY MECHANICS OF FLUIDS, Hunter Rouse. Classic undergraduate text widely considered to be far better than many later books. Ranges from fluid velocity and acceleration to role of compressibility in fluid motion. Numerous examples, questions, problems. 224 illustrations. 376pp. 5⅝ x 8¼. 63699-2 Pa. $5.00

AN AUTOBIOGRAPHY, Margaret Sanger. Exciting personal account of hard-fought battle for woman's right to birth control, against prejudice, church, law. Foremost feminist document. 504pp. 5⅜ x 8½.

20470-7 Pa. $5.50

MY BONDAGE AND MY FREEDOM, Frederick Douglass. Born as a slave, Douglass became outspoken force in antislavery movement. The best of Douglass's autobiographies. Graphic description of slave life. Introduction by P. Foner. 464pp. 5⅜ x 8½. 22457-0 Pa. $5.50

LIVING MY LIFE, Emma Goldman. Candid, no holds barred account by foremost American anarchist: her own life, anarchist movement, famous contemporaries, ideas and their impact. Struggles and confrontations in America, plus deportation to U.S.S.R. Shocking inside account of persecution of anarchists under Lenin. 13 plates. Total of 944pp. 5⅜ x 8½.

22543-7, 22544-5 Pa., Two-vol. set $11.00

LETTERS AND NOTES ON THE MANNERS, CUSTOMS AND CONDITIONS OF THE NORTH AMERICAN INDIANS, George Catlin. Classic account of life among Plains Indians: ceremonies, hunt, warfare, etc. Dover edition reproduces for first time all original paintings. 312 plates. 572pp. of text. 6⅛ x 9¼. 22118-0, 22119-9 Pa.. Two-vol. set $11.50

THE MAYA AND THEIR NEIGHBORS, edited by Clarence L. Hay, others. Synoptic view of Maya civilization in broadest sense, together with Northern, Southern neighbors. Integrates much background, valuable detail not elsewhere. Prepared by greatest scholars: Kroeber, Morley, Thompson, Spinden, Vaillant, many others. Sometimes called Tozzer Memorial Volume. 60 illustrations, linguistic map. 634pp. 5⅜ x 8½.

23510-6 Pa. $7.50

HANDBOOK OF THE INDIANS OF CALIFORNIA, A. L. Kroeber. Foremost American anthropologist offers complete ethnographic study of each group. Monumental classic. 459 illustrations, maps. 995pp. 5⅜ x 8½.

23368-5 Pa. $10.00

SHAKTI AND SHAKTA, Arthur Avalon. First book to give clear, cohesive analysis of Shakta doctrine, Shakta ritual and Kundalini Shakti (yoga). Important work by one of world's foremost students of Shaktic and Tantric thought. 732pp. 5⅜ x 8½. (Available in U.S. only)

23645-5 Pa. $7.95

AN INTRODUCTION TO THE STUDY OF THE MAYA HIEROGLYPHS, Syvanus Griswold Morley. Classic study by one of the truly great figures in hieroglyph research. Still the best introduction for the student for reading Maya hieroglyphs. New introduction by J. Eric S. Thompson. 117 illustrations. 284pp. 5⅜ x 8½. 23108-9 Pa. $4.00

A STUDY OF MAYA ART, Herbert J. Spinden. Landmark classic interprets Maya symbolism, estimates styles, covers ceramics, architecture, murals, stone carvings as artforms. Still a basic book in area. New introduction by J. Eric Thompson. Over 750 illustrations. 341pp. 8⅜ x 11¼.

21235-1 Pa. $6.95

TONE POEMS, SERIES II: TILL EULENSPIEGELS LUSTIGE STREICHE, ALSO SPRACH ZARATHUSTRA, AND EIN HELDEN-LEBEN, Richard Strauss. Three important orchestral works, including very popular *Till Eulenspiegel's Marry Pranks*, reproduced in full score from original editions. Study score. 315pp. 9⅜ x 12¼. (Available in U.S. only)
23755-9 Pa. $7.50

TONE POEMS, SERIES I: DON JUAN, TOD UND VERKLARUNG AND DON QUIXOTE, Richard Strauss. Three of the most often performed and recorded works in entire orchestral repertoire, reproduced in full score from original editions. Study score. 286pp. 9⅜ x 12¼. (Available in U.S. only)
23754-0 Pa. $7.50

11 LATE STRING QUARTETS, Franz Joseph Haydn. The form which Haydn defined and "brought to perfection." (*Grove's*). 11 string quartets in complete score, his last and his best. The first in a projected series of the complete Haydn string quartets. Reliable modern Eulenberg edition, otherwise difficult to obtain. 320pp. 8⅜ x 11¼. (Available in U.S. only)
23753-2 Pa. $6.95

FOURTH, FIFTH AND SIXTH SYMPHONIES IN FULL SCORE, Peter Ilyitch Tchaikovsky. Complete orchestral scores of Symphony No. 4 in F Minor, Op. 36; Symphony No. 5 in E Minor, Op. 64; Symphony No. 6 in B Minor, "Pathetique," Op. 74. Bretikopf & Hartel eds. Study score. 480pp. 9⅜ x 12¼.
23861-X Pa. $10.95

THE MARRIAGE OF FIGARO: COMPLETE SCORE, Wolfgang A. Mozart. Finest comic opera ever written. Full score, not to be confused with piano renderings. Peters edition. Study score. 448pp. 9⅜ x 12¼. (Available in U.S. only)
23751-6 Pa. $11.95

"IMAGE" ON THE ART AND EVOLUTION OF THE FILM, edited by Marshall Deutelbaum. Pioneering book brings together for first time 38 groundbreaking articles on early silent films from *Image* and 263 illustrations newly shot from rare prints in the collection of the International Museum of Photography. A landmark work. Index. 256pp. 8¼ x 11.
23777-X Pa. $8.95

AROUND-THE-WORLD COOKY BOOK, Lois Lintner Sumption and Marguerite Lintner Ashbrook. 373 cooky and frosting recipes from 28 countries (America, Austria, China, Russia, Italy, etc.) include Viennese kisses, rice wafers, London strips, lady fingers, hony, sugar spice, maple cookies, etc. Clear instructions. All tested. 38 drawings. 182pp. 5⅜ x 8.
23802-4 Pa. $2.50

THE ART NOUVEAU STYLE, edited by Roberta Waddell. 579 rare photographs, not available elsew'ere, of works in jewelry, metalwork, glass, ceramics, textiles, architecture and furniture by 175 artists—Mucha, Seguy, Lalique, Tiffany, Gaudin, Hohlwein, Saarinen, and many others. 288pp. 8⅜ x 11¼.
23515-7 Pa. $6.95

THE ANATOMY OF THE HORSE, George Stubbs. Often considered the great masterpiece of animal anatomy. Full reproduction of 1766 edition, plus prospectus; original text and modernized text. 36 plates. Introduction by Eleanor Garvey. 121pp. 11 x 14¾. 23402-9 Pa. $6.00

BRIDGMAN'S LIFE DRAWING, George B. Bridgman. More than 500 illustrative drawings and text teach you to abstract the body into its major masses, use light and shade, proportion; as well as specific areas of anatomy, of which Bridgman is master. 192pp. 6½ x 9¼. (Available in U.S. only) 22710-3 Pa. $3.00

ART NOUVEAU DESIGNS IN COLOR, Alphonse Mucha, Maurice Verneuil, Georges Auriol. Full-color reproduction of *Combinaisons ornementales* (c. 1900) by Art Nouveau masters. Floral, animal, geometric, interlacings, swashes—borders, frames, spots—all incredibly beautiful. 60 plates, hundreds of designs. 9⅜ x 8-1/16. 22885-1 Pa. $4.00

FULL-COLOR FLORAL DESIGNS IN THE ART NOUVEAU STYLE, E. A. Seguy. 166 motifs, on 40 plates, from *Les fleurs et leurs applications decoratives* (1902): borders, circular designs, repeats, allovers, "spots." All in authentic Art Nouveau colors. 48pp. 9⅜ x 12¼.

23439-8 Pa. $5.00

A DIDEROT PICTORIAL ENCYCLOPEDIA OF TRADES AND INDUSTRY, edited by Charles C. Gillispie. 485 most interesting plates from the great French Encyclopedia of the 18th century show hundreds of working figures, artifacts, process, land and cityscapes; glassmaking, papermaking, metal extraction, construction, weaving, making furniture, clothing, wigs, dozens of other activities. Plates fully explained. 920pp. 9 x 12.

22284-5, 22285-3 Clothbd., Two-vol. set $40.00

HANDBOOK OF EARLY ADVERTISING ART, Clarence P. Hornung. Largest collection of copyright-free early and antique advertising art ever compiled. Over 6,000 illustrations, from Franklin's time to the 1890's for special effects, novelty. Valuable source, almost inexhaustible.
Pictorial Volume. Agriculture, the zodiac, animals, autos, birds, Christmas, fire engines, flowers, trees, musical instruments, ships, games and sports, much more. Arranged by subject matter and use. 237 plates. 288pp. 9 x 12.

20122-8 Clothbd. $13.50

Typographical Volume. Roman and Gothic faces ranging from 10 point to 300 point, "Barnum," German and Old English faces, script, logotypes, scrolls and flourishes, 1115 ornamental initials, 67 complete alphabets, more. 310 plates. 320pp. 9 x 12. 20123-6 Clothbd. $15.00

CALLIGRAPHY (CALLIGRAPHIA LATINA), J. G. Schwandner. High point of 18th-century ornamental calligraphy. Very ornate initials, scrolls, borders, cherubs, birds, lettered examples. 172pp. 9 x 13.

20475-8 Pa. $6.00

THE DEPRESSION YEARS AS PHOTOGRAPHED BY ARTHUR ROTH-STEIN, Arthur Rothstein. First collection devoted entirely to the work of outstanding 1930s photographer: famous dust storm photo, ragged children, unemployed, etc. 120 photographs. Captions. 119pp. 9¼ x 10¾.
23590-4 Pa. $5.00

CAMERA WORK: A PICTORIAL GUIDE, Alfred Stieglitz. All 559 illustrations and plates from the most important periodical in the history of art photography, Camera Work (1903-17). Presented four to a page, reduced in size but still clear, in strict chronological order, with complete captions. Three indexes. Glossary. Bibliography. 176pp. 8⅜ x 11¼.
23591-2 Pa. $6.95

ALVIN LANGDON COBURN, PHOTOGRAPHER, Alvin L. Coburn. Revealing autobiography by one of greatest photographers of 20th century gives insider's version of Photo-Secession, plus comments on his own work. 77 photographs by Coburn. Edited by Helmut and Alison Gernsheim. 160pp. 8⅛ x 11.
23685-4 Pa. $6.00

NEW YORK IN THE FORTIES, Andreas Feininger. 162 brilliant photographs by the well-known photographer, formerly with Life magazine, show commuters, shoppers, Times Square at night, Harlem nightclub, Lower East Side, etc. Introduction and full captions by John von Hartz. 181pp. 9¼ x 10¾.
23585-8 Pa. $6.00

GREAT NEWS PHOTOS AND THE STORIES BEHIND THEM, John Faber. Dramatic volume of 140 great news photos, 1855 through 1976, and revealing stories behind them, with both historical and technical information. Hindenburg disaster, shooting of Oswald, nomination of Jimmy Carter, etc. 160pp. 8¼ x 11.
23667-6 Pa. $5.00

THE ART OF THE CINEMATOGRAPHER, Leonard Maltin. Survey of American cinematography history and anecdotal interviews with 5 masters—Arthur Miller, Hal Mohr, Hal Rosson, Lucien Ballard, and Conrad Hall. Very large selection of behind-the-scenes production photos. 105 photographs. Filmographies. Index. Originally Behind the Camera. 144pp. 8¼ x 11.
23686-2 Pa. $5.00

DESIGNS FOR THE THREE-CORNERED HAT (LE TRICORNE), Pablo Picasso. 32 fabulously rare drawings—including 31 color illustrations of costumes and accessories—for 1919 production of famous ballet. Edited by Parmenia Migel, who has written new introduction. 48pp. 9⅜ x 12¼. (Available in U.S. only)
23709-5 Pa. $5.00

NOTES OF A FILM DIRECTOR, Sergei Eisenstein. Greatest Russian filmmaker explains montage, making of Alexander Nevsky, aesthetics; comments on self, associates, great rivals (Chaplin), similar material. 78 illustrations. 240pp. 5⅜ x 8½.
22392-2 Pa. $4.50

THE EARLY WORK OF AUBREY BEARDSLEY, Aubrey Beardsley. 157 plates, 2 in color: *Manon Lescaut, Madame Bovary, Morte Darthur, Salome,* other. Introduction by H. Marillier. 182pp. 8⅛ x 11. 21816-3 Pa. $4.50

THE LATER WORK OF AUBREY BEARDSLEY, Aubrey Beardsley. Exotic masterpieces of full maturity: *Venus and Tannhauser, Lysistrata, Rape of the Lock, Volpone,* Savoy material, etc. 174 plates, 2 in color. 186pp. 8⅛ x 11. 21817-1 Pa. $4.50

THOMAS NAST'S CHRISTMAS DRAWINGS, Thomas Nast. Almost all Christmas drawings by creator of image of Santa Claus as we know it, and one of America's foremost illustrators and political cartoonists. 66 illustrations. 3 illustrations in color on covers. 96pp. 8⅜ x 11¼. 23660-9 Pa. $3.50

THE DORÉ ILLUSTRATIONS FOR DANTE'S DIVINE COMEDY, Gustave Doré. All 135 plates from Inferno, Purgatory, Paradise; fantastic tortures, infernal landscapes, celestial wonders. Each plate with appropriate (translated) verses. 141pp. 9 x 12. 23231-X Pa. $4.50

DORÉ'S ILLUSTRATIONS FOR RABELAIS, Gustave Doré. 252 striking illustrations of *Gargantua and Pantagruel* books by foremost 19th-century illustrator. Including 60 plates, 192 delightful smaller illustrations. 153pp. 9 x 12. 23656-0 Pa. $5.00

LONDON: A PILGRIMAGE, Gustave Doré, Blanchard Jerrold. Squalor, riches, misery, beauty of mid-Victorian metropolis; 55 wonderful plates, 125 other illustrations, full social, cultural text by Jerrold. 191pp. of text. 9⅜ x 12¼. 22306-X Pa. $6.00

THE RIME OF THE ANCIENT MARINER, Gustave Doré, S. T. Coleridge. Dore's finest work, 34 plates capture moods, subtleties of poem. Full text. Introduction by Millicent Rose. 77pp. 9¼ x 12. 22305-1 Pa. $3.50

THE DORE BIBLE ILLUSTRATIONS, Gustave Doré. All wonderful, detailed plates: Adam and Eve, Flood, Babylon, Life of Jesus, etc. Brief King James text with each plate. Introduction by Millicent Rose. 241 plates. 241pp. 9 x 12. 23004-X Pa. $6.00

THE COMPLETE ENGRAVINGS, ETCHINGS AND DRYPOINTS OF ALBRECHT DURER. "Knight, Death and Devil"; "Melencolia," and more—all Dürer's known works in all three media, including 6 works formerly attributed to him. 120 plates. 235pp. 8⅜ x 11¼. 22851-7 Pa. $6.50

MAXIMILIAN'S TRIUMPHAL ARCH, Albrecht Dürer and others. Incredible monument of woodcut art: 8 foot high elaborate arch—heraldic figures, humans, battle scenes, fantastic elements—that you can assemble yourself. Printed on one side, layout for assembly. 143pp. 11 x 16. 21451-6 Pa. $5.00

AMERICAN ANTIQUE FURNITURE, Edgar G. Miller, Jr. The basic coverage of all American furniture before 1840: chapters per item chronologically cover all types of furniture, with more than 2100 photos. Total of 1106pp. 7⅞ x 10¾.   21599-7, 21600-4 Pa., Two-vol. set $17.90

ILLUSTRATED GUIDE TO SHAKER FURNITURE, Robert Meader. Director, Shaker Museum, Old Chatham, presents up-to-date coverage of all furniture and appurtenances, with much on local styles not available elsewhere. 235 photos. 146pp. 9 x 12.   22819-3 Pa. $5.00

ORIENTAL RUGS, ANTIQUE AND MODERN, Walter A. Hawley. Persia, Turkey, Caucasus, Central Asia, China, other traditions. Best general survey of all aspects: styles and periods, manufacture, uses, symbols and their interpretation, and identification. 96 illustrations, 11 in color. 320pp. 6⅛ x 9¼.   22366-3 Pa. $6.95

CHINESE POTTERY AND PORCELAIN, R. L. Hobson. Detailed descriptions and analyses by former Keeper of the Department of Oriental Antiquities and Ethnography at the British Museum. Covers hundreds of pieces from primitive times to 1915. Still the standard text for most periods. 136 plates, 40 in full color. Total of 750pp. 5⅜ x 8½.

23253-0 Pa. $10.00

THE WARES OF THE MING DYNASTY, R. L. Hobson. Foremost scholar examines and illustrates many varieties of Ming (1368-1644). Famous blue and white, polychrome, lesser-known styles and shapes. 117 illustrations, 9 full color, of outstanding pieces. Total of 263pp. 6⅛ x 9¼. (Available in U.S. only)   23652-8 Pa. $6.00